DREAMING
DARKLY

DREAMING DARKLY

CAITLIN KITTREDGE

 KATHERINE TEGEN BOOKS
An Imprint of HarperCollins Publishers

Katherine Tegen Books is an imprint of HarperCollins Publishers.

Library of Congress Control Number: 2018941659
ISBN 978-0-06-266562-1

Typography by Catherine San Juan
19 20 21 22 23 PC/LSCH 10 9 8 7 6 5 4 3 2 1
❖
First Edition

For Grandma Hazel

I was eight years old when my mother tried to kill me.

One night, when we stopped outside Topeka, she held my head under the water of our motel room bathtub. I remember how warm her hands felt on the back of my neck and how the water chilled my skin. I heard nothing except the beating of my own heart.

I don't remember feeling afraid. I don't remember feeling anything.

When I woke up on the bathroom floor, my mother was gone. She came back later that night, sat on the sticky bedspread in our motel room, and cried. I've heard a lot of theories since then from school counselors and child shrinks about why mothers try to hurt their children, but that night, her tearstained face and heartbroken sobs told me everything.

There was something wrong with me—something bad in my blood, under my skin, deep as my bones. Something unnatural, something as dark and cold as the water I'd almost drowned in.

And my mother knew it.

Chapter I

The small boat churned through waves almost as high as the deck, rocking me so hard I lost my balance and fell into Officer Brant, who caught me and steadied me on my feet.

"You'll get used to it," he said. "Can't live out on the island if you don't have your sea legs."

I shook him off. I wasn't crazy about being touched, especially by a stranger. Except for me and Officer Brant, the only person on board was the captain, a woman with silver hair and orange waders who had introduced herself as Julia. That had been the first and last thing she said to me. From the way she was glaring out at the gray waves, it was clear she didn't want to be here.

That made two of us. I shivered when another wave hit the bow, salt spray soaking me all the way to my skin.

"When Simon called me and said he had a niece, I was surprised," said Officer Brant. "I thought all the Bloodgoods except him were gone."

My uncle, Simon Bloodgood, was the reason I was here, crammed in a stuffy cabin that smelled like fish, my one suitcase sliding back and forth across the deck. I'd never met the man, but I was pretty sure I already didn't like him. I was allergic to rich people, even if I was related to them.

Besides, where had this Simon guy been for the last sixteen years? If he and Mom had ever been close, she must have done a great job of alienating him. She'd had a gift.

"It'll be nice for him to have some company," Brant continued. I couldn't tell if he was totally oblivious or just loved the sound of his own voice. "I'm sure it gets lonely out there in that big old house."

I turned my back on Officer Brant and stared out the filthy window. He finally took the hint I wasn't into small talk and started fiddling with his radio.

The fog peeled back layer by layer, and I saw black rocks poking out of the water, hand-sized black seabirds clutching them for dear life. A white brick tower, thin as a finger bone, appeared above us, clinging to the promontory, and I got my first glimpses of the island. The granite cliffs below the lighthouse were pitted and eaten away, to the point where it looked like the tower could collapse into the waves any second. A foghorn blasted so close it rattled my teeth.

The headache I'd had since the social worker put me on the plane in Omaha started up again, throbbing inside my skull.

We passed by the cliffs, into a small harbor, boat engines winding down. Nearby in the channel, a rusty buoy bobbed, bell clanging in the boat's wake, over and over. I searched the shore for some sign that this might not be as bad as I thought, but all I saw were more black rocks, backed up by dark pines and fog.

I wrapped my arms around myself. I hadn't dressed for a cold that felt like winter even though it was only September. The boat lurched again as Julia swung us around to line up with the dock, and I felt my stomach lurch right along with it. I didn't like water. All I thought about when I was near the ocean was drowning.

A shadow flickered on the shore, and I squinted, rubbing a circle of clear on the dirty glass. I wasn't seeing things—a boy stood on a rock, watching the boat with an unblinking gaze.

I knew—*knew*—he couldn't see me through the salty glass, but I swore he locked eyes with me.

His skin was pale above the dark collar of his coat, and his hair shone blue-black even in the dim sunlight filtering through the fog. I couldn't tear my eyes away as we passed closer to the promontory he stood on. Close enough to make out his features, I saw his lips part and heard my own name.

Ivy.

"Ivy." Officer Brant touched my shoulder. "We're here."

I wriggled away from his touch again, and when I glanced behind me, the boy was gone. I must have imagined him. I was the only person under thirty on the island, as far as I knew.

Officer Brant walked with me off the boat and up a narrow dock that jutted into the harbor, wood planks slick with algae and rot under my combat boots. A woman as chunky and solid as the rocky shore stood waiting for us, wearing head-to-toe denim and a scowl. She was propped against a four-by-four so rusty I couldn't begin to tell what the paint color might have been. Everything around me was pitted and weather-beaten, dissolving slowly under the onslaught of the wind and waves.

Julia came after us, tossed my suitcase down, and swung back aboard without a word. Officer Brant winced. "Sorry. Locals don't like coming out to Darkhaven."

Looking around at the ramshackle boathouse and the empty beach, I didn't blame them. *I* didn't want to be here, so why should anyone else?

"Ivy." Officer Brant held out a small white card printed with his name and the seal of the town police department. "If you need anything, you can call me. Anytime."

I took the card and shoved it in my jeans, because I could tell he was just going to stand there holding it until I either took it or the rickety dock fell into the ocean.

"You'll be all right here. You might even like it," Officer Brant said. "And again, I'm sorry for your loss."

I must have given him an especially poisonous stare, because he backpedaled, waving his hands. "Your mother's accident, I mean . . . I got the gist from social services when they released you to my custody, but . . ."

"You don't have to try to say the right thing," I said, to shut him up. I grabbed my suitcase. The familiar grip of the worn plastic handle was the only thing that kept me from screaming. I could remember all the times I'd hauled it from motels to rented shacks to the trailer of whoever my mother was dating that month. When I held it I didn't have to think about anything that had happened in the last week.

"My mother killed herself," I told Brant. "She cut her wrists and I had to find her body. The only thing sorry about the whole situation was her."

All at once, acid boiled from my stomach up into my throat, like my shitty words were turning around on me. I barely had time to drop to my knees and lean over the dock before I threw up my breakfast into the harbor, my insides still rolling in time with the waves out on the ocean even though I was back on land. My head felt thick and hot, pain throbbing between my eyes, but I didn't close them. If I did, I'd just see what my mother had let me walk in on all over again.

I gasped, trying to pretend for the benefit of Brant I was just seasick, and swiped at my mouth. I didn't want this. I didn't want to think about my mother. She was gone, finally gone, and she couldn't make me feel like this ever again. I became aware of a pair of men's shoes, filled with a woman's feet wearing bright pink-and-green socks, standing next to me.

"If you're quite finished," said the feet's owner. "The car's just over there."

I made myself get up. There's no real trick to it, pretending everything's fine when you feel like you could never stand steady again. You can't think about what's happening. Lie to yourself, so you can lie to everyone else too. I was a good liar. Years of covering for my mother so nobody else would figure out she belonged in a psych ward had trained me well.

The woman in the denim shirt looked me up and down and sniffed before taking my suitcase from me and walking back to her Jeep.

Officer Brant followed us. "You're sure everything is all right? I can ride up to the manor, if you need me. . . ."

Manor? Oh, this was getting better and better. My uncle had a *manor* rather than a house, or even a mansion. I hated the idea of living with him more by the second.

"We're fine, Officer." The woman laid a glare on Officer Brant that should have made him burst into flames. "I'm sure you have real work to do back on the mainland. If we need someone to meddle in the family's affairs, you'll be the first person I call."

In spite of the utter suck factor of the morning so far, I

felt a tiny smile creep onto my face. I didn't know who this old broad was, but I kind of liked her.

She opened the passenger door of the Jeep. "Get in."

"I'm Ivy," I said as she gunned the engine and we pulled away from the dock, gravel flying.

"I know," she said. "If you're expecting a curtsy, you're going to be disappointed." Her voice was as flat and bleating as the foghorn, her accent pure Maine. I gave up on my one attempt to be friendly. One was all you got.

I glanced back toward the dock as Julia's boat pulled away. We were headed up a steep hill toward the cliffs, and I let my eyes wander to the rock where I'd seen the boy.

Nothing moved on shore but a few gulls, but as I watched the tree line, a dark shadow darted through the forest, following the path of the boat back out to sea.

"You may call me Mrs. MacLeod," the woman said. She jammed the Jeep into a lower gear as we crested the hill, and I turned around. I'd barely slept since Omaha. I wasn't seeing things—I just needed coffee.

"So where's Mr. MacLeod?" I asked. No response, not even a twitch. I tried again. "I thought my uncle was the only person living here."

"I am Mr. Bloodgood's housekeeper," said Mrs. MacLeod. "That does not mean I am your servant. I keep the house, I fix the meals, and I look after Bloodgood Manor and the gardens. I do not tolerate lying, stealing, using drugs or drink, back talk, or tardiness to meals. Do we understand one another, Miss Bloodgood?"

I forced myself not to roll my eyes. If the evil New England version of Mary Poppins thought she was going to order me around, she could go right ahead and enjoy her delusion. "You can call me Ivy, really," I said.

Mrs. MacLeod's mouth formed a tight little smile. "That was not the question I asked. I asked, can I expect you to obey the rules of the manor?"

I pressed my forehead against the cold glass, but it didn't help my headache. "Whatever. It's not like I have a choice."

"That is right." Mrs. MacLeod looked way too pleased with herself. I decided that I didn't like her after all. In fact, I sort of hated her.

I shut my eyes, hoping I wouldn't be stuck in the tiny car much longer since I was already feeling sick and smelled a little like puke. Rather than keep berating me, Mrs. MacLeod let out a curse and slammed on the brakes. My seat belt snapped tight, slamming my shoulders back against the hard seat. The Jeep fishtailed, gravel spraying against the back window. My eyes shot open in time to see a dark shape flash across the road and disappear into the woods on the other side. It was as tall as a man, black, and faster than a blink.

"What the hell was that?" I said, trying to catch my breath. The seat belt had knocked the wind out of me.

Mrs. MacLeod snarled, gunning the engine again. "That was the fault of those no-good Irish living up island, is what that was. If I've told 'em once, I've told 'em a thousand times to keep their animals to *their* side of the island."

I blinked at her. "There are other people living on Darkhaven?"

"Oh yes," she said. "And a worse group of degenerates and wrongdoers you won't find outside a jailhouse." She jabbed a finger at me. "This island is seven miles long, but for your purposes the road ends at three and a half. You stay on the Bloodgood side of Darkhaven, am I clear? The Ramseys don't like trespassers, and the state of Maine gives them ample right to shoot you if you cross the property line."

"Yeah, sure," I said, trying to hide my excitement. As soon as I could sneak out, I was definitely going to see what this Ramsey family was up to. Degenerates and wrongdoers sounded a hell of a lot more interesting than Uncle Simon's manor house.

"Told them once, told them a thousand times, letting those creatures wander all over the damn place . . . ," Mrs. MacLeod muttered again. I raised my hand.

"Am I supposed to believe that thing in the road was a . . . *dog* or something?" I'd spent most of my life in the Midwest. I knew a dog when I saw one, bigger animals too—whatever that was hadn't been a cow, a sheep, or a damn prairie dog.

"Mind your business, miss, unless you want that pert

nose clipped off for sticking it where it doesn't belong," Mrs. MacLeod snapped. I was going to snap back, but the Jeep rounded a curve and the land flattened out into the grounds of the manor house.

"Holy crap," I whispered. Perched at the edge of the cliffs I'd seen from the water, the place was made from granite blocks the size of Volkswagens, the same gray as the fog. A turret reached to the sky, while sprawling wings went in all directions. Windows made of tiny, lacy panes stared back at me, and we pulled up in front of iron-strapped main doors big enough to admit a bus.

"I'll take you through the main entrance, seeing as it's your first time here," said Mrs. MacLeod. "After this you'll be expected to use the servants' entrance, as Simon and I do. No sense in opening these doors every time you have a notion to take a walk."

I followed her up the broad steps, still not quite believing what I was seeing. All this time, while we'd been living in rent-by-the-week suites, my mother scamming strangers for pocket change, while I had two pairs of jeans and one pair of shoes to my name, my family had been living *here*. Not just rich like the kids I'd known in Omaha who got designer clothes and cars for their sweet sixteen. This was 1 percent territory: private island, murder-a-stripper-and-get-away-with-it rich.

Why would my mother have left this behind? She was

ruthless, and she loved money. I couldn't believe poor-little-rich-girl syndrome had driven her out of this spectacular house and away from the credit cards and clothes and cars that came with a family like this. Never mind the *inheritance*.

I thought about every time I'd had a Coke and a bag of chips from a gas station for dinner, and gone to sleep on a bench afterward because we couldn't afford a motel, and I wasn't sure who I was angrier at—Mom for running out on this or the uncle who'd never once, that I knew of, tried to track her down.

Whatever happened must have been bad. The only way Mom would bolt would be if she was angry and trying to make a point, and the only way she'd stay away was if somebody made sure she did. I wondered what could have put that kind of fear in Mom. For better or worse, she wasn't afraid of much.

Mrs. MacLeod opened the door from a ring of silver keys. The hinges screeched, and a flood of musty air rushed out at us.

It didn't matter now, I decided. I was here, Mom was dead, and I might as well enjoy the manor while I could. I only had a year and change until I was eighteen. I had a plan for that day—I was getting on a bus to California; I was going to San Francisco, the only place I'd stayed with Mom that I'd been sad to leave—and after that I'd figure it out. Fourteen months until I never had to go where I didn't want to again. I could survive until then.

"Come on, I don't have all day." Mrs. MacLeod shooed me inside and closed the doors. The rumble they made went all the way down to my feet, like the lid of a coffin slamming shut.

Chapter

2

My room looked over the cliff and a tiny rock-strewn beach at the foot of it. To the right, I could see the turret, which at this angle tilted alarmingly toward the ocean. The paint was peeling off the window frames, and the plaster on my walls was water-stained and dark. Despite the glowing hardwood floors, the Haunted Mansion–style furniture and curtains and portraits everywhere, and the general over-the-top size of the place, it was obvious the manor house was slowly decaying like everything else on the island. A blast of wind hit the window, and the glass rattled like loose teeth.

Mrs. MacLeod dropped my suitcase on top of the faded quilt covering my new bed and snapped it open before I could stop her, pulling out my clothes and tossing them into dresser drawers. "Don't get any ideas about going down to the shore," she said. "Those stairs aren't safe, and you'll be at the bottom with your neck broken before you can say boo."

She lifted out my mother's tarot deck, stashed under my clothes. The cards were wrapped in a blue velvet square she'd found at a thrift shop, but the deck itself had been with Mom since before I was born. "What's this, then?" Mrs. MacLeod asked.

I snatched it from her and shoved it into my nightstand.

"None of your business."

We locked eyes, and I found hers to be pale and smooth as pebbles, without any warmth at all. "You're at Bloodgood Manor now, miss," she said after a moment. "I think you'll find everything is my business."

She shoved my suitcase under the bed and pointed down the stairs. "Your uncle is waiting in the solarium. Put on something presentable and come down."

"This is as presentable as I get," I said, smoothing my hands over my damp jeans and my mom's old Nirvana shirt, one of the few things she'd owned I'd held on to. What could I say, I couldn't afford to throw out perfectly good clothes. "I must have left my party dress in my other bag."

Mrs. MacLeod narrowed her eyes. "It's fortunate you're not my child," she said.

I peeled off my wet, salty jacket and dumped it in the middle of the pin-straight quilt, water soaking it in a jagged circle. I looked at Mrs. MacLeod, daring her to keep talking. She stared at the jacket like she wished she could burn it, but she didn't say anything else. She didn't need to—I'd learned what I wanted to know. If I pushed her, she wasn't going to react with anything worse than snapping and glaring.

I picked up the jacket and hung it on the hook on the back of my door. "Let's meet the long-lost uncle," I said perkily.

Mrs. MacLeod grunted and led me downstairs without

another word, into a room with a wall of windows and droopy, half-dead potted plants sitting everywhere. Aside from some rusty iron chairs and a little rolling cart, I was alone. I turned to ask Mrs. MacLeod where my uncle was, but she'd vanished. Probably in a puff of smoke like the witch she was.

I pushed through the plants to the windows, which looked over the sea, into the roiling water and fog beyond. Rain started and streaked the glass, blurring out everything except my reflection. The wind cut around the corner of the house, howling and whining under the eaves.

"Beautiful, isn't it?"

I jumped higher than I'd admit to, feeling like I'd bitten into an electrified wire. A second reflection appeared next to mine, and I turned to see a skinny man in a tweed suit smiling at me. I shrugged. "It's okay, I guess."

"You really do look like her," my uncle said. "Myra, I mean." He picked a teapot off the little cart and held it up. "Tea?"

"I'm good." I stayed by the window. I could feel the chill coming off the glass. I really needed to find some long underwear or something if I was going to be staying on Darkhaven.

"I can't imagine what you've been through," Simon said. "But I'm so very relieved that you're home, Ivy. You have no idea."

He poured two cups anyway, and I sighed. Guess I had to get used to being ignored.

"Do you like your room?" he said. "I asked Veronica to put you in the best guest suite. Where *is* Veronica, anyway?"

It took me a second to realize he was talking about Mrs. MacLeod. I wouldn't have pegged old hatchet face for a *Veronica*. "Off polishing her broomstick, I think," I said.

Simon surprised me by laughing. He sounded like a seal. "Veronica is a dear woman, really," he said. "She just takes a bit of getting used to. But your room—you're comfortable? You feel at home?"

Never in a million years would I think of this rock pile as home. Not even if I *was* in the best guest suite instead of the glorified closet Spiteful McHagface had stuck me in. "It's fine," I said. "Listen, I'm really beat, so I think I'm just going to go hang out up there for a while."

All the plants were making me claustrophobic, never mind that I didn't want to be anywhere near my uncle. It probably wasn't his fault the first sixteen years of my life had been so crappy, but I wasn't used to being around family. "Family" was a weird way to think of Simon, anyway. If my mother had told me flat out he was a creeper, I would have felt less uncomfortable. It was the complete lack of information up until this moment—the fact that she'd never told me more than she'd had a brother and his name was Simon— that unsettled me. Simon was a void I couldn't read yet, and

I hated that. I relied on information to keep me ahead of other people, have the advantage. Simon was a black box, and that made him dangerous.

"I heard you were the one who found her."

That stopped me in my tracks. I opened my mouth, to answer him or scream, I'm not sure. Simon's expression gave me pause. It wasn't pinched or critical or angry. He didn't even look sad. He looked defeated.

Simon took off his glasses and squeezed the bridge of his nose. "I'm sorry, Ivy. I truly am. No one should have to see that, least of all a child."

"Yeah, well." I sat down on one of the little wire chairs, my legs inexplicably heavy. "That was far from the only crappy thing she did to me, Uncle Simon. I wasn't all that surprised." I didn't say anything else, especially about the incident when I was eight. I barely knew Simon, I didn't know how he'd react, and if I was being honest, I didn't want *anyone* to know about that. Not because I was embarrassed, but because there was a part of me that wondered, even now. Had she been right about me? Had she seen something in me that was just bad?

I wasn't normal, that much was for sure, and Simon would eventually figure that out. No point in spilling all of Mom's dark secrets and speeding up the process.

Simon sat down across from me and nudged the teacup in my direction. I sighed and took a sip. It was terrible, bitter and black on my tongue, but drinking it made me a little warmer, so I forced myself to down the entire cup.

"I can't say I'm surprised either, insensitive as that sounds," he said. "Deep down, I think I always knew Myra was destined to die young."

Finally, something we agreed on.

Simon put his glasses back on. "If you go exploring, please stay out of the turret and the east wing. This place is old, and it's not safe to wander around up there."

"That's it?" I said. "You're not going to spout a bunch of rules or try to make me like you by giving me presents?"

Simon's mouth lifted on one side. It was weird but sort of endearing, like a robot learning how to smile. "Would that work?"

"No," I said. "I've had about ten 'new dads,' so I know all the tricks. I'm unbribable."

"Myra never lost her penchant for hurting everyone she comes in contact with, then," he said, corners of his mouth turning down.

"She was damaged," I said. I didn't know why I suddenly had the impulse to defend Mom. Simon was only voicing stuff I'd thought for years. Maybe it was just that—his saying it out loud made it harsh, too real. After all, part of the "everyone" she'd damaged was me.

"You deal with your issues when a child is involved," Simon replied. "You don't pass them on."

I stayed quiet. I wasn't starting a fight five minutes after meeting the guy.

"You only have the one suitcase?" he asked as I pushed back my chair. "No boxes or trunks or family pets?"

"We moved too much for pets," I said. "No money for anything worth boxing up and taking with us."

"Okay then," Simon said. "Welcome home, Ivy."

I forced myself not to flinch. My last name might be Bloodgood, same as the brass sign bolted to the outside of the manor house, but this would never be my home, and Simon would learn quickly that I wasn't the kind of person he wanted as family. Sooner or later I'd cross some line that normal people knew to steer clear of, Simon would decide I was too much trouble, and I'd be gone. Even if he was the first person to treat me like a human being in quite a while, I was doing this for both of us. For my move to San Francisco as soon as I was old enough, and for sparing him the trouble of trying to "save" me when he couldn't do a damn thing. I tried to believe that as I climbed back to my room.

Chapter
3

I woke up in the woods. Darkness settled around me, no moon, no stars. Just the gray sheen of a foggy sky and the tips of the tall pines stabbing into its belly.

My bare skin prickled, and I felt mud squish between my toes. I knew I shouldn't be this cold, even wearing only a tank top and thin sweatpants. Sweat coated my skin. You didn't sweat in dreams, did you? This felt like just before a thunderstorm back in Omaha, when the air was so close and hot you could wrap yourself in it. When tornado sirens screamed louder than thunder, and you searched the horizon, waiting for those black clouds to funnel down and touch the earth.

Except it was cold. So cold my fingers were going numb.

I started to shake as moonlight shot through a tear in the fog, bathing the woods in silver. I had gone to sleep, exhausted from jet lag and everything else. In my bed. In the manor. And I was pretty sure this wasn't a dream. I'd never been in these woods, only glimpsed them from the boat. Mom had left Darkhaven while she was pregnant, and I was born on the mainland. I'd never seen the island with my own eyes before today.

But I was here, somehow. I glanced around, seeing shattered stumps of trees and flattened black vegetation. It looked like a foot had come from the heavens and tried to crush me, only I was still here, standing by a flowing stream, the scent of moss and mud and broken pine boughs filling my nostrils.

I turned back the way I'd ostensibly come, and saw the body.

I didn't scream. I felt my mouth open, felt the frozen air rush in, stinging my throat raw. I gasped, heart throbbing. My brain told me I was having a panic attack—I'd had them constantly as a kid, and they feel like you're choking and being hit by a truck at the same time. The last one had been years ago, around when I stopped having nightmares about the bathtub—but this time I couldn't stop it. None of the techniques a dozen school shrinks had suggested worked. I fell to my knees, hands sinking into the moss, and in the moonlight they were black up to the elbow.

Blood. I was covered in it. The front of my tank top, my cheeks, my arms.

The body was a man with dark hair, tall and muscular. Or he had been. He was covered in cuts, deep wounds, burns. I could barely see his face under the destruction.

I wanted to run, more than anything. Bolt into the trees and keep running until I hit the ocean. Why was I here?

Had I done this?

I remembered my mother sobbing, as she looked at me with that naked hatred after I shuffled out of the bathroom and started putting on dry clothes. I felt something shift inside me, that wrong thing I'd known deep down was there way before she locked the door and turned on the water in that motel bathroom. I was fully awake now, and my impulse was not to run back to the manor and call the cops. It was to stumble to the stream, wash the blood off me, and roll the body under the felled trunks of trees all around us.

My panic attack was stronger than the impulse, though, and my vision started to black out. The last thing I saw before I fainted were my hands, slick and gleaming black under the moonlight, bathed in someone else's blood.

I had managed to convince myself at the time, after that night, that it wasn't my fault. I read everything I could find about mental illness, and built the narrative that my mother was either seriously bipolar or some stripe of schizophrenic that made her detached from reality. That she'd taken it out on me because that's what abusive parents do. There was nothing wrong with me.

Nothing that my mother had recognized in me, and tried to get rid of.

I was a good liar, and I'd lied to myself right along with everyone else. I'd ignored stuff that didn't fit with my little story of how I was basically normal and I just had a screwed-up life.

But now, everything I'd told myself to sleep at night was gone, and as blackness closed across my vision, my only thought was maybe Mom had been right all along.

Chapter

4

I woke up in my bed. Light streamed in through the lace curtains. There was no forest, no bloody body.

I curled in on myself with relief. I hadn't had a nightmare that vivid in a long time.

All the racing thoughts that had boiled over the night before, that Mom had been right and I was sick, evil, a psychopath, a nutcase—take your pick, I'd heard them all—faded away in the crisp morning light. Of course she wasn't right. She was mentally ill; we lived in a country with crappy health care for poor people, and if somebody had dosed her ass with lithium before she stuck my head under the water, all of this could have been avoided.

I didn't know any of that for sure, but it was a theory I could live with. Any guilt I felt over what she did was just PTSD or something. I was normal—as normal as you could get being raised by an unbalanced grifter.

What I *did* know for sure was that I needed to get out. The manor was stuffy, and my bedroom was tiny and damp. The fog was still thick, but the rain had gone to a light mist. I realized I'd fallen asleep in the clothes I'd arrived in—not the thin nightclothes I'd worn in my dream. What had that been about?

I threw on my one jacket, my *other* pair of jeans, boots, and a tattered Stiff Little Fingers shirt I'd gotten from PJ, one of the few cool people I'd known in Omaha. He was a skinny punk in a party country town, had great tattoos, played guitar. I wouldn't call our thing dating, exactly, but I liked spending time with him, watching dumb Japanese monster movies from the seventies, going to underground shows, being somewhere that was not with Mom. She'd ruined it, though. Stole PJ's '69 Les Paul to ease our way to the next crappy town down Interstate 80. I should send him an apology now, or at least a check for the guitar. Hell, maybe a whole new guitar. I was suddenly rich; I needed to go on at least one wild spending spree.

It didn't take long to figure out how to escape the manor, not with an iron rose trellis outside my window. The longer I had to stay there, with nothing to think about except my horrible dream, the longer I had to think about how this was it. I lived here now. The "home" I kept equating with flat fields, dusty highways, and landlocked flyover states was gone. This place, like it or not, was home until I saved up my money and went to California, or until I got kicked out.

The garden that Mrs. MacLeod was so proud of was a tangle of overgrown lilac trees and hedges, surrounded by a stone wall that I climbed over to go to the forest. A cry sounded from somewhere ahead of me, high and echoing. I felt rain creep down the back of my jacket, the droplets like ice kissing my skin.

Soon I couldn't see anything except trees and snatches

of the sky. I kept walking, because it was better than being back at the house. For such a big place, it felt overstuffed, all crammed with crap over every inch of floor and wall, the damp that never went away, and the view of nothing but ocean from almost every window making me feel like I was stuck on some kind of alien planet with no way off.

Just like she'd never told me about Simon, Mom never talked about this place aside from telling how she'd left when she was six months pregnant and was never going back. She would repeat that when things were especially bad for us—we might be broke and homeless, but at least we weren't stuck back in Maine. We were free, she always said, over and over. She made money reading tarot cards and scamming morons, and I tried to stay out of her way. Especially when she had dark moods and would stare at me like I was a stranger, flipping those damn cards over and over in her hands. *I should throw them out*, I thought as I walked. They were antiques, had been hers since she was a little girl, and I guess I'd had the idea that I'd sell them, or give them back to Simon when I found out I was coming to live here. I sure as hell didn't want them. They carried a lot of bad memories.

But Uncle Simon clearly wasn't a tarot guy. He couldn't be more different from my mother, from us. He didn't even look like Mom. She and I shared rich auburn hair, hers more red and mine more brown. We both had pale skin and freckles, but Simon was just pale, or whatever came after pale—sallow. His thinning blond hair clung to his head like it might run away any second. He was small and nervous, where my mother was imposing, almost six feet tall in her motorcycle boots, with shoulders like an Amazon in a Harley jacket.

Or maybe that was just the way I remembered her. She could work a room—that was for sure. On a good weekend, if there was a convention or a trade show in whatever rear end of nowhere we'd landed in, she could rake in thousands of dollars. At least until the local cops caught on to the fact she never bothered to get a permit for her tarot readings and cloned credit cards whenever she could.

The cry rang out again, saving me from plunging my foot into a swollen brook while I was lost in thought. It sounded much closer, almost like it was next to me.

Just a bird. Had to be. I'd never lived deep in the woods, and I didn't know anything about Maine wildlife. There had to be all kinds of birds and small fuzzy animals hanging around, making noise.

I walked along the thin trail through the pines and let myself zone out, enjoying being outside somewhere that didn't smell like a stockyard. Big swathes of Nebraska stink. There was damp here, but not the enveloping humidity of the Midwest. The air tasted different—salty, sharp, a little sting when you breathed it in. This island was clean, like few places I'd ever lived. Clean and ancient, untouched by the few inhabitants. The trees and the thick ground cover spoke to that.

I looked back after what felt like no time and saw that the manor had totally disappeared. I was in a clearing, the trees thinning out into a small circle covered in moss and flat rocks. The light had changed, and I realized I must have been gone much longer than I thought.

Just as I decided to turn around, because I had no idea where I was on the island and didn't want to get shot by the neighbors Mrs. MacLeod had mentioned, a shape slithered across the corner of my vision. Just a blink and then it was gone, quicker than the raindrops shimmering in the air.

"Hello?"

Another shape, this one off to my right. I wasn't just spooked by the woods. There was something out there.

A branch cracked, and the pines rustled. Scratch that. There was something *big* out there, and it had brought at least one friend.

"Okay," I said out loud, because if there *was* something there I didn't want to seem scared, "enough of this Red Riding Hood bullshit."

"So is this the part where you say, 'My, what big teeth you have'?"

I screamed, so loud and sharp that a flight of crows lifted from the pines, squawking in response. The boy from the rocks grinned at me from a few feet away, the skin around his near-black eyes crinkling.

I hit him. With a closed fist, of course. I wasn't a debutante. I didn't slap openhanded. "You think that's funny?" I yelled. "What kind of jackass are you, sneaking up on people?"

"Whoa!" He held up a hand, putting the other to the blossoming red bruise on his jaw. "You're the one who wandered onto my side of the island, girlie. I'm the one who should be pulling the angry-yet-still-smoking-hot bit."

"I'm not angry," I snarled. "You're just an ass."

"But you don't deny I'm smoking hot?"

I raised my fist again, but he caught it. His hand was rough against my tender knuckles, warmer than it had any right to be in this freezing, drizzly hellhole. "Take it easy," he said. "I was joking."

Fury bubbled in my gut. I don't think I've ever met someone who'd made me hate him in thirty seconds flat, but this guy had won the prize. And he had the nerve to stand there, smirking at me from under his fall of black hair like I'd swoon at his feet any second.

"Why don't you go piss up a rope?" I finally blurted. *Good job, Ivy*, I thought. That definitely put him in his place in a way that didn't, at all.

I jerked my fist from his grasp as I turned to storm back to my side of the island, but he caught me again, swinging me around so we were pressed chest to chest. Up close he smelled good, a more intense version of the pines and the wet, dark earth all around us. Since I was human, I also had to admit that he wasn't totally wrong—objectively, he was kind of hot. I tried to ignore that, though, in light of his being a smug douchebag.

"Tell me your name," he said. His voice rumbled against my rib cage.

I sighed. "If I do, will you let go of me?"

"I'll let go of you either way," he said. "I don't look forward to getting kneed in the balls."

"Hey," I said. "You're marginally less stupid than you look."

He laughed and let go of my arm, smoothing down my jacket lapels and brushing off a few pine needles. "There. Good as new."

I stepped out of reach, swatting at him. "Free advice: I don't like being touched."

"Well, I don't like being punched in the face, but I'm dealing with it," he said, starting to smile, then flinching when his bruised jaw muscle twinged.

"You have a serious lack of boundaries, dude," I said.

"I'm sorry," he said, holding up his hands, palms toward me. "You're right, you don't know me, and I shouldn't have grabbed you. But to be fair, you did start it."

I looked back at the way I'd come, then at the boy again. *Boy* was probably the wrong word for somebody who stood about six foot three and was built like a small backhoe, but he seemed to be my age and acted about half it, so *boy* it was.

"I'm jumpy," I said. "And you scared the crap out of me."

I did feel sort of bad, as the bruise on his jaw got bigger and darker, so I sighed and dropped my defensive posture. "My name is Ivy."

He smile-flinched again, no doubt an evil scheme to blind me with his perfect teeth. "Ivy what?"

"Ivy Bloodgood."

His grin dropped at that, replaced by a spark in his dark eyes that got my stomach flipping in a way no amount of grabbing my arm ever would. "So it's true," he said. "Simon did bring you back to the island."

"You know my uncle? Or about me, for that matter?" I felt my eyebrow go up. The boy returned my look.

"News travels fast. Julia—the boat captain—told one of my cousins a few days back that Simon had a niece coming into town to stay on the island. And Simon is one of the only two people on the island besides my family so . . . yeah. Why wouldn't I know him?"

I shrugged. "You seem . . . I don't know . . . alive? And interesting?"

He laughed, rough and low. "Simon's an okay guy. By Darkhaven standards, anyway."

I started to ask what he meant by that, but he stuck out his hand.

"I'm Doyle. Doyle Ramsey."

"Can I ask you a question, Doyle?" I shook his hand in return, noticing again that his grip felt like it could crush rocks. He held my fingers gently, though, almost carefully, like I might break apart. I squeezed a little harder. The last thing I needed was some arrogant rich kid thinking I was fragile.

"You can ask me anything," he said, moving closer, definitely starting up the flirty crap again.

I rolled my eyes hard, letting go of his fingers. "Dial it back, Twilight. I'm serious."

Doyle spread his hands. "I'm offended. I'm much hotter than a vampire covered in stripper glitter." When I didn't smile, he dropped the cutesy-banter tone. "You're serious, okay. I am too—ask." He never took his eyes off my face, and I finally looked over his shoulder, where one of the crows had landed on a branch once again.

"Were you watching me from the rocks yesterday?" I said.

He shrugged. "I hear there's a girl my age coming in on the boat, I figured I better check it out."

"See, that's the thing," I said. "When I saw you out there, you said my name."

His grin never wavered. "How could I? You only just told me."

I pulled my soaked jacket tighter around me. "I'd better head back. I have no idea how far I walked."

"Nearly four miles," he said. "That stream you crossed is the property line."

"Yeah, like I said . . ." I shivered, imagining picking my way back through the woods. "Better get going. It was made pretty clear I wasn't supposed to be on your side of the island."

"Oh, come on," he said. "It'll take you an hour to get home, and my house is right over there. Come dry off and I'll drive you back."

I narrowed my eyes at him, and he cocked his head in return, hair falling in front of those dark eyes. He was still looking at me like he wanted to eat me, but he didn't seem like an ax murderer, just a cocky high school boy, and those I could handle. I'd even dated a couple of them. Just because I didn't let anyone in on my crappy home life didn't mean I hid in my hair and rambled on about not being like other girls. I liked boys sometimes, and generally they liked me back. Doyle wasn't the only one who could turn on the charm. Besides, Doyle sort of reminded me of PJ, if you gave PJ a haircut and six inches of height and made him really into something like lacrosse instead of punk music. "This wouldn't be a ploy to get my clothes off, would it, Doyle?"

He grinned again. "I wouldn't be that obvious, Ivy." He stripped off his jacket, which was made out of some water-resistant material, and draped it around my shoulders. "Come on."

I followed him, grateful to be warm for the first time since I'd gotten to the island. I couldn't help looking back as we left the tree line, but the shadows had gone. The woods were just woods. They resembled the ones from my nightmare, the brook and the clearing and all, but they weren't. I hadn't been covered in blood. There was no dead guy lying among the pine boughs.

That didn't change the fact Doyle Ramsey was a liar, and a pretty bad one. He'd known who I was, from the moment he'd seen me on the rocks. When I'd told him my name just now, it hadn't been new information for him. *Why* he was lying about it was anyone's guess.

Still, he was about to save me a long, wet walk in the gathering fog, and that was definitely worth ignoring what I hoped was just a white lie. I followed Doyle, leaving the forest behind.

Chapter
5

Doyle's home was the opposite of my uncle's in every way except that they were both crumbling— the Ramsey house rambled away into wings and additions, paint rotting and peeling at the edges, gingerbread trim covered with withered wisteria vines creeping over every flat surface. It was low and comfortable, nestled into the landscape rather than jutting out of it. Two trucks that had at least thirty years on me were up on blocks in the front yard, and I heard music blaring from a red barn beyond the house.

"Come on in," Doyle said as we stepped into a front hall made of dark wood and plaster, with more holes than the roof of the trailer my mother and I had rented in Missoula. "And if you're a vampire, I've just totally screwed myself, haven't I?"

"Yup," I said. "Consider your blood drunk."

Doyle accepted his windbreaker back, and took my jacket besides, leading me into a kitchen lined in yellow-flowered wallpaper and full of the smell of fresh bread. He inhaled and made a growling sound in the back of his throat.

"Sorry," he said when I raised an eyebrow. "Skipped breakfast."

So you could spy on me? I kept that to myself and stood with my hands shoved in my jeans pockets, listening to the plastic cat clock on the wall tick, until Doyle realized I wasn't going to fill the silence to be polite.

"I'll grab you a towel and run your coat through the dryer," Doyle said. "Sit tight."

I wandered around the kitchen while he was gone. The shelves were groaning under canned jams and fruits, mismatched plates, and novelty mugs decorated with slogans like MAINE: VACATIONLAND and WICKED GOOD LOBSTAH. Beyond the Ramseys' barn, the land sloped up sharply to a hilltop, where a blackened brick chimney and the remains of a wall glowered over the rest of the property.

"Old homestead," Doyle said, handing me a blue towel with frayed edges. I mopped the rain out of my hair. I was probably going to look like a bag lady when it dried, but I wasn't trying to impress anyone, least of all him.

"Believe it or not, we used to live in the lap of luxury," he said. "That place was even bigger than Bloodgood Manor."

"What happened?" I said.

"The usual," Doyle said. "Big fire in 1801. No money to rebuild, so they knocked together this heap and called it a day." He pulled a pitcher of iced tea from the fridge and offered me a glass.

I shook my head. "It is way too freezing for that. Is it always this cold?"

"It's Maine, sweetheart," Doyle said. "We're all a little cold-blooded up here."

"Don't call me *sweetheart*," I said. "Has that 'let me help you get warm' line worked for you on any girl, ever?"

Doyle drained the glass and set it in the old porcelain sink, reaching past me to do it. "It's working on you right now and you know it."

"On second thought," I said, tossing the now-damp towel back at him. "Maybe I will walk home."

"Suit yourself," Doyle said, still smiling. "I'm just trying to be a good host."

I snorted. Who did Doyle think he was kidding with this crap? "You know, Simon and his creepy housekeeper aren't your biggest fans." I briefly considered that maybe Simon had this rule for a reason, and I'd just gotten so used to ignoring anything adults told me to do I'd walked myself into trouble. I brushed the thought away, though. I had way too much experience keeping myself out of bad situations to get taken in by some backwoods Ted Bundy.

Doyle didn't offer a smile or a crack in response to what I'd said, like I expected. He just got closer to me, filling my nose with that piney scent all over again. "I could say some things about your uncle too, Ivy. Things you probably wouldn't like."

"What happened to him being an 'okay guy'?" I said, raising an eyebrow.

"I was being polite," Doyle said. "Because I thought you were too. Now I don't care so much."

"You know, it's been fun meeting the local weirdo and all, but I really do need to go home now." I knocked his arm away from me and pushed into him, forcing him to move.

Doyle just looked at me with a line between his black eyebrows, like I'd started speaking a foreign language all of a sudden. "Shit," he said at last. "You really *don't* know, do you?"

"Know what?" I threw up my hands. "Are you going to give me a ride home or not?"

"I mean, you came onto our land, and you came to my house," Doyle said. "I thought Simon told you, or you found out on your own. . . ." He shook his head, and when he looked at me again his eyes were shadowed, full of ink where they'd been full of flame a moment before, when he'd been close to me. "It's my fault, probably. I shouldn't have invited you over here, or followed you in the woods. But I figured if you'd come to our side of the island you didn't care. . . ."

"I'm confused," I said. I got the table between us, just in case I'd miscalculated and he *was* some kind of handsome, square-jawed, tea-drinking serial killer. "What is it that I supposedly know and don't care about?"

"About your family," he said. "About the Ramseys and Bloodgoods, about the murders that happened in the 1940s. About how all the Bloodgoods are cursed."

Chapter
6

I don't know what Doyle was expecting, but he looked surprised when I started laughing.

"Okay," I said. "I get it. Freak out the new girl. Consider me unsettled. Good work. Can we go?"

"I'm totally serious, Ivy," Doyle said. "Ask your uncle about the Bloodgood curse." He gestured out the window. "Ask why we're the only two families on this godforsaken rock."

"Because of a curse," I said. I thought the stress of the week had gotten to me, because I couldn't stop giggling. "Listen, my mom and I made a living off selling spooky crap to locals, and as spooky crap goes, this is amateur hour. Gold star, you tried, but I'm gonna go home now." I walked to his front door and opened it. It felt good to be back in the real world, where you laughed at the people who believed in dumb stuff and, if you were Mom and I, took their money. The ten minutes or so I'd spent in Spookyville were more than enough for me.

"I'm not joking," Doyle said, following me.

I laughed again. "You're cute, but *man* are you weird, Doyle. I can find my own way home. See you at the next coven meeting, okay? And please, *please* consider befriending some normal people before you go completely off the rails.

Get on Snapchat or something, at least."

He slammed the door, putting his body between me and the outside. "I'm *not joking*."

"And neither am I, so move!" I said, shoving him aside and opening the door.

"I bet you're only here because your mother died!"

I stopped at that, swiveling my head to glare at him. He clearly didn't recognize a warning when he saw it, because he barreled on.

"She died violently, right? Well, so has everyone else in your line, as far back as either of our families can remember. You're cursed, Ivy. You should get out of here before it's too late for you."

"Two things," I said. "First, don't talk about my mother unless you want me to do a lot more than pop you in the jaw. Second, since it's the twenty-first century and we stopped burning people at the stake a while ago, I don't believe in curses." He looked a little put out at that, but I ignored him and stormed down his driveway.

"Wait!" he yelled. "Let me drive you back! It's not safe out there!"

"Safer than it is here!" I yelled back, and then didn't look behind me again. Doyle didn't chase me, and eventually, as I tromped down the muddy road, I came to the turn I recognized as leading up to the manor house.

I was out of breath by the time I climbed the hill, and barely made it back up the trellis to my room before I collapsed on the braided rug. I was going to have to get in better shape if I wanted to keep sneaking around. Although from now on, I was definitely staying on the Bloodgood side of the property line.

I was more jarred than I wanted to admit by what Doyle had said. Clearly he was either super far into the freak forest with this curse story or he was just trying to scare me, but it had worked on some level. Guessing my mother had died was a cheap cold-reading trick—one I'd learned when I was still mastering spelling my own name—but his insistence was what got to me. He looked like he really believed it.

I made myself get up and stop thinking about Doyle. If I bought into this, Darkhaven would make me wacky too, and I'd barely been here a day. I was starving from my hike-slash-weirdo encounter, and I went downstairs to see if Simon had anything in his fridge worth raiding. At least that's where I was headed until I heard voices coming from behind a closed door off the main hall.

"And she didn't have anything with her?"

"Nothing." Mrs. MacLeod's brogue was loud and clear. "Just some tatty clothes and a pack of her insufferable mother's tarot cards."

"Have a little respect," Simon said. "Myra did just pass away."

Mrs. MacLeod gave one of her grunts. I heard a clink of crystal against glass, and Simon coughed a bit. "Is that your first one today, Veronica?"

"And a hell of a day it's been, Simon. Like I said, the only thing she has of Myra's are those stupid cards. I went through her bag; I went through everything she came with. I didn't miss something, if that's your implication."

Now *that* was interesting. Definitely wouldn't be leaving anything in my room I didn't want Mrs. McSnoopy knowing about. If I'd had a more normal existence, I probably would have been pissed about the invasion of privacy, but not trusting people was second nature to Mom, and so it became that way for me. I'd have been more surprised if Veronica hadn't searched my things.

"She's Myra's child," Simon said. "It *has* to be with her. Myra dying made her part of it. Even if she doesn't know yet."

"And who's to say the father doesn't have it, for safekeeping?" Mrs. MacLeod sounded way too happy with herself. "Myra went and got herself a bastard, from who knows what kind of low-class hoodlum who'd likely do anything to get his hands on what Myra was set to inherit. Who's to say he's not sitting on the mainland waiting for his adorable little felon to call him over and slit our throats?"

"Remember who you're talking to, Veronica." Simon's voice suddenly had a sharp edge I was surprised he was capable of. "Ivy is a Bloodgood. Doesn't matter who her father is. She's my blood. Don't call her a bastard again."

"That's what I'm afraid of," Mrs. MacLeod muttered. "That she *is* a Bloodgood, through and through. You remember as well as I do what Myra was like when she—"

"I said enough!"

I didn't even have to eavesdrop for that one. Simon was yelling. "I know what could happen with her being here. I can handle it. And if you'll remember, Veronica, you're in this up to your neck."

Mrs. MacLeod gave a laugh that sounded like gravel crunching. "Just because you've got yourself a sword to hold over me doesn't mean I'm wrong, Simon."

"For the love of everything, Veronica, I'm not turning her out. That would be the opposite of what I want." A chair pushed back, and I retreated down the hall. I could just hear Mrs. MacLeod reply.

"That's not what I was talking about."

I was sitting in a front parlor overlooking the sea, eating a ham sandwich, when Mrs. MacLeod came in carrying an armload of firewood. "How much of that did you hear?" she said, dumping it into the grate.

I didn't bother trying to look innocent. She wasn't anyone who could punish me. "Enough," I said. "How did you know I was there?"

"I came to this house when Simon and Myra were barely ten. I'm well aware that the less you want children to overhear, the harder they'll try. None of your sneaking about goes unnoticed," Mrs. MacLeod snapped.

I raised a hand. "I heard a lot, but don't worry. I get why you don't want me here. And for the record, I have no idea who my father is, and if I *did*, I'd be living with him a long way away from this island, not conspiring to murder the two of you. You're so not worth the effort."

Mrs. MacLeod shook her head, shoving crumpled newspapers in between the logs. "Dear God, girl, what did Myra do to you to make you this hard at sixteen?"

I shrugged. "Sounds like you knew her pretty well."

"Nobody ever knew Myra. Not really. She was locked up tighter than a tomb even as a girl." She sighed, sitting back on her heels. "Regardless of how you and I started, I have no desire to be rid of you. You've got no one but Simon now. I would never try to sever that bond."

"Please don't act like you care about what happened to me," I said. "I can tell when you're faking it."

"Ah, but I do care," Mrs. MacLeod said. "I care that Simon cares about you, because I don't want to see him hurt. So I care that you understand exactly what being a Bloodgood means, Ivy. I care that you realize your blood carries a weight."

I don't know why I decided to tell her. Maybe I wanted

her to show her true self, to get pissed and yell and threaten me. I could deal with her being mean—this about-face into awkward compassion was just uncomfortable.

Maybe I just wanted to tell someone else about Doyle's story and get confirmation that he was out to lunch and the whole bit about people in my family dying violent deaths was just his trying to creep me out. "I met a guy today," I said. "He told me the family was cursed."

Rather than yell, Mrs. MacLeod touched a match to the paper, watching as fingers of flame worked their way over the wood, leaving sooty bruises in their wake. She breathed in, out, a rattling sigh that mimicked the wind outside. "I did tell you not to go near those Ramseys, did I not?"

"Since you're here alive and talking to me, I somehow think you're not my mom," I said.

Mrs. MacLeod pursed her lips. "Lord, even Myra never gave me that sort of mouth," she said. "It was Doyle you met, wasn't it? The youngest one, with a touch of the devil in him?"

"A little more than a touch," I said. "And, you know, nuts. You'd think he could come up with something scarier than 'You're cursed, ooo.'" I waggled my fingers, casting spooky shadows in the firelight.

Mrs. MacLeod smiled at me, and it was so creepy I prayed she'd go back to the usual hatchet face. She took the other chair opposite me in front of the fire, picking up the poker and jabbing at the logs, eliciting a rush of flame and smoke.

"The first man on Darkhaven was your ancestor Connor Bloodgood." She used the poker to point at a portrait above the mantel. The guy in it resembled a male version of my mother, dressed up in clothes I usually associated with the Pilgrims. He also looked like he might cut you for looking at him sideways, so that was consistent with the profound emotional instability that seemed to be my family's one defining trait.

"What a charmer," I said.

"Aye, charm and looks to spare, but that wasn't enough for him." Mrs. MacLeod stared at the flames. They caught her face and made it hollow, until I couldn't see her eyes, just black holes. "Connor sold half his land to a pair of brothers, Declan Ramsey and his younger brother, Sean. Irishmen with more money than sense. Declan was salt of the earth, but his brother was another story, a thief and a silver-tongued rogue. Sean had a pretty wife, Aislinn, and he left her a widow inside a year. Washed up on those rocks right below your window, dead as a doornail."

I hoped I looked encouraging, because this was actually halfway interesting. Mrs. MacLeod settled back with a sigh, and I leaned forward. "That's it? The brother died and the wife just hung around with her brother-in-law?"

Mrs. MacLeod waved her hand. "It's just the history of the island. Nothing so exciting as a film or even a ghost story. All the interesting bits are just hateful gossip the mainlanders spread over the years."

I tucked my feet under me. "I can get on board with hateful gossip. I know literally nothing about my family. When I had to fill in those genealogy trees in elementary school I'd use the alias names of superheroes." If you stick to the second-tier Justice League, it works pretty well. Barry Allen and Hal Jordan had each been my fake dad more than once.

Mrs. MacLeod sighed. "I'm only telling you so you'll understand what it means to be a part of this island. *Not* giving credence to silly stories." She pointed a stubby finger at me. "And don't repeat this to your uncle. The terrible things people over in town say about the family upset him."

I made the lip-zipping motion and she finally continued.

"Some say Sean Ramsey fell from the cliff in a storm. And some say Connor Bloodgood pushed him. Connor loved Aislinn, you see. She was a fair woman in a rough land, and that's a prize better than gold."

If Doyle was anything to go by, his great-great-whatever had been a looker, for sure. My dour-faced great-great-whatever with the crazy eyes hanging above the mantel was a serious downgrade. Poor Aislinn.

"Aislinn knew the old ways, the magic of the *daoine sídhe*," said Mrs. MacLeod. "That's the fairy folk back in the old country. White magic, likely just herbs and ways to ease childbirth and such. You could be called a witch for any damn thing back then." She pursed her lips, and I nodded encouragingly.

"It totally sucked being a woman in the olden times, got it."

"She was a good woman," Mrs. MacLeod said, "and she came to love Connor with all the force of her power. But Connor wanted more than Aislinn. He wanted the riches Sean Ramsey brought with him to the island, the money and the fine things the Ramseys got through their business on the mainland. Connor wanted more than that, always more."

"What a tool," I said, and Mrs. MacLeod flicked the poker toward me. "Sorry," I said. "I'm listening."

"Some say Connor Bloodgood made a pact with the devil," Mrs. MacLeod said. "Some say that the dark power was merely Aislinn whispering in his ear. But as he used Sean's nest egg to blackmail, kill, and steal his way into an earthly fortune, Aislinn's eye strayed. A mistreated woman's will, eventually. I don't blame her one bit." Mrs. MacLeod bit her lip, and I noticed the hand holding the poker was shaking, ever so slightly. "She came back to her former brother-in-law, Declan, and together they made plans to rob Connor of all the gold and riches he'd plundered from Sean's estate, to restore the Ramsey fortune. But when they arrived, the coffers were empty. Connor had hidden his wealth some-where on the island, somewhere only one of his bloodline could find it. Aislinn was with his child, you see. She could go back to life as his wife, rich beyond belief, trapped in a loveless marriage with a violent man. Or she could give up her child to be with Declan, and bear the disgrace of being an adulterer. Connor's rage forced her to make a terrible choice."

I didn't want to say anything now. All I could hear was the snap of the fire and the wind wailing outside.

Mrs. MacLeod shook her head. "In the end, she chose neither. She followed Sean Ramsey over those cliffs. Connor arrived in time to cut the baby out of her, but it was too late for his wife. With her dying breath, Aislinn cursed Connor. He wanted to possess both her and his wealth, so she cursed him to have one or the other but never at the same time. Every generation of Bloodgoods will either slay another or die by their own hand. Always wealthy, but always spilling blood to stay so. Always close to the one they love, but always forced apart by death. The Ramseys were destitute by comparison after Connor stole Sean's estate, but they never left this island, and the Bloodgoods never really let them be. Generations of bad blood, of killings and suicides and backhanded thieving, all because of one silly man and his selfishness over one poor woman who never asked for any of it. The Ramseys' fortune died out, but the Bloodgoods' only grew, to the point where it's rumored that Connor filled an entire cave with riches, starting with what he hid from

Aislinn. That part's bunk, obviously. Even if it existed, no amount of money could buy back the few moments of happiness that miserable man ever experienced." She sighed and looked at me. I realized my heart was pounding, and tried to act like the story hadn't bothered me. "And now you and Simon are the only Bloodgoods left. It's said when the line is broken, the curse will be ended, and your family can find peace at last."

My mouth was dry, and I licked my lips, my voice coming out a whisper. "So it only ends when we're all dead? You're saying you believe all of this?"

Mrs. MacLeod stood up, smoothing her hands over her denim shirt. "I'm not a Bloodgood, Ivy. I don't have to believe anything. But rest assured the Ramseys do. Even if you don't believe, your family and theirs have been feuding for so long that there's more than a few in their clan who would like nothing more than to see you dead."

Chapter
7

Simon didn't have a television, of course. I'd have been surprised if the manor even had a radio, since he and Mrs. MacLeod were clearly happy to live like they were Amish, passing the time by freaking me out with ghost stories.

I managed to find a library, which was mostly stocked with history books, all of them mildewed and dusty, and a shelf full of legal thrillers marked with *V. MacLeod* inside the flap.

I put them all back. I was bored, not stupid enough to take Veronica's property without asking. Besides, I couldn't stop thinking about her story, and even though I didn't believe in magic and curses and whatnot, I did wonder a little about the violent-death-and-murder part. Rather than poor Aislinn's curse, maybe there really was something wrong with all of us, something medicine at the time couldn't explain, and still couldn't.

It sure would explain a lot about Mom. And me.

Finally I found a trove of Dark Shadows novels. Set in Maine, the copy told me, based on the TV show, so I took an armload to my room. Vampires and witches and a campy Bela Lugosi–looking guy on the covers were about what I could handle right now. Silly vampire books were always easy to find at thrift stores and book sales, and I'd pretty much read them all at one time or another—*Interview with the Vampire*, *'Salem's Lot*, *I Am Legend*—if it involved blood drinking and brooding, it was the perfect distraction from real life.

Reading didn't work this time, though. When I was really upset, I couldn't focus on print or much of anything else. My solution used to be to go for a walk, but it was just before full dark outside. Gulls screamed, and I watched the black dots of their shapes track back and forth from the lighthouse as they wheeled over the sea.

Stupid gulls. They were free, able to fly away from here at will.

I threw the book back into the pile on the floor. Campy vampires weren't going to help me stop thinking about the weird shit that had started happening since I'd gotten to this island. About Doyle clearly knowing who I was before he met me, about my uncle, even that story about Aislinn and Connor.

I looked at the drawer of my nightstand and then sighed and yanked it open. Yeah, they held bad memories, but if I admitted it to myself, I knew why I'd kept the tarot cards. When I'd had bad dreams, my mother and I would look through the cards, at the major arcana, and she'd tell me the meanings and the stories, tracing the faded drawings with one of her thin fingers, nail spotted with the remains of black or purple or crimson polish until I drifted off again.

I could recite them in my sleep: the Fool, the Hanged

Man, the Tower, the Magician. One of the only times my mother used a calm voice, spoke to me like she cared, even held me if I'd had a really epic nightmare. Ignoring that her comforting me over a nightmare caused by her own actions was kinda fucked-up, I remember it as one of the few good times we had.

I pulled at the drawer again, but it wouldn't open wide enough to get at the cards. Damn damp manor house. I might as well live in a cave.

Reaching under the nightstand, I tried to knock the drawer loose. Instead, my fingers brushed cloth, and I pulled out a crumple of white fabric, jammed behind the drawer, hidden from all sight.

I knew what it was before my shaking fingers smoothed it out, but I still couldn't accept it. I stepped back like it was a snake, my foot kicking over the pile of books and sending paperbacks slithering around the room. It couldn't be, but it was, sitting on my bed, real as everything else in this ratty bedroom. This time, I was definitely awake.

The thing hidden in my nightstand was my tank top. And the front was covered in dried blood.

I grabbed the plastic bag out of the trash can beside my bed before I could spend time thinking things over. Like how my nightclothes were covered in blood, and how they'd gotten hidden. The tank top went in the bag, and I went out the door, making myself slow down and walk like I wasn't about to go find a place to dispose of what could easily be called evidence. Of what, I had no idea, but nothing good left you covered in that much blood that wasn't yours.

Once I was outside, I froze. The woods were out—after what had happened earlier, I couldn't risk one of the Ramseys seeing me. The landscaped gardens wouldn't work. I was sure Mrs. MacLeod watched the entire grounds like a hawk.

I didn't even consider telling anyone. Who would I tell? *Sorry, Simon, it turns out the delinquent teenage niece you took in out of the goodness of your heart is off hacking up woodland creatures, serial killer—style.*

At least I thought it was animal blood. It had to be— there was nobody unaccounted for on the island as far as I knew, unless you counted the dead guy in my dream, which I certainly didn't. And while my mother might have been convinced I was evil incarnate most days, homicidal blackouts would be a new wrinkle.

A gull screamed out over the water, and I headed for the steps to the beach, crumpling the bag between my fingers. Mrs. MacLeod had said the steps weren't safe, but if it were between breaking my leg and somebody finding the bloody shirt, I'd risk a limb any day. I didn't know either Simon or Veronica, not really. I had no idea how they'd react if they found this, except that it wouldn't be good. I wasn't ending up in juvie or some ward for disturbed teens, not when I was

so close to being on my own. Destroying the bloody cloth-
ing anywhere in or near the house was way too much of a
risk, given how damn nosy Mrs. MacLeod was. So I sucked
up my fear of the creaking steps and started down.

I would dispose of the tank top, I told myself. That was
step one. Step two was figuring out what the hell was going
on. One step at a time. That's how you keep from losing
your cool, panicking, and getting caught. Don't think too
far ahead.

I tested the first tread, and when it held my weight, I
picked my way down the cliff face. The beach was a good
fifty feet below me, and the stairs swayed with every step.
The wood was slick and rotten, and I clutched the railing.

One almost-fall and a bunch of splinters later, I found
myself on a small strip of rocky sand. The waves pounded
the cliffs around me, hollow booms that sounded like thunder. There was a cave entrance off to the right, and I headed
for it.

I couldn't even see the house anymore. It was just me, the
fog, and the waves. It was unsettling, to say the least, especially coming from places where you could see the horizon
in every direction.

I'd never thought I'd miss Kansas, or Minnesota, or New
Mexico—any of the places my mother dragged us—but it
had to be better than here.

I climbed up a flat rock at the cave entrance, perfectly

smooth like a table, with four smaller rocks set on top. There was even an indentation in the middle for some kind of fire pit. Maybe when the weather didn't suck, some long-ago owner of this place had actually had fun; picnics on the beach, back in the era of giant hats and those weird woolen bathing suits that went down to your shins.

I looked at the swirling tide pool before I slid down the other side of the rock, and that cold stole over me again. The wind was turning all my exposed skin numb, but this was more than that. Bad memories always made me cold, ever since the time my mother had shoved my head in the bathtub.

It caught me hard—black swirling water, salt in my mouth, cold bottomless ocean waiting to accept me and keep me.

I fell hard, landing on my butt inside the mouth of the cave, salt water soaking into my jeans. If my phobia of water had gotten to the point where I couldn't even look at it, I was sort of screwed. Maybe now that I had a rich relative, I could get some pills to help out with that.

Either way, I buried the tank top in a corner of the cave, deep under the sand and pebbles, down past where the tide would pull it out. My hands were red and my nails were bloody by the time I finished, but I breathed deep for the first time since I'd found the top in my drawer.

The climb back to the house was long and slow. I crept

back up to my room and stripped off my wet clothes. I showered to get warm, slapped some bandages on the worst of the cuts, and tried to come up with a convenient excuse if someone asked me what had happened. "Joined a fight club" was right out. Maybe Simon would believe I was just a really intense nail-biter?

I didn't need to worry, though—nobody bothered me, not even when I went back to the kitchen to forage for a real meal; after covering up evidence of a violent crime, another ham sandwich just would not cut it. Mrs. MacLeod had left a note on the kitchen table: *Gone to the mainland overnight for shopping. Please do not leave dirty dishes in the sink. Don't disturb Simon.*

The adrenaline had worn off a long time ago, and now I was more bored than anything.

I tossed what had happened earlier around in my head. Point in my favor: I'd never blacked out and lost time before. Point against: the shirt was definitely real, and something had definitely happened. But I'd never had any urge to kill anything. I didn't even eat the venison Mom's boyfriends brought home, if they hunted.

I couldn't even be *sure* it was blood. I'd freaked out and buried the thing—not exactly waited to do a lab test. It was dried stiff and felt a little sticky and looked like blood, but if I'd gotten that much on my shirt, there'd be some on me, on my shoes, *somewhere.*

Which circled back to the idea I was sliding into delusions or hallucinations. I didn't like that idea much, but technically it was better than covering myself in blood with no memory of it.

I groaned, and dumped the leftover casserole I'd found, minus a few bites, into the garbage. It was really terrible—I was almost nostalgic for truck stop hot dogs.

Before, I'd been able to stay busy to keep these thoughts away. There were parties to go to, people to hang out with, weekend trips if I knew somebody with a car. Even though my life with Mom kept us isolated in a way, in practice I'd spent very little of my life alone. Sharing a motel room or a bus-station bench or a tiny trailer with someone for sixteen years doesn't really equip you for the profound silence of an empty house.

I was about to sneak out and see if Doyle wanted to hang—he might be a certified weirdo, but I couldn't exactly be picky—when I saw someone leave the servants' entrance that I was supposed to use, to avoid embarrassing Simon in front of the nonexistent neighbors, and walk through the garden to the woods.

I scrambled to the window and peeked through the crack in the velvet drapes, which puffed dust into my face. The blond hair was familiar even in the moonlight, and I watched Simon disappear into the tree line. I had to get better about learning the sounds of this place. I didn't like thinking somebody could be creeping around within a couple of rooms of me and I'd have no idea. I'd figured Simon was upstairs, in his room. I hadn't even heard the outside door shut. Simon moved like a cat burglar. I waited about thirty seconds, until he wouldn't see me leave the house, and then followed him out the servants' door. It was truly freezing, now that the sun was down; I shoved my hands into my pockets, turning in a slow circle until I saw Simon's blond head bobbing through the trees.

This is weird, Ivy, even for you, I thought as I followed him. Simon was probably just taking a walk—he looked like the kind of dude who'd go for strolls around his estate.

But then why wasn't he wearing walking shoes? Or walking on a trail, or out in the open? Or, I don't know, doing this all in daylight instead of by the moon, with no flashlight?

I had an idea of where he was heading even before I heard the whisper of the stream that divided us from the Ramsey land.

Simon stopped at the end of the clearing, and I tucked myself behind one of the massive pine trees, feeling the damp bark scrape against my cheek and my palms.

A sliver of silver light peeked through the fog, and then it was dark again. Simon pulled out a small flashlight and checked his watch, sighing and picking at his jacket.

"You look more nervous than a jackrabbit in a dog run,"

said a voice from the other side of the stream. I watched a tall guy with silver hair emerge from the trees. He wore one of those padded jackets that hunters like, jeans, and a plaid shirt open at the neck. He was as huge and swarthy as Simon was skinny and pale, and he towered over my uncle.

"Liam," Simon said. "If it's all the same to you, why don't you tell me what you want? The less time I spend in your dog run the happier I'll be."

The Liam guy glared, taking a hard step toward Simon. I wondered if I was going to have to save my uncle from getting his ass kicked. Maybe that would help us bond.

"Neil's dead," he rumbled. "Something caught him while he was out rabbit hunting, and he's dead. You wouldn't know anything about that, would you, Simon?"

Simon rolled his eyes. "You mean when he was out poaching on my side of the island?"

Liam's face twisted up like a rough stretch of road, and he let out an actual growl, taking a step toward Simon. Simon held up a hand to halt him. "What reason would I have to hurt any of you? That would be like cutting my own throat."

"Well, *someone* did it," Liam snarled. "And I'm going to find out who."

"Clean up your own house, then," Simon said. "You know what kind of people your nephews deal with—or should I say try to rob and cheat. Neil never did know when to back off." He didn't seem to care that this Neil person was dead, whoever he was.

I wished I felt the same way. I was thinking about the bloody shirt again, about my dream of the dead guy in the clearing. At least that had been a dream. This wasn't the same clearing—the one I'd been in had been hacked out of the forest, it wasn't natural like this spot. And as much blood as it was, if I'd killed an actual person, there would be more.

If I'd killed a person, I told myself, I'd know. Simple as that. I trusted myself, if almost nobody else, and I knew what I'd seen had been a dream. And whatever the bloody shirt pointed to, it wasn't this Neil guy dying by my hand.

Simon turned to leave when Liam called out to him. "My boy met your niece today."

Simon stopped, his skinny shoulders bunching up. I pressed back into the shadows, afraid he'd spot me, but he spun around. "You tell your mutt of a son to stay away from Ivy."

"When Doyle listens to a word I say the sky will be falling," said Liam. "And the way I hear it, she trespassed."

"To trespass, she'd have to go somewhere that wasn't her birthright," Simon said. "And she doesn't know about all this. Not yet."

"You telling me everything, Simon?" Liam took another

step. "Is she going to play her part? Or do you have plans for her you're keepin' to yourself?"

Simon shook his head. "Your kind doesn't understand mine, and that's the way I like it. Keep Doyle away from her. I mean it."

He walked past me, and I had to dive to the ground when Liam shouted again. "We will find out what happened to Neil, Simon! You mark my words."

Simon smiled, and it wasn't a nice smile. It was thin and nasty, completely at odds with his bland, pasty face and the laid-back guy who'd given me tea. "Good luck with that, Liam," he said, and walked back toward the manor.

I waited until I couldn't hear Liam crashing through the trees anymore and then followed Simon, shivering from more than the cold wind.

Chapter
8

Simon knocked on my door a few minutes after I'd crept back inside and up to my room. He held out a steaming mug when I cracked it open. No china service this time, just a plain blue chipped coffee mug with faded yellow letters on the side. SMILE. That was rich.

"When I used to sneak out, I went down the old fire escape at the end of the hall," he said. "You're going to get tetanus on that trellis."

I took the mug, feeling my face turn red. At least my cheeks warmed up when it did. I wasn't used to normal people, people like Simon, who didn't scam and con people as a way of life, figuring me out.

"Not used to being the one on the spot, are you?" Simon invited himself in and sat in the little chair next to my vanity. I flinched seeing how close he was to the drawer where I'd found the bloody shirt but forced myself to stay calm. I hadn't done anything. I had nothing to feel guilty about.

"What gave me away?" I said. I tried the tea. It was some kind of herbal blend and stirred with enough sugar to give me type 2 diabetes.

"Myra was the same way," he said. "Always watching people. Hanging back. Getting a read on them so she'd know how to manip—how to act around them."

"She was manipulative," I said. "You can say it. I know

she played people. She would have been a crappy psychic if she wasn't."

Simon tried to smile, but it looked pained, like he'd just realized he was sitting on a pin. "I don't mean to imply she was malicious, Ivy, I really don't. She and I both had our share of baggage, even as kids. Growing up here wasn't easy. In a way, you're lucky you got out of it."

It was my turn to flinch. I managed not to pour the mug of hot tea on my uncle's head, so that was something. He had no idea, none at all, about what it was to grow up without enough food, without a real bed, knowing that acquiring those things depended at least partly on you. "Figured she left because she didn't get a pony for her birthday," I said, to cover the stab his words had aimed into me.

Simon's unpracticed smile turned back into a grimace. "Trust me, Ivy, there are dark places even in lives that look perfect from outside. If your mother didn't tell you much about her past, I have to assume she had her reasons." He stood, smoothing the wrinkles from his khakis. "Have a good evening."

I wanted to stop him, to blurt out everything she'd done, starting with the bathtub. I wanted to hurt Simon like he'd just hurt me.

But I fought the impulse. I had more control than that. I had, after all, had a great teacher. Whatever else Mom was, she never ever miscalculated and got emotional when she was dealing with people outside our family.

"I'm tired," I said. "I'll probably just go to bed."

Simon came back and patted me on the shoulder. His grip was firmer than I expected from his spindly arm and hand. "Of course you are," he said. "I'll leave you be. And, Ivy?"

He paused in my open door, and I kicked off my boots, letting my sore feet and general exhaustion win out over the shit fit Mrs. MacLeod would surely throw when she saw the mud on my floor. "Yeah?" I said, flopping backward on the bed.

"Next time you're tempted to follow me, don't," he said. "The Ramseys don't like our family, they like outsiders even less, and they're firmly dedicated to the second amendment." He brushed his hand across his forehead, putting his glasses askew. "Liam Ramsey is a paranoid hillbilly who thinks the government listens in on everyone and is out to get him specifically, and the rest of his family isn't much brighter."

"I get it," I said. "Although, technically the government does listen in on everyone."

"Go to sleep," Simon said. "Julia will be here at seven to take you over to get registered at the high school. I filled out all the forms online, so all you have to do is show up."

I expected to have a terrible time falling asleep after everything—with the bloody shirt, and what I'd overheard about Neil, and Simon turning out to be way more observant than I'd calculated—but I'd barely flicked off my light when sleep hit me like one of the waves pounding the cliffs below my window, pulling me deep into its undertow and blessedly shutting off my thoughts for the night.

Chapter

9

Cold crept up and wrapped me from head to toe. It kissed my bare skin, and left crystal droplets in my hair and eyelashes that glimmered like tears when I opened my eyes.

I was barefoot, wearing gym shorts and a thin T-shirt that didn't stand up to the bone-deep chill all around me. Sharp points scraped against my heels, and I made the mistake of looking down.

Nothing was under me. I could see straight to the bottom of the cliffs, or at least to the blackness where the bottom should be. The water hissing between the rocks drifted up to my ears. The only thing holding me up was a rusty iron balcony, floor studded with small points to keep someone from slipping and plunging into the ocean.

My toes were on the edge. If I looked straight ahead, I could see the lit windows of the manor, glowing amid the fog as if the entire house were floating.

Everything in me stopped, from blood to breath. For a second I just stood there, like a dumb cartoon coyote right before she realizes the road has run out and goes splat off the cliff.

Then it all came rushing back in a wave of panic. "Oh shit," I whispered, afraid anything louder than exhaling would dislodge me and send me tumbling. "Oh shit, oh shit, oh shit . . ."

I felt myself start to sway as a gust of wind buffeted the lighthouse. It whined through the broken panes surrounding the giant light bulbs, and a tear slipped out of my eye as my vision ricocheted wildly from the rocks below to the silver-bellied clouds above.

There wasn't time to ask how I'd gotten here. I was going to fall. I was going to die.

There was no way except straight down. The platform swayed and creaked when I so much as shifted my weight, and the wind threatened to peel me off the platform. Even the ground on the back side of the lighthouse, facing away from the cliff drop, had to be forty feet down.

I was stranded, as far away from help as if I'd been on the moon.

I blanked out then, from the gut-wrenching but not unfamiliar feeling of being one step from death. I tried to twist my neck and look behind me for a way back into the lighthouse—the way I must have come up—but all I saw was the sheen of shattered glass in the moonlight, the huge panes encasing the beacon lamp reflecting my terrified eyes back at me from a hundred jagged angles.

"Help," I tried. My voice didn't even rise to my own ears over the howling wind. "Help me. . . ."

I was shaking so hard I was worried I'd plunge off the

platform no matter how I tried to stay put, and my mind started to jump frantically, like a jittery screen catching flashes of picture through static.

I could hear my own screams inside my head, not from now, standing in the cold, but from a long time ago, walking along a rainy sidewalk in Portland, Oregon. Mom dragged our duffel bag and her sack of tarot cards, candles, and all the other set dressing she used in her act. I hauled her folding chair. We'd made almost sixty bucks with her fortune-teller act, and I'd pulled two credit cards from women who left giant, gaping purses slumped next to them while Mom stroked their palms and told them what they wanted to hear.

"Will you look at this crap, now," Mom said, pointing at a short woman hunched over a folding table. We were at a farmers market–, street fair–, hipster walkabout–type place that Portland had everywhere on the weekends. This woman didn't fit in. She was old, and not in the soft, friendly hippie way most of the older women who worked the fake fortune-teller circuit were. She looked like she'd seen some stuff, face all lined, eyes bright as beads and sunken into her head like one of those apple dolls. Her hair was white streaked with black, like dirty snow, and wrapped in a faded red scarf.

Mom snorted. "Fake Gypsies are so old-school," she said, shouldering her bag again. Mom was a great cold reader—

she could take one look at you and tell you all sorts of stuff that sounded like she must have an inside track to all the bullshit psychic powers she claimed. But I thought she was wrong this time. The woman at the table was flipping plain playing cards, one after the other, playing the fastest game of solitaire I'd ever seen. Her scarf wasn't affected—it was as faded and old as the rest of her. Her skin was dark and weathered, and I thought she probably wasn't a fake but the real thing—a Romani who'd somehow ended up reading cards for yuppies on a rainy street corner.

"I'm hungry," I said, wanting to change the subject. I didn't want Mom's poisonous tongue turned on this old lady, who clearly had enough shit to deal with. Mom shrugged, like, *What do you want me to do about that?*, and walked on. I would have followed her, except the old woman looked at me. I don't mean glanced up to see if I was a mark or on the job like her, but looked at me, burned a hole right through me with her black eyes.

"You," she whispered, almost like she was telling me a secret. Her hands faltered and stopped on her cards. "You can't see darkness, but it's all around you." Her accent was sharp and from somewhere in the neighborhood of Brooklyn, not Eastern Europe like I'd guessed, but no matter where she was from, that didn't change the fact she made me intensely uncomfortable.

I glared at her. *She's just trying to scare you,* I told myself.

It's just a hard sell, and it doesn't work, because marks don't like feeling scared.

"Well, could you tell the darkness to back off?" I asked. "Because I need to go with my mother."

She moved so fast she almost jerked me off my feet, grabbing my wrist and pulling me to her. The cards went flying all over the sidewalk, fluttering around me like dead birds.

"You and your mother are fakes, but I'm not," she grated. "And I tell you, death will come for you three times. Once in your past and twice more in your future."

"Lady, *back off!*" I snapped, pulling away. I was a lot bigger than her, but she had one of those wiry old-lady grips that's like a handcuff. The big glass globe sitting on her folding table fell off and shattered on the sidewalk as we struggled.

"I'm trying to help you!" the woman barked. "You're just a girl, you don't deserve what's coming!"

"Hey!" Mom dropped our bag and ran back to me, trying to wrestle us apart. My legs tangled with hers, and I fell. I could have told her not to bother; the old woman, who looked frail, was Hulk strong.

She shoved Mom off, sending her sprawling on her butt, and then grabbed my hand again so it was palm up, snatching one of the shards from her glass globe with her free hand. Before I could even react, she'd scratched an X into my palm, deep enough that the pain made my eyes water and that my blood flowed freely, like I'd dipped my hand in a jar of red paint. "That's a mark against the evil eye," she hissed in my ear as I yelped in pain. "Use it to ward off what's coming."

"Get away from my daughter, you crazy bitch!" Mom screamed, taking the old woman to the ground, slapping and clawing at her. The old woman's scarf came off and her hair spilled out, soaking up rainwater.

Somebody in the crowd let out a long whistle, universal grifter signal for "Cops!" Mom and the woman let go of each other, panting, and Mom pulled herself up, grabbing her stuff.

"You are fucking dead, I see you again," Mom snarled at the old woman. "I mean it."

Mom grabbed me with her free hand and pulled me along, the two of us fading into the crowd as a pair of Portland bike cops came flying up. I looked back once at the old woman as Mom dragged me away toward the Greyhound station. She still lay on the ground, breathing hard, cheeks red. Her clothes and hair were soaked and clung to her skinny body. She looked wispy and defeated, but when she locked eyes with me I could still feel her words echoing inside my head.

Use it to ward off what's coming.

I walked behind Mom, hand wrapped in her pajama bottoms to the stop the bleeding, still dragging the chair with my good arm, and feeling numb. She made me wait until we got all the way to Ashland to get stitched up in a free clinic, and in the intervening few years, the X-shaped scar had smoothed and faded, but it was still there.

That was the same numb feeling I had now, the feeling of being so completely cut off from anything I recognized as real that I couldn't begin to think my way out of it. Usually I was good at that—getting myself out of trouble, but that was regular trouble. Getting caught shoplifting, forging excuse notes, boosting Mom's boyfriend's Chevelle and driving it out to the desert when Mom and I lived in New Mexico to get drunk and smoke pot around a bonfire with the other burnouts and losers from my latest school.

I heard a sound behind me, a voice.

"Ivy, don't move."

Doyle.

I tipped and felt one foot slide off the edge of the platform.

For a heartbeat, I touched nothing, suspended in the air as I finally lost my balance and fell. Then a scream ripped out of me as Doyle's hand clamped on my arm. He pulled me toward him, but it was too late. We plunged together, and the ground flew at us. The roaring of the waves blended with the roaring in my ears, and I went limp, waiting for the impact.

There was none. I hadn't moved. Doyle and I had tipped back, landing hard on the iron deck, me on top of him. Doyle's skin was fever-hot against mine, clammy and burning.

He coughed. "I told you not to move."

I rolled off him, staring down at him as he winced, a thin trail of blood working its way from the corner of his mouth. "God, why did you do that?" I groaned.

"I might not have if I'd known you were going to flip the fuck out when I touched you," he grunted, pushing himself up and swiping at his bloody lip. "What the hell were you doing up here in the first place?"

I tried to help him up, but I was shaky and he was sweaty and I lost my grip. He sat down hard again and let out a moan, clutching at his side.

"I'm sorry," I said. My voice had gone from nothing to sounding awful and bellowing inside my own head. The world still spun slowly, as the adrenaline from my imaginary fall worked its way out of me. "I don't know what happened. I woke up, and I was on the ledge. . . ." I started shaking and couldn't stop. I thought I was going to chip my teeth, they were rattling so hard. My vision tunneled down until all I could see were my muddy toes, which had started to turn blue.

"Sounds like you were taking a little midnight stroll courtesy of the Ambien fairy," Doyle muttered. He stripped off his heavy canvas jacket and wrapped it around me, rubbing my arms until I stopped shaking. "I'll get you home," he said.

I stayed quiet as we picked our way back down the rusty

metal stairs of the lighthouse, Doyle's boots making a booming clang that got my head throbbing again.

"I don't take sleeping pills," I said once we were outside and I could see the faint porch light on the back side of the manor sending out a struggling halo in the mist kicked up from the waves below the cliffs.

"Well, maybe you should," Doyle said. "Avoid any more sleepy-time adventures." I started to tell him that, no, he didn't understand, I could sleep like a rock anywhere—a bus, the back seat of a car, a motel with paper-thin walls where you could hear every inhale and exhale of the people in the next room, but he grabbed me before I could.

I let out a sound I wasn't proud of—I'd like to say it was a yelp but it was more of a ladylike squeak, the kind an actual lady would let out if a mouse ran across her foot. "Easy," Doyle grunted. I could tell his ribs were bothering him, but he slung me up in that damsel hold guys do, like I weighed less than nothing. "Rocks are sharp," he said by way of explanation. "Don't need to bloody your feet on top of the night you've had."

Normally I'd fight, as much as I hated being touched, but I couldn't muster the strength. Nor did I want to—my legs were rubbery and my calves screaming from the trip up and down the hundred lighthouse steps, and my feet were already bruised from the metal deck. As the shock of waking up drained out of me, I felt my eyelids fluttering, and I tucked my head against the warmth of Doyle's chest.

"What are you doing over here?" I asked him as he deposited me under the sagging roof of the manor's back porch. The granite blocks that made up the floor were wet and freezing, but smooth enough that they soothed the pain in my feet.

"I can't sleep." Doyle shrugged. I handed back his jacket, and he tucked it under his arm. "I like to walk at night. It's peaceful. You feel like you're the only person in the woods." He flashed me a grin. In the half-light, I could see only the white of his teeth. "Except the cursed ghosts of all the Bloodgoods buried on the island, that is."

I wrapped my arms around myself, chilled all over again. "You're freaking hilarious with that crap. You afraid I'm going to wig out and kill you?"

"Nah," Doyle said. "Your family's crazy, but the last couple of generations have leaned more toward offing themselves, like your grandmother."

I blinked at him. "What?"

Doyle took a step back. "Shit. You didn't know?"

I spread my arms. I wasn't so cold anymore, my heart pounding. "At the risk of sounding like a broken record, know what?"

"Never mind," Doyle said. "That is really not my place to tell you. You should get inside. You'll catch a cold being out here."

He backed off the porch and ran, slipping past the hedge-row and turning into a slice of darker space against the darkness before he vanished from my eyes entirely.

I huffed out a breath that clouded in front of my eyes, shaking my head as I tried the back door. It was locked, but I found a loose window in the laundry room and popped the old-fashioned latch, sliding it up and climbing inside.

I landed in a heap next to a basket of clean sheets, just glad I hadn't landed in them. The last thing I needed capping off a night of sleepwalking to my death was Mrs. MacLeod having a conniption about dirt on her laundry.

I made myself get up again and tried to wobble back to my room. I couldn't even start to process what Doyle had said—although if my grandmother *had* killed herself, it was hardly a surprise. Whatever was off-kilter about Mom's chemistry could be genetic. With my luck the same time bomb was ticking away in my own head. I'd had all the psych tests—you get shrinked a lot when you're the troubled child of an itinerant single mother—and nothing too weird had shown up, but who knew? Underpaid school psychologists weren't exactly brilliant profilers. You can't even be diag-nosed with a lot of stuff until you turned eighteen. I knew from my reading I was right at the age when a lot of schizo-phrenic people had their first breakdown. And here I was, losing time and sleepwalking and seeing things— *No*, I told myself sternly. I had already decided that was just a dream.

Either way, whatever the truth, it was too much for me right then. My sight wavered, and I collapsed right there on the kitchen floor, feeling the cool kiss of linoleum on my face before I passed out.

Chapter
10

Simon shook me awake. He was wearing a blue satin robe with gold trim and pajamas that looked like he might have hit up Truman Capote's estate sale. He sat back in relief when I opened my eyes. "I wasn't sure if you'd hit your head."

"I . . ." Sunlight made me crinkle up my face. My head hurt. Everything hurt. And I was covered with rust and grime, feet caked in sandy mud. Almost like I'd run to the top of a five-story building and had then been tackled to a hard surface by the nosy neighbor boy . . .

"Did someone do this to you?" Simon helped me sit up and went to the stove, rattling around pots with an unholy clatter.

"No," I said. I covered my eyes, massaging my forehead. I'd had hangovers before, but at least I usually got to have fun first. "It was just a stupid accident," I said. Once my head stopped throbbing and I stopped seeing halos any time I opened my eyes, I'd figure out exactly what sort of accident I'd purportedly had to explain this situation. Now I just pulled my knees to my chest and groaned.

Simon started water boiling and then took a first aid kit out of a cabinet. "Care to elaborate?"

"I . . . uh . . . tangled with an angry possum? You have those on the island, right?" I flinched. The last twelve hours were really messing with my ability to lie.

"Cute," Simon said. He soaked a pad in antiseptic and swiped at the cuts on my hands and forehead.

"Ow!" I jerked my arm away but not fast enough. Simon frowned at the scratches, turning my arm back and forth in his thin, cold fingers. I realized there was an outline of a hand where Doyle had yanked me away from the ledge, and I shut my eyes, waiting for Simon to freak. Right on cue, he did.

"Did Doyle Ramsey do this to you?" he demanded.

I blinked. That sure was a fast jump. I guessed the animosity Doyle had for my uncle was mutual. "No, he didn't. I would have been really hurt if he hadn't grabbed me. He was trying to hold on to me, not harm me."

I didn't want to rat Doyle out for trespassing, but I figured that was better than Simon thinking he was some kind of maniac who'd attacked me.

"And just why the hell were you outside in the middle of the night?" Simon demanded.

Or maybe Doyle wasn't the one I needed to worry about.

"I, uh . . ."

Simon held up his hand. "I wanted to give you time to settle here. Feel like you could stay in one spot for more than a few months at a time. But if it's already happening . . ."

"What?" I shouted. My head kicked like a mule in

response and I winced. "What is going on here? What is everyone afraid to say to me?"

Simon sighed and pulled out a chair at the kitchen table. "Sit," he said when I didn't move. I hauled myself into the chair, whimpering softly as I sat and agitated a whole new group of cuts and bruises. Simon got a couple of chippy mugs and a little silver ball that he packed full of tea. "Earl Grey all right?" he asked. I shrugged.

"Doyle didn't do anything wrong," I said again. "I was sleepwalking. He tried to help me."

Simon pursed his mouth up. He looked so parental, even after two days. Disapproving and about to chew my ass out. "The last thing the Ramseys want to do is help you, Ivy." He took the tea strainer away and blew on his cup.

"I'm getting the sense that's the last thing you want too," I said, staring at him. "Or you'd tell me the truth right now instead of making tea."

Simon smiled in response. The light caught his glasses and reflected two Ivys back at me. I looked like crap. I was scratched up all over my cheeks, smeared with dirt, and I had sticks in my hair.

"You're a lot like your mother," he said. "Resilient to the core."

"That's not the word I'd pick for her," I muttered, taking a sip of tea. It was hot and bitter, but it warmed me up, so I downed it.

"Ivy, there are people and things in this world that fall outside the understanding of the average person," Simon said. "Such as our family. That curse the locals whisper about may be a fairy tale, but there is something in our blood that leads to madness. A particular kind of madness. It comes on in late adolescence, and it . . . well." He licked his lips. "Needless to say, I was relieved when it passed me over and devastated when it consumed my sister."

I put my mug in the sink and ran water over my scratches, the blood dissolving and running down the drain, staining the spotless porcelain pink. "Okay," I said, turning back to my uncle. "I get that there's something seriously fucked-up swimming in our gene pool. If you could just fill me in using small words, that'd be awesome."

Simon wrinkled his nose at my swearing, but he stood and faced me. "I'm afraid I don't know a great deal more. Myra left before doctors could do much work with her, and in our parents' day mental-health problems weren't much talked about . . ." He trailed off and spread his hands. "All I know is it doesn't correspond to any disorder in the *DSM*, it doesn't respond to medication, and it tends to affect the women more than men. My sister—your mother—was the worst in a long while. But I never believed she'd do harm to anyone except herself, and I'm glad to see I was right."

I wanted to tell him how wrong he was, to pick up the mug I'd just rinsed and smash it. I didn't, though. I just stood there shaking, even though the radiator in the corner was hissing and clanging as it poured out waves of warmth.

"I wanted to ease you into this, keep an eye out for any signs before I even brought it up or scheduled any doctors' appointments for you," said Simon. "But Doyle Ramsey made that impossible. His whole family are animals. They loathe us, and you *cannot* trust them."

"Is the loathing because of the whole penchant-for-murder thing that runs in our family?" I said. Simon grunted.

"In the 1940s, my grandfather—your great-grandfather— walked to the other side of the island. He picked up a hatchet from the Ramseys' woodpile and he massacred everyone in the house. Everyone except Liam's father, Colin, who was just a boy at the time. The police eventually found my grandfather dead in the ruins of the original Ramsey mansion. My mother was also just a girl, and she was never the same after what her father did. She went looking for him the morning after the murders. She saw what he'd done. She was the one to wash the blood off Colin Ramsey and the one to wait for the boat to the mainland, to fetch the police. She was all of twelve years old."

Both of us went quiet. Only the radiator kept up its clanging, like tiny hands hammering to be let in. "My grandfather was insane, and it wasn't anyone's fault but his, but you coming here has stirred up a lot of issues for Liam, to say the least," Simon murmured at last. "And now with that drunk idiot nephew of his, Neil, turning up dead . . . Stay away from the Ramseys, Ivy. I mean it. Just because we share this island doesn't mean they won't decide to take out on you what a Bloodgood did all those years ago."

I stayed quiet. Doyle didn't seem so bad—he had saved me from being a human pancake, after all—but I wasn't about to start a fight with Simon when he was finally being open with me.

"You can ask me anything, even though I don't know much," Simon said, picking up his tea. "We can discuss this more later as well, but right now I need to continue my morning, and you should go shower and get ready for school."

"Am I for sure going crazy?" I whispered. I thought again of just telling him about Neil and the bloody shirt and my inability to shake the feeling I'd done something really terrible. The bottom line was he was being honest for now, but I'd known him less than a week. I'd be an idiot to trust him with something like that when I wasn't even sure what happened.

Simon gave a sad shrug. "I don't know, Ivy. Your mother went through something very similar, starting around your age. All we can do is wait, watch, and hope."

That was a bullshit answer, and we both knew it, but I decided to let it slide. I'd had enough information thrown at me for me one sucky morning. The second thing he'd said registered with me, and I cocked my head. "You seriously expect me to go to school now?"

"I seriously do," my uncle said, picking up a newspaper from the table and tucking it under his arm. "Today and every other school day. The boat leaves in an hour."

Chapter

II

Mrs. MacLeod was silent when she returned the next morning and drove me to the boat, which was good, because I had no clue what to say to her. I held my old leather book bag close on the boat ride over, like I hadn't since the fifth grade.

When the boat pulled up at the town pier and I saw the beat-up school bus waiting, I made my fingers relax. I wasn't going to be the weirdo new kid, especially at whatever hillbilly high school they had going on in the town of Darkhaven, which from what I could see looked small, ugly, and run-down, like a million other rotted-out, zombie-apocalypse-by-way-of-Norman-Rockwell towns in the poor and rural corners of the country. I made a point of either fitting in or not giving a crap at the schools I went to, sometimes monthly if Mom was feeling restless. It was a lot easier than sparring with every bully and mean girl in whatever fresh hell our constant moving around landed me in.

A crowd of kids was getting off the big white ferry that came from some other island, where I bet they had the internet and nobody tried to murder anybody. They were all laughing and jostling. Tight friend group. Best to not even try to infiltrate those.

I was the only person getting off a private boat, and I

sped up to be the first one on the bus. The driver barely looked at me. I sat in the back and put in my earbuds. I didn't turn on my music, but at least it kept anyone from doing more than stare.

We stopped at a long string of weathered farmhouses and crappy little one-story cracker boxes, collecting more kids. The only one who sat next to me was a guy in a hoodie that had Pikachu ears. He spent the entire ride farting.

In sight of the school, we paused at a cluster of rusty little trailers—not double-wides, which I knew well, but the kind that looked like space pods from an old sci-fi movie. They were all more brown than silver, and laundry flapped sadly from a line strung between them.

A girl came flying out the door of the closest and jogged to the bus, getting there just as we started to pull out. She stumbled down the aisle and flopped into the seat directly ahead of me.

"Hi!" She stuck out her hand, and I blinked at it. "I'm Elizabeth. Elizabeth Tyler. Not Taylor. Everyone calls me Betty."

"I didn't know this was a garbage truck," said a female voice from a few rows up. "But sure enough, we just stopped to pick up trash."

I looked back at Betty's hand. The last thing I needed was being seen making best friends with the school reject.

But she looked so hopeful, like a cute, dumb puppy. Maybe I was still punchy from the night before, but I gave her a nod. "I'm Ivy."

"That's a pretty name! Are you new? I'm new. I mean, we moved here over the summer, but this is my first year of school. I'm a junior. I skipped a grade. My dad is a mechanic. Boats mostly. My brother works at the Bay View, that restaurant on stilts down by the pier. I worked there too, but I quit because of school. Where are you from?"

The bus jerked to a stop, and I held up my hands. "Betty, if we're going to be friends, you are gonna have to take it down at least three notches. Okay?"

She nodded, smiling happily. "Sorry! I know I talk a lot. My mom used to say I could talk the hind leg off a horse. She's dead. My mother, not the horse. I'm allergic to horses and most large livestock."

A burst of laughter erupted from the same seats as we all got our stuff and shuffled off the bus. I shot a redheaded girl a glare that could strip paint. Loser or not, laughing at someone's dead mom is shitty. If Ginger up there had been laughing at me in Betty's spot, she'd be missing a big chunk of that hair and probably a few teeth, but it wasn't my job to protect other people from the queen bee and her squad. If Betty wanted to handle it passively, that was her business. I still glared, though. Just to make sure Ginger knew I didn't like her.

"What are you gonna do?" she said as we started up the wide stone steps of the school. "Cast a spell on me?" Her evil little pod of girl-thugs snickered.

"If I do, the first one will make all of your snaggleteeth fall out," I said. "Which would actually be doing you a favor, since it'd detract from the freckles—oh no, sorry. My bad. Those are pimples."

Girls like her are everywhere. They're just insecure and paranoid, like most teenagers who are middle class enough to have no real problems and live in towns small enough where things like who's the prettiest girl at the prom still matter. I stopped worrying about them at least five schools ago.

I thought I might shake Betty in the crowd, but she was right there with me, like a chirpy shadow or an incompetent stalker. "I can't believe you talked to Valerie like that. What did she mean by *cast a spell*? I hope she doesn't decide to pour bleach in my locker again."

"People in this backwater apparently think my family made a pact with Satan for evil powers," I said. "And I thought you said you were new. How can you already have a nemesis?"

"Summer school," Betty said. "We move a lot, and I was really behind. Valerie was here for extra credit. She wants to be a doctor. We got along this summer, but when her real friends came back from vacation she decided she hated me."

"Where's the office in this place?" I broke in. Darkhaven High was in an old building, the high ceilings and stained glass mostly hidden under gross linoleum floors, harsh lights, and dented, rusty lockers. A faded football banner hanging in the front hall proclaimed it was the *Home of the Moose.*

I'd been a Wolverine, a Jayhawk, a Patriot, and, memorably, a Fightin' Bearcat, but those schools had at least picked team names that used plurals. What were we collectively? Mooses? Mooseii?

"I'll show you!" Betty was clearly gearing up for another string of non sequiturs, so I cut her off.

"Just tell me."

She pointed mutely to a wavy glass door, and I ran for it before she could start talking again. "I'm Ivy Bloodgood," I said to the secretary. "My uncle registered me late, so I don't have a schedule."

She harrumphed but looked me up in her computer and gave me a schedule, my locker combination, and a student handbook. "Sit there until I can find someone to show you your homeroom," she said, and went back to pecking on her keyboard.

"I'll take her." I snapped my head up and saw Doyle looking down at me. This day just couldn't get any better. Maybe a meteor would smash through the roof and squash me, or the undead would rise from their graves and school would be canceled. That was the only way it'd improve at this point.

"Fine," said the secretary. I followed Doyle back into the hall. He gave me a sideways glance as we walked and then sighed.

"You want to talk about what happened?"

"Hey," I said. "I get it. My great-grandfather murdered your grandfather's family, vendettas, curses—it's all a big party on Darkhaven Island. And while you're at it, you don't have to tap-dance around my grandmother's suicide. Very sweet of you and all, but as a person with now two female relatives dead by their own hand, it just makes me feel even more like there's something wrong with me when people act like that. Not saying it can't change what happened."

"I meant about you," Doyle said. "You were on top of the lighthouse. I thought you were about to jump."

I stopped and stared at him, feeling flush creep up my face. "No! I was sleepwalking. I wasn't . . ." I trailed off, words eaten up in a tangle. I wasn't somebody who threw herself off towers. I didn't have the demons my mother did. I was strong; she was weak. That's why I was here and she wasn't.

After the last few days, that was patently crap, but I sure wasn't showing any cracks to Doyle. Emotionally unstable mopey girls don't fit in, don't get anything but ridicule or pity, and I was not letting myself in for a year of stares, whispers, and eating lunch with only Betty for company.

"I'm just glad you're all right," Doyle said. "And I'm glad I was there. And I'm sorry. About your grandmother, and your mom too. You're right—people don't talk about shit they should say out loud, and it's crap."

I lifted my chin. He was tall, but so was I. I looked into his eyes. "Thank you," I said. "To set the record straight, I was not and am not trying to kill myself."

"Good to know," he said. "I'll sleep better knowing I don't have to repeat that lighthouse gig. I hate heights."

"Why *were* you there?" I said. "Walking at night, fine, but trespassing in my backyard?"

Doyle cocked his head, a smile breaking out. His whole face warmed up when he smiled, and went from hard, carved chin, cheeks, and nose to something you could touch, someone you could trust. "Come on. Like you've never broken a rule?"

I tilted my head. "You just happen to show up when I'm about to sleepwalk myself off a creepy old lighthouse," I said. "If I was a suspicious sort of person, I'd wonder if you had known what was going to happen."

Doyle let out a low, skin-prickling chuckle. "Your side of the island has the best view out over the water. I like to stand on the cliffs and watch the mainland at night. And while we're at it, you're welcome."

"I'm grateful you saved me from falling," I said. "But that doesn't mean I trust you."

The bell rang, and the halls cleared out. We were suddenly all alone, and Doyle took a step closer. "You're going to have to trust someone sometime, Ivy."

"What the hell's that supposed to mean?" I whispered. "I'm not that easy to scare, so either say something real or leave me alone."

Doyle's eyes went dark. "Fine. You want specifics? You need to leave. Today, if possible. Don't get back on the boat. Go to the bus station and get out of town."

"Uh, yeah, I'll just skip town with my Black Card and trust fund," I said. "Get real, Max."

He looked confused, and I sighed. For a guy who played at being Mr. Coolest and Smartest, he sure didn't know much. "Max, the creepy guy from *Rebecca*? It was a movie and a book. I've decided that's your nickname."

"I'm serious." Doyle pulled me close, but after last night, when that closeness had kept me from falling to my death, I didn't mind it as much as I had before. "Darkhaven isn't the place for you, Ivy. Please, please find somewhere else to go before it's too late for you too. You must have some other family you can stay with."

"No, actually," I said. "This is it for me. And you still haven't told me *what* I'm in danger from. The only one here who's made me uncomfortable so far is you, Doyle."

He sighed. "It's not like that. I'm trying to help you. Save you, even."

"Look, sleepwalking up a lighthouse aside, I'm not really in the 'needs saving' category," I said. "And even if my uncle is freaky weird, considering it's here or foster care, I'm gonna be staying, if that's all right with you."

A teacher carrying a sheaf of test booklets approached us and glared at Doyle over his glasses. "Get to class, Mr. Ramsey. This is not the way you want to start a new year."

"Sure thing, Mr. Armitage," Doyle said with a wide, white smile. "Dick," Doyle muttered when he moved on. "Armitage is a total hard-ass. I gotta go, but promise me you'll at least be careful around your uncle?"

"Because let me guess, he's really part of a blood-drinking sacrifice cult and the whole nerd thing is an act to keep me around until the next full moon?" I said.

"You were the one who wanted a reason to go," Doyle snapped. "I gave you one."

"No, you actually gave me nothing except more reasons to think you're a super-extra weirdo," I muttered as Doyle jogged off down the corridor. He never did show me which homeroom was mine. I wasn't going to run away, like he'd so charmingly suggested, but I decided I could use my time off the island to figure out some stuff about my family, find some answers that came from an impartial source. I scooted into the homeroom my schedule identified and took a seat as the bell rang.

This day wasn't any different than my other first days. Homeroom was in a dusty high-ceilinged classroom with old maps pasted all over the walls and giant windows that looked down a hill to the harbor. If the fog hadn't rolled in, I could have seen Darkhaven Island. I moved from class to class, sat in the back when I could, and tried not to talk.

The lunchroom had the wood paneling and weird cherub-infested wallpaper of a formal parlor, and the sticky orange tables bolted to the floor made the place look like the day room at Arkham Asylum. Doyle was sitting in the far corner with a group of other tall, good-looking boys, and I watched Valerie sashay from the steam table with a tray and sit on his lap.

"They're dating." Betty landed beside me like an unwanted hummingbird. "Have been since last spring fling. She told me all about it when we were friends. He won't let her meet his family. Apparently they're like hermits or repulsives or something."

"Recluses," I said.

Betty stuffed a tater tot in her mouth and shrugged. "Isn't it weird, though? All of them out there on that island?"

"It's not too weird," I lied. "I live out there."

"Shut the front door!" she exclaimed, the shortest sentence she'd managed yet. It didn't last—she peppered me with questions for the rest of lunch. I told the truth where I could, and lied when I couldn't. Betty ate it up, clearly so grateful to have *anyone* talk to her she was practically vibrating.

I looked at Valerie and Doyle again. She brushed the hair off his forehead and smiled down at him, while he grinned like having a hot girl in his lap was the way every lunch period went. It probably was. If I'd met Doyle for the first time today, I'd have rolled my eyes so hard at the sexy-alpha-male-jock routine.

"Do you have TV? Do you have electricity?" Betty said. I looked back, frowning at both her and what passed for lunch in this place. The tater tots looked radioactive, and for all I knew, the shapeless lump of casserole could have been made from people.

"Yes, Betty, we have electricity," I said. "This isn't *Pride and Prejudice*."

"I love that book," she sighed.

I zoned out again, unable to keep from sneaking looks at Doyle. According to my schedule and the dog-eared book sticking out of Doyle's backpack under his lunch table, we had one class together—world literature, taught by the aforementioned hard-ass, Mr. Armitage, who right that second exited the steam line and came at me like a tweed-covered missile. He looked down at me over his half glasses as he dropped a copy of *Jane Eyre* on our lunch table.

"You, new girl. Have you read this before?"

"Yeah," I said, ruffling the dog-eared pages.

"Good," said Armitage. "I had the other students preread over summer break, so plan to refresh yourself by tomorrow. For today, just sit in the back and be quiet."

He stalked in the direction of the teachers' lounge, and I had to agree with Doyle—this guy was a dick. My opinion of him didn't improve in class that afternoon. Armitage spent a minute slamming the sliding blackboards around and then turned on us. I looked over at Doyle, but he was grinning at Valerie, so I turned around again. It wasn't like he had to talk to me. Just because he'd saved me from falling didn't make us best friends. I tried not to let that sting. Being ignored is never awesome, even if I wasn't entirely sure where I stood with Doyle.

Not that I was gonna cry about it. "Some boy ignored me" was wayyyy down my list of current problems. I didn't need a boyfriend distracting me this year, anyway—I needed to graduate on time, so I could get a job and save up money for the few months between the end of high school and me turning eighteen. A real job that didn't involve conning people. Once I'd saved up enough for a ticket and a deposit on a place in San Francisco, I could finally stop. Stand still. Be in the place I actually wanted to be. I could do whatever I wanted, with nobody looking over my shoulder, asking me to stay with them, to do this and do that and never leave their side. I'd be *on my own*, not just *alone*. No more Dark-haven, no more Bloodgood family drama. I stuffed *Jane Eyre* into the bottom of my bag as the bell rang and headed for my next class. Just a little over a year, I told myself. A measly four hundred something days, and I'd be free. Surely I could last that long.

Chapter

12

"Somebody talk to me about the symbolism of the chestnut tree," said Armitage the next day, with even more acid in his tone than in our first class. Everyone stared back with a blank face, except Doyle, who didn't bother looking up from the distinctly not *Jane Eyre* book he was reading.

Normally I would have been super happy to do just as Armitage had said for me to do and stay quiet. Not just today but permanently—because it wouldn't be long until Mom got itchy feet and I was the new girl all over again. But that wasn't happening here. I was stuck here for the entire year. I knew the answer. And I already didn't like this guy. What the hell.

I raised my hand. "The tree is struck by lightning and split apart but still connected at the root. It's telling us Jane and Rochester will be torn apart but ultimately their bond, not only of love but of shared hardship, will keep them connected."

Someone—probably Valerie, the ginger witch—let out a small, ladylike snort. "What is this, *Twilight*?"

"Shut up, Valerie," Mr. Armitage said. "When you have something meaningful to contribute to the class discussion, that's the day I cash out my 401(k) and retire, because the end times are clearly upon us."

I blinked, surprised that anyone would take my side, never mind Armitage, who was leading the pack for meanest burned-out teacher I'd ever run into.

"And you," Armitage said. I flinched away from his finger. Maybe I'd hold off on jumping up on the desk to recite poetry in his honor for now.

"This isn't some soppy love story where true love conquers all," Armitage snarled. "This is love cast in the harshest light. Lightning strikes the tree because love is a destructive force. Love shatters what's good and pure in Jane's world. It does nothing but bring her misery."

I felt heat creep up my cheeks, and the words flew out before I could make myself be quiet. "That's your opinion. Maybe Charlotte Brontë wanted to show how sinister forces are conspiring against Jane but she's stronger than they are. You can destroy the branches of a tree, but if the root survives, it can grow back."

We glared at each other. Finally Armitage sniffed. "Fair enough, Ms. Bloodgood. Since you're so convinced you're right, you can write me a paper for tomorrow defending your evidently very strong opinions about Ms. Brontë's intentions in this scene."

Valerie snickered. I stared at the back of her head and wished I could shoot deadly lasers out of my eyes and into her brain. We moved on, and I didn't raise my hand again. I should have learned by now trying to impress teachers never ended well. You either came off as a kiss-ass or an over-achiever, neither of which would make my life at Hell High any easier.

After last bell, I went outside and saw Valerie and half of her posse heading down toward the field in bright shorts and tank tops, even though to me it was practically winter. I saw another group of girls stretching and lacing up shoes, and against my better judgment I followed them. Being on a team was the easiest way to fit in, and it'd get me off the island on weekends. So what if Valerie was the queen b-word of the track as well as the school?

I set my stuff down and approached. "Hey. This is try-outs, right?"

Valerie gave me a pitying look that somehow managed to be toxic and condescending at the same time, which was a feat. "Mascot auditions are in the gym. Since I assume you're looking for something that will save everyone from having to look at you."

I took off my jacket and pulled my running shoes out of my bag.

"No sassy remarks this time?" Valerie pushed. "Am I upsetting you? You going to go home to your freak family and cry about the mean girl?"

I looked up at her and gave her a wide smile. Smiling con-fuses people if they're expecting you to get all upset. "That's an idea," I said. "But I'd rather stay here and kick your ass on the track."

More girls showed up in civilian running clothes, and Valerie stomped back into the crowd. I followed the other hopefuls into the locker room, changed, and went back out to stretch. I got the feeling of eyes on the back of my neck as I worked on my quads. Turning, I saw Doyle watching me from the shadow of the bleachers. He gave me a little wave and beckoned me over.

"Are you sure your girlfriend won't bite your face off for talking to me?" I said when I jogged up.

He laughed. "I think you're doing a fine job pissing her off on your own."

I heard a whistle blow and shifted my feet. "Did you want something, or . . . ?"

Doyle handed me a folded piece of paper. "Just wanted to give you this. In case you change your mind about getting out of here."

I shoved the paper into the pocket of my shorts. "Thanks, but I'm good." He still didn't leave, so I reached for the first reason that sounded halfway plausible. "Unless you want to give me a real, concrete reason, I'm kinda reluctant to run out on the first home without wheels I've lived in since grade school."

His jaw twitched but he sighed. "Fine. I can't stop you."

"No," I agreed. "You can't." I jogged back to the group on the track, and I felt like I'd swallowed a rock when I saw the track coach was Mr. Armitage. He raised one eyebrow when he saw me.

"You do know this is a team sport, Ms. Bloodgood? You're expected to get along and support the other girls."

"Is *that* what this is?" I said. "I thought this was the club where we go into the woods and fight each other Hunger Games–style."

A few of the girls snickered, and even Valerie cracked a smile.

"If you're so tough, give me your fastest mile," Mr. Armitage said. "Valerie, since, unlike English literature, this is your arena of expertise, try not to beat her too badly."

We lined up, and Valerie streaked ahead of me on the whistle. I caught up by the end of the first lap and felt my heart throb and my blood pound. This wasn't like waking up on the lighthouse, though. I was warm and alive, and I dug my toes into the damp red clay of the track, letting my longer legs pull me just ahead of Valerie. If I could tire her out, I could shut her down in the finish lap.

Valerie was faster than I'd expected, though, and more important, she hated me, and she pulled ahead—way ahead. I watched her bright copper ponytail swish away from me, and I pushed myself again. My calf muscles burned, and I could hear my lungs making saw-blade sounds, but I wasn't letting her beat me. This wasn't a school I'd stay at for a few months and get to move on. I was here for who knew how long, and I wasn't going to be dealing with some wannabe Regina George dogging my every step.

Gray thunderheads piled up as Valerie and I rounded the last turn, close enough to touch. My vision was blurring around the edges, and I saw a bright tongue of lightning flick the underside of the clouds over the bay. Two more steps, that was all I needed to get ahead. There was a flashbulb, and a thunder crack, and then my feet skidded across the chalk line at the end of the lap. Valerie came up a half second later and almost plowed into me. She doubled over, wheezing, and Armitage tossed her a bottle of Gatorade. "Walk it off," he ordered, and then turned to me. "Seven sixteen. Not terrible." He fished a jersey—blue with a bright yellow *D* on the back—from the mesh bag at his feet and tossed it to me. "Welcome."

The sky opened and rain poured down on everyone, freezing droplets that washed all the sweat off my skin. Mr. Armitage called off the rest of the tryouts until the next day, and we ran for the gym.

Valerie caught me after I'd showered and headed for the bus. "Hey," she said.

"Hey," I said, eyeing her warily.

She sighed. "Look, you're really good. We need more strong distance runners. Can we just call off the Game of Thrones?"

I shrugged. "I'm willing to stop being a bitch if you stop calling me a witch."

Her mouth lifted at the corners. "Fair enough. Where did you go to school before Darkhaven? Not many people can just walk on the team with a seven-sixteen mile."

"All over," I said honestly. "Track is the one sport almost every school has, so it was easy to keep up even if we moved." And running didn't cost more than shoes and sweat, whether it was on the rainy, spongy ground of Portland or concrete-hard New Mexico high desert. It also gave me a ready-made excuse to get out and away from Mom, who would only run if the cops were chasing her.

"I'm jealous," Valerie said. "I had to train all summer with a coach to shave my time down to under seven thirty."

"Don't be," I said. "You have a long stride for somebody your height. I bet you kick ass cross-country." I guessed I was serious with this olive branch extending, because I felt almost happy when Valerie held up her phone.

"Add me on Instagram and I'll add you back, and I'm usually on Google chat. I'm Valirun98."

"Cool," I said, because "I don't own a smartphone and live on a island where wireless signals go to die" would have made me look very much like some kind of boring time traveler from the past.

Valerie started to walk over to a red SUV idling at the curb and then turned back. "One more thing—stay away from my boyfriend. I know you guys are neighbors, but he's mine, and we're serious."

"Yeah, I'm not his type," I said. I wanted to roll my eyes at Valerie virtually peeing a circle around Doyle, but he *was* the best-looking guy I'd seen in this shallow gene pool of a town, and she was probably counting on the two of them moving someplace where restaurants stayed open past eight when high school was over. She could do her doctor thing, like Betty had said, and he could sit around being attractive. They'd be a perfect couple.

She could have her fantasy. Aside from the superstitious crap, I'd met a dozen guys just like Doyle. None of them had a clue what the real world was like. The first time being an upper-middle-class male didn't get them what they wanted, they melted down.

The note he'd passed me crinkled inside my shorts pocket when I pawed through my bag for my water bottle, and I pulled it out and unfolded it while the bus rumbled down the hill to the pier.

> I was tossed on a buoyant but unquiet sea, where billows of trouble rolled under surges of joy.

I smirked. *Somebody* was lying about never having read *Rebecca*.

Doyle's number was scribbled below it, with a note.

Call me if you change your mind.

I crumpled up the note and shoved it into the bottom of my bag. I couldn't figure Doyle out. One second he was all into me, the next he was practically dragging me to the town line and shoving me over it to get me away from him.

Rain lashed the bus window and lightning lit up the harbor, light then dark then light again. I wrapped my coat around me and ran for the boat. I never thought I'd be glad to be going back to the island, but cursed family lineage, mystery illness or not, it was better than high school.

Chapter
13

S imon and Mrs. MacLeod were both out when I got back to the house, so I showered and spent an hour or so padding through the various rooms. Most on the upper floor were guest rooms, shut up and chilly, their radiators as silent and sheet-shrouded as the rest of the furniture. Some were entirely empty, deep drag marks in the wood floors where heavy objects had been taken away. I hoped they'd gotten to go somewhere a little less moldy and dank.

Only one room, one that looked out over the top of the greenhouse to the ocean, wasn't a total tomb. It was dusty, but still full of stuff, as if the owner had just stepped out and forgotten to come back for twenty years. Old makeup and perfume were dried to dust on the vanity. Dresses and shoes spilled out of a closet, and I'd left the same mess behind myself enough times to recognize the signs of someone taking off with only what they could carry. I opened and closed drawers, coming across some jeans and tees that smelled like they'd spent the last decade marinating in a damp cave and a small leather book with the cover falling away. Most of it was blank, but yellowing Polaroids were pasted into the first twenty pages or so.

I saw Simon as a teenager, wearing swim trunks, sitting

on a rock in the sun and glaring at whoever was taking the picture. He was pale as ever, but with a lot more hair and a lot fewer lines on his face. Same dorky glasses, though. I flipped through the rest of the photos. Most of them were random shots of the beach, the house, and Darkhaven, all featuring peeps in bitchin' nineties fashion that dated things a few years before I was born. I looked around the room again, at the curious emptiness, even though it had more stuff in it than most. The unmade bed had black sheets, and the faded gilt wallpaper was covered with posters and tear sheets from concerts, rusted thumbtacks spreading brown stains across the plaster. Siouxsie, the Clash, the Pixies, and Nirvana, just to start.

I closed my fist around the book. I never saw the photographer, but it had to be my mother. This was her room, her stuff. Before she got pregnant and decided to run away. And whoever had been left behind—Simon, I guessed—had just left this room like a tiny museum to her deserting the place. I doubted it was sentimentality, but maybe a tiny part of him missed her. They sure seemed happy in the photos. Mom had that effect on people—you couldn't stand to be around her, but you missed her when she was gone, and she'd bolted on Simon just like every other close relationship she'd had since I'd been around. That kind of behavior could lead to the exact mix of resentment and regret Simon seemed to hold toward his sister.

He hadn't even bothered to erase the chalkboard hanging on the wall above her desk. The writing reminded my twenty-years-ago mother to BE EXCELLENT TODAY.

All at once, even though it was freezing, the room was too hot and too small. I ran out and slammed the door behind me. I couldn't reconcile the happy, messy, teenage girl whose bedroom that was with the hateful, bitter, selfish woman I'd known. The fact that I'd never gotten to meet this facet of Mom made me angry, but something else choked the anger out, something heavier and harder to deal with.

It wasn't just Mom's room—the whole manor house suddenly felt too small. I needed sound, something to distract me, but there was no TV and my music player's battery was dead. I'd left my charger in Omaha.

I went to the kitchen and used the ancient wall phone, punching in Doyle's number. Rain pattered like cat feet against the glass, leaving streaks that gleamed in the last rays of daylight. The phone hummed and buzzed for a good ten seconds before it deigned to actually ring, and I sighed impatiently. Landlines didn't work any better than anything else on Darkhaven, apparently.

"Yeah?" Doyle said.

I gripped the receiver. I felt stupid for calling him. If there had been anyone else to talk to, I wouldn't even be doing this. But it was too late now. What would I say—seeing my dead mother's room had made me not want to be alone in the place where she'd grown up, the last place she'd been happy?

"Ivy, is that you?" Doyle said. "Are you okay?"

"Can, uh . . ." I swallowed and got a hold on myself. Whatever my flaws, I could talk to people. That was one of my few good qualities, even though I'd mostly used it to scam unsuspecting social workers, cops, and anyone else who had something I wanted. "Want to hang out or something? A few days away made me forget how boring this place is." I held my breath after I said that. Reminded myself he had a girlfriend, and now that I knew that, I had to remember his flirting wasn't going anywhere.

But I hadn't called to feel him out romantically, I'd called because he was the only person I'd remotely connected with, or trusted, since I came to Darkhaven. Even if he was off-limits dating-wise, having an actual friend close by would be a big relief. So what if I had liked him a little? I could keep that to myself. I wasn't interested in stealing anyone's boyfriend.

There was a second of silence, and I got the feeling it wasn't because of me. Doyle's voice was lower when he spoke again, like he was trying not to be overheard. "Meet me on the beach."

After he hung up, I got my jacket and a heavy wool scarf I'd found in the closet of my bedroom. There was a big steel flashlight hanging by the kitchen door, and I grabbed that too before stepping into the rain.

Doyle was waiting when I finally fell-climbed my way down the rotting steps, wearing a green canvas coat and hiking boots like he was taking a break from a freakin' L.L.Bean ad. His hair was wet and blown across his forehead in inky streaks, a stark contrast to his skin, which had a faint blue-silver glow in the near night. "Took you long enough," he called above the muted roar of the waves.

"The stairs from the manor are a compound fracture waiting to happen. You want me breaking my damn ankle?" I said.

"Shouldn't worry you." Doyle grinned. "You can just fly down here on your broomstick, right?"

I stuck my tongue out at him. "Screw you."

Doyle shoved his hands into his pockets, hunching against the wind. "So what's up?"

I looked down, kicking a trough in the rocky beach with my feet. "I don't know. Nobody's home and I just . . . I'm not used to living somewhere that big. Back in Nebraska or wherever, I was lucky if I got my own bed."

Doyle glanced up at the house, then at me. "Come here," he said, stretching out his hand. I took it, finding his grip still callused and strong. It surprised me again. He didn't look like the kind of guy who'd be into manual labor.

He led me back toward the small cave I'd visited. I felt my stomach flip in panic as I glimpsed the spot where I'd buried the shirt, but we moved past it, deeper into the dark. The tide was low now, and Doyle ducked and took a sharp left. I saw what I hadn't before—a set of steps carved into the rock, covered in seaweed and clusters of mussel shells, waiting for the tide to return.

"Bootlegger cave," Doyle said. "We just have to make sure we go back before the tide comes in." I followed him up the steps, using his hand for balance, and found myself on a dry rock shelf in the shape of a half shell, evidence of some ancient lava flow that had carved through the rock. A sort of arch, braced up with railroad ties so rotted they were green with algae, led away into blackness.

"Supposedly the tunnels go all the way to the other side of the island," Doyle said. "Drop the booze off on the ocean side, roll it over to a lobster boat moored on the bay side, take it to the mainland."

"Was that your family or mine?" I said. Doyle felt around in the dark and came up with a pack of matches.

"Mine, of course," he said with a grin. "The Bloodgoods were way too prissy to be criminals."

"Yeah, I think my uncle would literally faint if he knew some of the stuff I've done," I muttered.

Doyle lit an old Coleman lantern, the squat red body

pitted with rust from the salt in the air, and frowned. "He's not as wimpy as he looks."

I saw a couple of old footlockers stacked to one side in the light of the lantern, and Doyle flipped one open. "My brother and my cousins stored some stuff here. They used to sneak onto the beach and go drinking and partying. We're not supposed to be on this side, but that never stopped them."

He spread out a sleeping bag that was mildewed around the edges and patted the spot next to him. I sat cross-legged, watching Doyle's profile in the harsh silver light of the lantern.

"This is so bizarre," I murmured. "I spend my entire life thinking it's just me and Mom, and now there's all of this . . ." I held out my arms to encompass the cave, my uncle, everything. Doyle cracked a half smile.

"Honestly, if I were in your position, I'd be losing my head. I don't know how you're so calm."

"Trust me," I said. "Almost taking the plunge off that lighthouse was not the worst moment of my life. Far from it."

The waves hissed on the rocks, and I tried to leave everything else outside the mouth of the cave. I wanted to just let it be Doyle and me for a while. I didn't want to think about how before I came here, spending any time near the ocean made me sick to my stomach. How I could hear the water rushing into my ears and the slow, ebbing throb of my own heartbeat getting slower and slower if I watched the waves for too long.

Doyle sighed. "I'm glad I met you, but I wish to hell you hadn't come here."

I rolled my eyes at him. "Come on, Doyle. You keep harassing me about it, I'm gonna find it creepy."

He snorted, stretching his arms above his head and lying back on his elbows. "You want creepy, talk to that uncle of yours."

"Simon isn't any creepier than your relatives," I said. "I saw your dad talking to him out in the woods. He didn't seem all that happy."

Doyle went quiet for a minute, and I wondered if I'd ticked him off. Then he sighed. "He's upset and on edge. We all are. My cousin was killed a few nights ago. Dad spent most of today planning his funeral."

"Killed like murdered?" I already knew the answer, but figured playing dumb wouldn't hurt for now. Did Doyle think Simon was somehow responsible? My uncle had made the feud sound like a simmering, passive thing just below the surface of his relations with the Ramseys, but maybe it wasn't.

I watched Doyle closely as he sat up again, leaning on the damp rock of the cave. Aware for the first time how utterly isolated I was, if some of the other Ramseys *did* show up to take out Neil's death on a Bloodgood.

I was pretty sure Doyle wouldn't let them hurt me, but I didn't want to find out for sure.

"Let's just say he didn't accidentally walk in front of a bus," he said. "He was out hunting, and someone killed him."

My heart started to beat faster. If I hadn't hurt Doyle's cousin, then whose blood was it? Why couldn't I remember? Simon had said the signs of the Bloodgood sickness started showing up in my mother around now. And she'd definitely been violent. I wished now I'd thought to ask, *Hey, Mom, are you prone to blackouts? I've had two and one may have ended in a man's death, so, what's the 411?*

"You never said anything," I murmured. "Your cousin dies and you just . . ."

"Look, no offense," Doyle said. "But it's family business, and we don't generally share it with outsiders. Any outsiders. And . . ." He frowned. "This is just my family being idiots, and mainlanders being petty, but there have always been rumors about the Bloodgoods. To hear some of the locals talk, your family mansion is a real-life murder house. I've heard that crap my whole life, and I still catch myself thinking, *Don't tell her anything; she's a Bloodgood, and she might use it against you.*"

My heartbeat picked up, but I didn't know if it was from Doyle's words or my anxiety at knowing I was sitting so close to my buried secret. "If there were bodies stacked like cordwood in my house, I think I'd know about it, Doyle."

"Me too," he said. "Neil owed a lot of people money, and he had a bad habit of getting drunk and sleeping with their women, so I'm thinking somebody from the mainland came on over to settle a score. But I also think you owe it to yourself to be aware of what kind of danger you're in, staying in *his* house."

I got up, pulling my jacket around me. Water was starting to swish across the sand below us, leaving lacy patterns that looked like the shredded hem of an old dress. Whatever Doyle held against my uncle, Simon had made an effort with me. He'd been up front about my mother's mental state. He'd tried, albeit poorly, to comfort me. That counted for more than Doyle's vague insinuations right now. "Tide's coming in. I should go."

Doyle brushed his fingers lightly over mine. "You sure you're going to be all right?"

I shrugged. I was still shivering uncontrollably, even inside my jacket. "I always have been before." I started to walk away, then stopped and turned back. "Do you really think my uncle is a murderer, or are you just trying to get at me?"

"I don't know," Doyle said. "But I'd be careful of Simon. My dad's known him a long time. Nothing I can prove, but to hear him talk, your uncle is not a nice guy. You can't trust him. He's dangerous. I don't know what he wants from you but it can't be good."

"I thought all that was just locals gossiping," I said, words coming out louder than I meant and echoing off the cave walls. "So it's not? You really do think I'm related to killers and psychopaths?" I knew I was being reactionary, but Doyle was hitting a nerve without knowing it.

"I'm trying not to take sides here, Ivy," Doyle said, his voice holding a snarl that made the skin all up and down my back prickle. "But I'm a Ramsey, and you're a Blood-good. Family is family, and you better hope you're right in trusting Simon. Because if we find out your uncle *did* do something to Neil, *my* family will kill him."

I got so cold then I couldn't feel my hands anymore. The tide rushed around me, the water bubbling until it turned to white foam. "I have to go," I whispered, and ran, my shoes digging into the wet sand. I heard Doyle shout after me, but I kept running until I was up the cliff face and back in the kitchen. I shut and locked the door behind me and sank down on the muddy linoleum floor. It took me a long time to stop shaking.

Chapter 14

I tried to calm down after that, go up to my room and do my homework, but I couldn't concentrate.

I'd been mad enough to kill someone a few times, but not to the point I'd actually, physically use my hands to beat someone to death.

Although if I were, as Simon so delicately put it, ill, would I even know if I'd gone past the point of no return, to the point where I'd hurt anyone who got in my way?

It occurred to me as I stared up at the water-stained ceiling in my tiny room that if Doyle and his family found my bloody shirt during one of their cave parties, or got any hint I'd been in the woods that night, none of the stuff about me not being strong enough to kill a full-grown man armed with a hunting rifle would matter. The Ramseys clearly had it in for Simon. They'd never believe I didn't have something to do with it.

I jumped up, determined to go back to the cave, dig up the shirt, and get rid of it for good. Somehow. I grabbed my copy of *Jane Eyre* as cover—I could be going for a walk to clear my head and planning how to write a pointless paper. Definitely not destroying evidence.

I opened my door and almost smacked into Simon, his fist raised to knock. "Oh, you startled me," he said, grabbing at his sweater vest with his other hand. It was chunky and striped in blue and brown. I was going to have to chat with my uncle about what exactly was acceptable attire for full-grown men who were not attending a snooty 1950s prep school.

"Sorry," I said. Simon tilted his head to examine the book in my hand.

"*Jane Eyre*," he said. "You know, I find her so tiresome. If she'd just minded her own business, none of that nonsense with Rochester would have happened."

I tossed the book back on my bed and tried to smile. "Jane's pretty nosy."

"Girls nosing into secrets that aren't theirs to know never ends well in the real world," Simon said. "If any of our nannies had gone exploring in our family possessions when your grandmother was alive . . ." Simon pulled a mock-horrified face. "The bay would run red with blood. Anyway, I came to tell you supper is ready."

I followed him downstairs, silent, unable to stop thinking about the bloody shirt. Dinner was a nightmare, Mrs. MacLeod glaring at me every time my fork clinked against my plate. I practically ran back to my room, only to have Simon show up again.

"I thought you might like some tea," he said, offering me a mug. "It's herbal, to settle the stomach. You weren't looking well downstairs."

"Thanks," I said, taking it and starting to shut the door.

Simon stuck his arm out and stopped me.

"Are you all right, Ivy? Did something happen at school today?"

"Just tired," I said. "I have this paper to write, so . . ."

Simon smiled, not taking his hand off my door. For such a skinny guy, he was really strong, and I gave up trying to push against it and just let him come in. He looked at all my stuff, examining all the old stickers on my suitcase, and smoothing the ratty quilt on the bed.

"I hope our conversation yesterday didn't bother you."

"That's one of the least crappy parts of my day, believe it or not," I muttered.

Simon pulled out my desk chair and sat down. "There's something else we should discuss."

The tea that touched my tongue was bitter and hot. I was starting to think that when Simon said "herbal" he just meant "kinda gross," no matter what type of tea he was offering. I still kept the mug at my lips, a barrier between me and whatever bad news my uncle had.

"The police in Omaha have released your mother's remains," Simon said. "I know this is hard, but I'm having her interred here, in our family cemetery, and I think we should have a small service." He studied me, the lenses of his glasses reflecting my desk lamp. "That is, if this isn't all too overwhelming for you."

I knew what the right answer to that question was, so I

swallowed my tea and said, "Okay. Whatever you want."

"It won't be anything involving priests or anyone else at all, really." Simon stood. "Just a few words in my sister's memory. Anything you want to say, that feels appropriate."

I rolled the warm mug of tea between my cold fingers, thinking that Simon *really* didn't know what he was asking. He reached out and squeezed my shoulder when I didn't say anything.

"I don't want you to lie or sugarcoat. But we both need to say goodbye. Even if you don't realize it now . . ." He trailed off, staring out my window into the dark. "Saying goodbye is a privilege. Many of us never get that."

I bit back anything else I might have had to say about my mom. Simon was right. He'd never gotten a chance to say anything to Mom as an adult—he'd been not much older than me when she bolted. The least I could do was grit my teeth and get through the only goodbye my uncle was going to get. Even if it turned my stomach to keep my mouth shut.

"I guess you're right," I said.

Simon gave me a limp, benevolent smile, like I was one of those little purse dogs and I'd done a trick. "Sleep well, Ivy."

He left, and I drank the rest of the tea. I tried to keep my eyes open to read and make notes for my paper, but I couldn't do it. I fell asleep in my clothes and woke up just as dawn was starting to peer over the eastern line between the sky and the water. My room was lit by an eerie blue, and I swung my feet to the ground to grab my notebook and write the world's worst paper on romantic love in *Jane Eyre* in the few hours before school.

Something sharp and crunchy bit into my sole, and I yelped. I looked down and saw a litter of broken ceramic on my floor, little white chips scattered everywhere like fragments of bird bone. One chip protruded from my foot, and I pulled it free, wincing as dark blood welled up and dripped onto the braided rug.

I wrapped a sock around my foot and slid into boots sitting close by my bed. My desk lamp was trashed as well. Everything in my room that had been on a surface was on the ground. My few clothes were thrown in the four corners of the room, and one of my shirts had been shredded. I tried the switch, and electricity popped and fizzled. The bulbs in the ceiling light were shattered, little more than smoking stumps.

As I stared at the chaotic swirl my room had become, I clued in to the fact that the stuff scattered everywhere wasn't mine. My backpack had vanished, along with the few things I'd brought with me. My stomach plummeted just as it had when I opened my eyes at the top of the lighthouse.

My room was different in every way—the furniture was new and polished, the walls were covered in bright, flowery paper, and as it strobed my eyeballs, I saw the lighthouse on the promontory was whole and working, a bright white spike poking into the barely morning sky.

I breathed in, out, in again with a panicked weight settling in my chest. I had to be dreaming, but it was like I wasn't fully there, like I was just a passenger in my own body, in these strange clothes, long black dress, pointed lace-up boots. I was definitely rocking the OG Goth look instead of my usual jeans. My breath made a pale fog—it was freezing, ice crystals creeping over the windowpane.

I heard a faint sound from outside my door and without any intention on my part, moved down the hall, down the broad front stairs, past the solarium, and toward Simon's office. I wasn't in control, and I got the feeling that even if I could have made my lungs work to scream, I couldn't have made a sound.

The choking gasps that I'd guessed to be a radiator at first got louder, and I passed into the library, only to take a sharp turn through a narrow door into a room that was all odd angles and lines, ceilings that sloped down to almost touch my head on one side and rose at least ten feet above me on the other. I was in some slice of the house left over when everything else was finished, and I skidded to a stop when I saw a girl bent over on the carpet, sobbing. Her back heaved inside her blue-and-white-striped dress, the white lace collar stained and spattered just as her pale skin was.

She'd collapsed in front of a wall of portraits, most of them those old, muddy-colored photographs you see in antique stores.

The girl looked at me, her green eyes wide and rimmed in red, hair even lighter than Simon's tumbling in perfect barrel curls over her shoulders. She looked about my age, but in the way that you can't really tell with folks from way back, when sixteen was an adult and twenty-one was practically old.

Reaching out, the girl unfolded her fist. Blood soaked both her arms up to the elbows, the small curved blade between her fingers black with it. She choked, rocking.

"Look what I've done," she moaned. "Look . . . look . . ." She threw the blade aside and began clawing at her cheeks, yanking her hair, tearing at the collar and hem of her dress.

"Look!" she screamed. "Look at me! Look what you've done!"

Strong hands grabbed me and yanked me out of sleep. Waking up felt like crashing into a wall, and I thrashed, cracking Mrs. MacLeod across the nose.

"Settle down, Ivy!" she thundered. I jerked away from her. I was covered in sweat, a deep V soaked through the neck of my shirt, and shaking so hard I felt like I'd been shocked. Still, I was back in my room. I was really awake, and for that I was profoundly grateful.

"Saints wept." Mrs. MacLeod slumped into my desk

chair. Her hair had come loose from its bun, and thick curls flew around her face. "You were screaming to wake the dead. What's gotten into you?"

I rubbed my hands over my arms until I thought I'd bruise myself, but I couldn't get warm. "I'm sorry," I managed to chatter. "I had a nightmare."

"I'll say." I felt her rough hand reach out and squeeze my shoulder. "Real or imagined, it was just a dream, Ivy. Let it go now."

I was so surprised that she'd actually been nice to me I stopped shaking. Maybe that was her evil plan all along. "I've always had them," I said. "I'm—I'm sorry if I woke you."

Mrs. MacLeod pursed back up into her trademark hag-face. "Get dressed and come downstairs," she said. "It's not just me who'll be awake the way you were carrying on."

I showered under the hottest water the groaning pipes in my bathroom were capable of and threw on one of the sweaters I'd found in my mother's closet the day before. It was gray and shapeless but warmer than anything I owned. It smelled like cedar and clove cigarettes and dust.

The dream flowed back to me, and I realized I'd breathed in that same smell when I'd been wearing the other clothes, the long dress and granny boots that were oh so retro . . .

They were my mother's clothes.

I gagged, ripping the sweater back off and flinging it across my room. At least I hadn't really trashed anything.

My books and bag were still on the desk, dirty clothes piled in the hamper, tarot cards and crappy vampire paperbacks in the nightstand. My foot ached when I pulled my boots off, and I peeled my sock back off, finding a neat red puncture on my sole, an almost perfect circle in the center of a bruised purple halo.

Despite the scalding shower I'd just taken, I was freezing again, the blood rushing out of my head.

There was no way that dream had been real. Maybe I'd stepped on an errant nail or something and then . . . what? Sleepwalked around cleaning blood off the floor and sterilizing my cut?

I bent down and examined the rug, where dozens of fat blood droplets had landed in the dream, but it was pristine. I crouched and peered under the bed. It was clean, of course—any dust bunny that tried to take up residence in this place clearly died a quick death.

I was about to stand up and try not to worry I was losing my mind when the faint sun caught a small fragment of white under the bed, far away against the wall. I squirmed under the tiny bed frame, rough timber scraping my back, and grabbed for it.

The tiny arrow-shaped piece of mug had a tip of red, where it had pierced my foot. I stared at it for a moment, wondering if there'd been an LSD chaser in that chamomile tea I'd had before bed.

"Ivy!" Mrs. MacLeod hollered from somewhere in the bowels of the house. "Your breakfast is going cold, girl!"

I shoved the fragment into my pocket, grabbed a hoodie from my suitcase, and ran downstairs, ignoring the pain in my foot. The rambling, mall-sized manor house seemed too small again, and I just wanted to get out.

Mrs. MacLeod plunked a bowl of oatmeal and a cup of hot chocolate in front of me when I came into the kitchen. "Eat," she said. "Warm yourself up."

I looked down at the bowl. "Is it poison?"

"It might be if you keep up like this," she said, pouring herself coffee from the old-style silver percolator. She sipped and stared at me. I tried to eat, but my stomach bunched up every time I thought about the girl crying, and the blood, and standing in front of her, a strange little child holding her strange little knife.

"Do you have episodes like that often?" Mrs. MacLeod asked.

I let the spoon clatter back into my bowl, glaring at her. I didn't have the energy to deal with her crap, not after the last few days.

"It's a fair question," she went on. "Especially since Simon has decided to welcome you into the fold. I look after him. I need to know if you're going to be a harm to this family and this house."

"You mean am I going to come at him with an ax from

the woodshed?" I snapped. "I don't know. You seem to be intimately familiar with all of my family's mental issues, so why don't you tell me, Dr. Veronica?"

I pushed back my chair so hard the linoleum shrieked, grabbed my bag, and stormed out the door. My heart thumped like a fist trying to beat its way out of my rib cage as I stomped down to the boat dock. It was a long walk even downhill, but I needed it to try and get myself under control, so I wouldn't show up at school with my face looking like I felt. Twin spots of hot tears worked their way down my face, and I hated myself way more than Mrs. MacLeod then. I was losing it. I never used to cry unless I had a damn good reason and the tears were a means to an end. Uncontrolled crying was useless and made you look weak, and whatever else I might be in light of the blackouts and the bad dreams, I wasn't that.

While I waited for the boat and tried to get hold of myself, I saw a sleek black cabin cruiser slip out from the bend in the harbor and head for the mainland. It wasn't fair Doyle got a nice warm cabin and I got the rust-bucket express. Still, I was glad he hadn't seen me. I didn't want to have to explain why I was crying.

I looked back up at the house. It squatted at the top of the cliffs, gray and rocky, like it had always been a part of the island. I wonder if my mother had ever felt like it was crushing her, holding her under the rocks, down in those caves Doyle had shown me. I knew she'd run away the second she could.

I wondered if she'd already been crazy, or if living here had pushed her into it.

I wondered if it was doing the same thing to me.

Chapter
15

I managed to avoid Doyle all day at school, mostly by keeping Betty at my side whenever we were between classes. I kind of wished I could take her home with me, wind her up, and just keep her chatting all night. Maybe then I'd stop dreaming about creepy bloodstained girls.

"So are you game for that if I can get my dad to let me borrow his truck?" Betty said.

I realized I'd totally tuned out, staring into the depths of my locker but really seeing that weird little cave of a room, the girl's blood-soaked hands reaching out to me as I stood in the doorway. "What?" I said, grabbing my track uniform. Valerie was standing by the doors to the gym, giving me the stink eye.

"I said, there's this really awesome revival house in Camden. They're showing *An Affair to Remember* tomorrow, and my dad won't let me go alone but if *you* came we could see it. It was one of my mom's favorite movies. She'd watch it and we'd make popcorn. You and I could get popcorn, unless you're allergic to peanut oil. I'm allergic to shellfish. My throat won't close up or anything, but I get a rash."

"Um," I said, reaching for an excuse. It wasn't like me to stumble on those, and I made the mistake of looking at her while I did. She'd already deflated like a parade balloon sprayed with buckshot. "That sounds like fun," I heard myself saying, although sappy old movies on a big screen sounded like waterboarding-level torture.

Betty scuffed her shoe across the floor and said shyly, "Maybe you could even sleep over?"

"Can't this weekend," I said, thankfully recovering my ability to say no. "Some other time."

"Okay!" she chirped. "But not next week. Next week is *A Clockwork Orange*, and I don't like violent movies. They make me agitated, and then I wouldn't be able to fall asleep."

"Week after for the sleepover, then," I sighed. "See you Monday." I followed Valerie into the locker room.

"Word of advice?" she said while we were lacing our shoes. "Stop hanging out with Betty Tyler. She's a freak."

"You think everyone is a freak." I rolled my eyes. "Yesterday, you were convinced I was some kind of Satan-worshipping deviant."

"That was yesterday," Valerie said, glaring at me. "Betty's been weird the entire time she's lived here. I tried to be nice, but I had to cut her loose after summer school because she's got her phasers set to maximum cling, twenty-four/seven. Who wants that?"

"I have a pretty high tolerance for weird," I said. "And I get the feeling you're not gonna rush to put me on the prom committee."

"Whatever, I tried. Keep on being freak fodder if you want," Valerie sighed. We clustered outside on the grass with the other girls and started stretching. "I'm just warning you—her family is even worse. Her dad is über-religious and looks like the Unabomber, and she's always wandering around with like a Bible and stuff in her backpack. I think she's one of those saving-it-for-marriage chicks, even."

"Like anyone would *want* it before marriage," said one of Valerie's girl-thugs—I think they called her Mandy or Tandy or something else that fell short of a real name.

Valerie turned her back on me and started gossiping, so I concentrated on shaving down my mile. I didn't mind that my foot was on fire by the time I was done—it was at least real, something that had actually happened and hadn't been a figment of my imagination. I managed to shower and change without any more social faux pas, and I was almost on the last bus when Doyle caught up.

"Are you hiding from me?" he said. "Not that I'd blame you."

I shrugged, shoving my hands in my pockets. "I wasn't sure you'd *want* to see me."

"You were the one who ran off," Doyle pointed out. The bus driver tapped the horn and gestured angrily at me when I looked.

"I need to go," I said. "I've had a crappy day and my mom's funeral is tomorrow, so that pretty much guarantees today was a walk in the park by comparison."

"Ivy, wait!" Doyle ran to catch up with me.

"Stop following me," I said. "Stop acting like we're friends and then not and then getting upset when I get fed up. Either you want me around in spite of what your family thinks of mine or you're toeing the party line and we can never be friends."

"Look, I'm sorry," he said. "You're right, I've been kind of a jackass. I don't really know how to act around you."

"Not like this?" I suggested, and Doyle chuckled.

"Believe it or not, I'm usually pretty charming." He reached out, hand hovering over my arm before I gave a small nod and he touched my shoulder. "Ivy, seriously. I don't put that much stock in old family legends, but there is some very bad blood between your family and mine, and if we're going to be friends it's always gonna be there. I'm never going to be your uncle's biggest fan, and we can't exactly parade in front of my dad."

"Fine by me." I shrugged. "I'm not your girlfriend. I don't have to meet the parents."

"My father doesn't like Valerie either," Doyle said. "He doesn't like anyone who isn't family, and even some of them would probably just as soon shoot him on sight."

"I have to go," I said again as the horn sounded a second time. "But I'm glad you decided you didn't want to ditch me for our family feud."

"Me too," Doyle said. He watched me as I got on the bus and kept watching until we turned out of the drive, like he'd watched the boat from the rocks the day I'd come to the island. Unlike then, his black stare didn't unsettle me now—knowing Doyle was watching out for me made me feel safe, for the first time in longer than I could remember.

It was almost dark by the time the boat docked at the manor's slip. The days were getting shorter, and the air bit at my exposed skin with a relentless cold. The manor house looked like it was floating alone in the clouds, windows glowing in a jagged pattern of light against the iron-gray sky.

Simon called me into the solarium when I came in. I had a feeling even before he made me sit that Mrs. MacLeod had ratted me out. In a way I was glad. I had a few choice things to say about old Hatchet Face myself.

"I hear you and Veronica had an argument earlier," he said. "Ivy, you know I can't have you disrespecting her. Veronica and her entire family have worked hard for the Bloodgoods."

"She started it," I grumbled. "She said something really shitty and uncalled for. She apparently thinks I could snap at any moment and go postal on you."

Simon flinched, then took off his glasses and started polishing them. "I see you found Myra's room."

"Was I not supposed to? It didn't look like anyone would care. Her stuff was just sitting there." It wouldn't make much difference if he told me I couldn't go in there. She was my mother, and I knew next to nothing about her.

"Of course you can look through her things," Simon said. "I probably have some pictures from high school some-where. A yearbook or two. I can try to dig them out of the attic if you like. I couldn't bring myself to pack everything away but I did box up the photos and other things that were too painful for me at the time."

I nodded, surprised he'd let the thing with Mrs. MacLeod go so quickly. "Am I grounded or anything?"

"No," Simon said. "Just try to get along better with people, all right? Your mother had the same problem with authority, and it didn't do her any favors."

He stood, looking at his watch. "I can't exactly order up a pizza, but I think I have the frozen variety if that's accept-able. I gave Veronica the night off."

I wisely didn't say she probably took the extra time to bake children into pies, and just nodded instead.

"I'll call you when it's ready," my uncle said.

I jumped up from my chair, making the iron legs scrape across the stone floor. "Do you know who my father is?"

Simon stopped. His shoulders knotted up like I'd yanked on a string attached to his spine. He tipped his head from side to side before he faced me again, like he was getting ready to take a punch. "No, Ivy. I'm sorry. She never told us."

"She was pretty young, right?" She'd been seventeen, not all that much older than me.

"Our mother had just died," Simon said. "I have to think Myra's getting pregnant was in some way a reaction. Your grandmother was disturbed for many years, Ivy, ever since she had to see the aftermath of what my grandfather did to the Ramseys. She was in and out of institutions her entire life. That hurt all of us, but Myra by far the most. She was becoming unstable even before she got pregnant, and I honestly thought that she'd died a long time before that social worker called me from Omaha and told me what happened."

I was two out of two for being a jerk tonight, and I decided to cut my losses. "I'm sorry," I said. "I know this isn't exactly a light topic for you either."

"It's perfectly normal to want to know who you are." Simon came back to me, looking like he wanted to hug me but was a little afraid I'd bite him. "Did your mother ever tell you anything? Any detail that I might be able to interpret? She talked to our mother, but she didn't make much sense. Your grandmother's nurse at the time encouraged me to commit your mother as well, and I've always regretted not doing it. But I was fifteen, and it's not like I had any legal standing. Your grandmother died with no provision for any of our affairs, and your mother wasn't exactly in a position to take care of me or herself. Our family lawyer had to manage things until I turned eighteen and even then, I had to learn a lot about being an adult the hard way, like when your sister is in the middle of a psychotic break, you move heaven and earth to get her hospitalized before it's too late."

"It's not your fault," I said, realizing with a little start that Simon might not know that. He hadn't spent the last sixteen years with Myra. He didn't know the level she'd sunk to. "Even if you had managed to lock her up, I'm pretty sure we still would have ended up here."

Simon gave me that sad smile. "You're much too young to carry all this tragedy, Ivy. But you're right. It isn't my fault, or yours either. As for your father, if she gave you any details at all I'll try my best to narrow it down based on the friends of hers I knew about."

"She yelled that me and my dad were both worthless and evil a lot," I said. "Beyond that, I'm guessing he was tall and had green eyes, since yours and Mom's are both blue. You guys friends with any shiftless, green-eyed buff dudes about sixteen years ago? I mean, I'm guessing shiftless. Based on her later taste in boyfriends."

Simon gave his odd robot smile. "I can't say I was. But if anyone springs to mind, you'll be the first person I tell. We're family, Ivy. You can ask me anything."

Doyle's words slithered to mind then, unbidden and unwanted, like something that crawls up through your shower drain. *You can't trust him. He's dangerous. I don't know what he wants from you but it can't be good.*

I brushed them away. Doyle had always had a family, at least one parent who as far as I could tell wasn't an unemployed grifter, always gone to sleep knowing he'd wake up in the same place. "Thanks, Uncle Simon," I said softly.

Simon reached out his hand and laid it on my shoulder. "I'm . . ."

The lights pulsed and went out with a low groan. Somewhere far off in the house a bulb shattered. Simon cursed under his breath. "Stay here. We've blown a fuse."

He moved away from me, fumbling near the plants for a battery-operated lantern.

"Does this happen a lot?" I asked. I felt tingly, as if the darkness had brought the cold from my nightmare with it.

"A fair amount," he said. "This house is ancient and it badly needs upgrading, but try getting any of the toothless hicks from the mainland to come work on the home of the cursed Bloodgood family, and soon you get used to living with bad wiring and lukewarm bathwater."

He found a second flashlight and moved off, but I got bored sitting, so I took the lantern down the halls, wandering past rooms that looked foreign in the dark. I turned into the library at last, on the far end of the house from my bedroom, and shivered a little. It probably wasn't such a great idea to go poking around now, when I still couldn't quite shake off the nightmare. It had been way more than a normal dream, and I was just scaring myself for no reason.

I held up the lantern, to assure myself the door was shut, and instead saw the same seamless green wallpaper printed with small pink flowers that encased the rest of the library, an oval mirror with a chipped gold frame hanging in the spot where a door should be.

In a way, it was a relief. There had never been a room. It was a dream; it was over; I never had to feel that choking disconnection from my body again.

On the other hand, that meant I'd come up with it entirely from my own mind . . . a mind that my mother had started losing right around the age I was now.

The mirror glass threw the lantern light back into my face, until it looked like I wasn't there at all, just a smear of a hand and my hoodie and a ball of light where my face should be. I could hear Simon banging around, muttering to himself, and the clunk of old-style plug fuses being changed.

I sighed and lowered the lantern. Nothing to do now except go see if I could make myself useful, and if not, eat some cereal for dinner instead of the promised pizza and go to sleep.

As the dazzle disappeared from my eyes, I swore that I saw someone standing in the door of the library watching me, a white shape just barely visible in the black. Fast as I saw it, it winked out of view, and when I spun around, the lantern fell out of my hands and clattered on the wood floor.

"Ivy?" Simon called. "I think we'll be back in business shortly. Only one fuse blown, and I have a spare." After another few seconds, the lights flickered once, twice, and then burned steadily, flooding the house with light again.

Nothing. There was nothing there, and never had been. I picked up the lantern and switched it off. I needed to get a grip.

"Ivy?" Simon called again. I stopped at the library door, in the spot where I'd seen the shape. I turned back to the mirror. Just my own reflection, complete with frizzy hair and deep rings under my eyes. I looked more terrifying than anything I could dream up. I dropped my gaze, feeling a headache starting.

Next to my boot, a set of small, wet footprints marred the wood floor, floating on the surface before they turned away and traveled down the hall toward the front door, each one perfectly delineated, a wet, gleaming trail under the dim old-style light bulbs in the tarnished brass lamps.

Wet and red. Not water or mud but bright, red, still-gleaming blood. Girl's shoes, heel and toe, the kind girls wore back when bloomers were also in fashion. Girl's footprints in blood.

I screamed, pasted against the wall, feeling my nails dig

chunks out of the wallpaper and plaster. I screamed until Simon showed up and grabbed me, and then I shut my eyes, feeling the full body shakes envelope me until I could barely stand up.

"It's all right," Simon said over and over. "Tell me what happened. It's all right."

I couldn't tell him. I didn't even know why I'd started screaming, if it was out of fear or if I was just so overloaded my mind couldn't take it anymore.

"Ivy," Simon murmured. "Open your eyes. Everything is all right."

I made myself do what he said. I wasn't afraid of the dark, or anything in it. I was tougher than that. I was a Bloodgood, after all—we were the people everyone *else* was supposedly afraid of.

The footprints were gone. Everything was normal, real, just a dusty old house and the uncle I barely knew holding me up so I didn't collapse. I stopped shaking then, and started to cry, sobbing silently and violently into Simon's shirt. He wrapped his arms around me tight, and didn't ask me why I was crying. I don't think either of us knew for sure.

Chapter

16

I managed to hold myself together after that. My uncle and I ate dinner in silence, neither of us wanting to bring up what had just happened. Simon, I assumed, because he was as crappy at handling the emotions of others as I was, and me because I didn't have anything to say.

That was a lie. I did have something to say, but it wasn't anything I was ready to admit. If I spoke up, I'd have to ask Simon to call a doctor, get me an MRI, a psych eval, something. I couldn't deny it anymore—there was something wrong with me, and it had started going wrong the second I set foot on the island.

I couldn't even *begin* to deal with that after what had happened in the library, so I just kept my mouth shut. It felt weird, just eating and not talking, like a normal dysfunctional family where nobody hallucinates a little girl's bloody footprints, but it was better than either of us bringing up what had just happened.

The painfully awkward silence was broken by the sound of tires pulling into the drive. Simon looked up. "That's Veronica. Do you mind putting the dishes in the sink?"

I shook my head, going one better and actually washing them. I was on my way upstairs to do homework when I heard my uncle and Mrs. MacLeod talking in the front hallway. I tiptoed to the edge of the staircase in my stocking feet, staying out of sight against the wall so they wouldn't see me if they looked up at the landing.

"It can't happen soon enough," Simon said. "You should have seen her, Veronica. It wasn't pretty."

"I still think you're full of it," Mrs. MacLeod grumbled. "She's not going to be able to handle it, Simon. She's weak, just like her mother."

I bristled, fighting the urge to stomp down there and tell her off again. Simon held up a hand before I could. "Enough, Veronica. It's not your call."

"No, and it's not *your* only problem," Mrs. MacLeod snarled. "I ran into Liam Ramsey on the mainland today, and he was even less charming than usual. They want their pound of flesh for that dead boy, Simon, and if you waffle much longer, they're not going to be too particular about who they cut it out of."

"You let me worry about Liam," Simon snapped.

Mrs. MacLeod huffed. "Your mother—"

"—knew when to keep her mouth shut, and I'd appreciate it if you learned before I lose my temper!" Simon bellowed.

The dusty crystals in the chandelier hanging over the foyer rattled, like a wind had rushed through the house. The lights dimmed and then flared, and I heard a faint exhale of terrified air from Mrs. MacLeod. Then her footsteps retreated, at a brisk clip, without another word.

I backed up into the shadows on the landing. I just hoped

Simon never screamed at me that way. He sounded way too much like my mother.

The next morning being Saturday, I woke up ready to stop telling myself lies and actually face up to what was going on with me. Maybe do some more careful poking around by asking Simon more about Mom and my grandmother.

Then reality crashed over me. I wasn't doing anything like that today. All I was doing was getting dressed and meeting Simon outside the manor house's back door. The sky was crushingly crystal blue, but along with the clear weather came a snap of cold that took the breath out of my lungs the minute I went outside. I'd found a black coat in the hall closet, and put on my darkest jeans and shirt, turning it inside out to hide the band logo.

The boat delivered the casket early. I skipped that part. Let Mrs. MacLeod drive my mother to the cemetery. I'd already said everything I ever wanted to say to her. *Simon*, I reminded myself as I shoved my hands into my armpits to thaw them out. *This is for Simon. Not her.*

I had thought about calling Doyle to at least talk about how messed up this DIY funeral was, but the memory of blood on my skin, the bloody footprints, the dream that had somehow still cut my foot open, stopped me. I wasn't in any state to be confiding in anyone right now. I walked behind Simon along the gravel road, away from the mansion, my chest getting tighter with every step, like what waited on top of the little hill was yanking me in.

"Nearly there," Simon said as we turned the opposite way from the forest along the property line, climbing past the lighthouse to the highest point on the cliff, where thorny wild roses and brambles sheltered a small plot hemmed in by an iron fence. Simon opened the gate for me and gave me a kind smile, pushing his glasses up his nose. He was so far from the screaming lunatic I'd seen last night I had to think Mrs. MacLeod had just pushed him over the edge. "It's nothing to be afraid of."

I lifted my chin. "Do I look like I'm afraid?"

"No," he said. "Like my sister, I doubt you're afraid of much." He snapped off one of the last live roses from a nearby bush and walked ahead of me. The grave had been dug by hand, no doubt Mrs. MacLeod's work, and the casket rested on two sawhorses. It was silver, metal, with airline shipping stickers still clinging to it. I was surprised. You always think of ornate coffins, organ music, that kind of thing. But my mother was going to be buried in what she'd blown into town in from the Omaha morgue. That was fitting, I guessed.

Simon placed the rose on the lid of the coffin, his pale hand resting next to it. "My sister always loved the outdoors. She loved this spot, high on the rocks. Looking out over everything. Loved music, loved animals, loved her life.

Right up until she got sick." He looked at me, his eyes red behind his glasses. I knew my eyes matched his, in spite of my best intentions not to shed one more tear over her. "Did she pass any of that on to you, Ivy?"

I shrugged. "We moved around too much to have pets, like I said. We didn't even have plants."

Simon sighed. "I thought as much. I wish I could ask my sister why she did things the way she did."

"Not much mystery there," I muttered. "No offense."

Simon lifted his glasses off the bridge of his nose, rubbing the red mark. "I wish I knew why she turned against us. She and I were close, especially after our mother . . . well."

"Also went crazy?" I supplied.

Simon winced.

"I'm sorry," I said instantly, my stomach knotting for reasons that had nothing to do with the coffin a few feet away. Usually I had a better sense of when I'd crossed the line with a mark. Maybe that was the problem—Simon wasn't a mark; he was family. I wasn't supposed to read him and figure out how to manipulate him into telling me secrets and giving me all his cash to supposedly get in touch with his dead relatives. That wasn't how normal families behaved. It wasn't my uncle's fault I didn't know how to be a part of one.

"Mom really messed up," I said. My throat was tight, burning. I could still taste that metallic, overfiltered bathwater.

A strong wind caught the rose, and it slid off the coffin, slamming into the ground and scattering its petals over the muddy turned earth. "She wasn't happy," I whispered. "But at least all that's over now." I sucked in a breath, looked at Simon. He was holding it together, but his cheeks were wet, and his shoulders trembled. I knew from watching other people's grieving families that he was about two seconds from losing it. So I got control of my own shaky voice and spoke in the smooth, unruffled one I'd practiced over and over, and told the biggest lie I'd fed Simon yet.

"I don't know what happens after this," I told Simon. "But I hope wherever she is, she's at peace."

Simon swiped at his cheek with a gloved hand and slid his other arm around me, squeezing my shoulders with that surprising, wiry strength of his. I didn't pull away—I didn't even have to hold myself still. I was glad for the support. We lingered silently while Mrs. MacLeod used the winch on her Jeep to lower the casket the rest of the way into the grave. Simon picked up a handful of dirt and threw it on the casket. I did the same. Then it was over.

Simon poured himself a mug of coffee the moment we were back in the kitchen and filled his mug to the rim from a bottle of supermarket bourbon he pulled from the back of a cabinet. He took a swig, winced, and then tipped the bottle to an empty mug, looking at me. "Ivy?"

Normally I'd have been jazzed to have an adult offer me booze, but it just felt wrong, Plus, it was barely 10:00 a.m. "I'm good." I said. "But I will take coffee."

"I know that you don't feel much now," Simon said as he handed me coffee and went back to sipping and wincing between sentences. "But when it eventually hits you, you can talk with me, or I can arrange for you to speak with some-one else. A professional."

"I don't need grief counseling," I said sharply. I'd held it together in the cemetery, but if Simon kept going over and over this I was going to lose it.

"I have no doubt your anger toward Myra is justified," Simon murmured. "But she's dead, Ivy, and holding that bit-terness now only hurts you." He drained his mug. "There's a saying: resentment is like taking poison and expecting the other person to die. Whatever she did . . ."

I lost it. I couldn't keep quiet another second. Weirdly, it was because Simon had been so good to me, last night when I broke down and today at the funeral, that I started yelling, words barely separated by breathing. He was a truly decent person. He didn't deserve the illusion about his sister, that she was damaged but basically okay. That the person he'd loved was still alive in her in any way, shape, or form the day she'd killed herself.

"She tried to kill me!" I slammed my mug down, coffee sloshing all over the kitchen table. "She wasn't confused or just angry. She was so calm when she did it. She held my head under water in a bathtub, and I think she regretted not going through with it every day after, because she *never* treated me like I was human again, much less her daughter." I was shaking, body and voice. I'd never been this honest with anyone, and it was terrifying. "You've treated me more like family in the past week than she did in sixteen years."

Simon stared at me, eyes unblinking behind his glasses. I shut my own eyes, waiting for the yelling to start, for the rage I'd seen the other night. He'd call me a liar, a trouble-maker, want to know why I had to stir up drama. Why was I ungrateful? How dare I speak that way about his dead sister?

I jumped when arms wrapped around me, but I didn't fight. Simon pulled my head down onto his shoulder, his free hand rubbing my back. "I'm so sorry, Ivy," he whispered. "I had no idea."

I sniffed hard. I'd had enough of crying over Mom, but I couldn't stop. "I knew she was sick, but you have to believe if I had an inkling she'd tried to harm you, if you'd ever contacted me for help, I would have taken you in years ago, no questions asked."

"I do," I said very softly. For all his awkwardness and temper, I really did think Simon would have helped me. It wasn't his fault Mom had kept me hidden.

"I am so very sorry," Simon whispered.

I pulled back, using the hem of my shirt to wipe my face. "It's okay, Uncle Simon. It's not your fault."

"I can't change the past," he said. "But going forward, maybe you and I can give each other what we didn't get from our family until now. I want you to stay here, Ivy. Not just until high school is over. I want this to be your home. You can go to college all expenses paid, make a life for yourself— if not on Darkhaven, at least close by. Let me do that for you."

"Uncle Simon," I said. My voice was rough from the yelling and the crying. "You don't have to overcompensate. Really. We're good."

He managed a real smile this time, not a robot smile. "You're a good kid, Ivy. I know you haven't heard that much, but I mean it. I'm very glad you came here."

Even though we'd just buried my mother and I'd finally told the worst secret I'd ever kept, I felt strangely light. I wasn't holding everything so close anymore. I'd dropped a tiny piece of the baggage Mom had left me. I smiled back at Simon. I actually meant it too. "It doesn't totally suck here," I allowed. Simon barked a laugh.

"That's my girl. Why don't you go wash your face and relax? If you have homework, just tell the school you were sick on Monday. I'll back you up."

I didn't argue. I was exhausted, like I'd run around the entire island a dozen times. I went back upstairs, changed into sweats, and after a moment of debate, shoved my clothes from the funeral into the trash can next to my desk. I wasn't going to wear them again.

I went to root around in the fridge as night fell, but Mrs. MacLeod loomed out of her apartment and stopped me. "No snacks before supper," she said. I caught a glimpse of a tight studio off the kitchen, with a hot plate, a twin bed, and, miracle of miracles, a sleek white laptop sitting on a small desk. Just as I was about to ask if she'd let me use her Netflix account, she slammed the door and locked it with a fat skeleton key.

"So the whole 'my mother just died and today was her funeral' exception isn't gonna cut it with you?" I asked her.

"We've all lost, miss," she said. "All you can do is carry on, and part of that is sticking to routine. Indulge yourself once, and you'll be indulgent right along, any time the slightest wind shakes your boughs."

I narrowed my eyes at her. "Just what exactly is your problem with me?"

Mrs. MacLeod shrugged. "Where do I begin? I didn't care for your mother either."

"In case you hadn't noticed," I hissed, "I'm kinda going through something. So maybe back off the anti–Mary

Poppins routine for one day, okay?"

Mrs. MacLeod bared her teeth slightly. "Rude. Like mother like daughter, I suppose."

"You have no idea what I'm like," I snapped. "So instead of being awful, why don't you take up a useful hobby, like renting yourself out at Halloween to scare kids?"

"You . . ." Mrs. MacLeod started to reach for me but stopped when Simon came into the kitchen.

"Could I speak with you privately, Ivy?" he said.

"You could be about to give me the Talk, and it'd be better than this," I said, rushing to put him between Mrs. MacLeod and me.

Simon guided me to the door of his office and slid it open. Inside, it looked pretty normal, if you were either a big fan of scary movies or Hannibal Lecter. Bones, human and animal, were everywhere. The animals and people were displayed on bases or strung together with thick black wire and hung on the wall. Birds flew in ghostly formation from the ceiling. Behind a giant desk that was carved with all kinds of mythical creatures across the front, taxidermy heads that still had their fur studded the deep red wallpaper.

"It's a little much," Simon said. "My grandfather was a biologist and a big-game hunter. He collected most of these. Before he lost it and committed multiple murders, obviously."

I felt my shoulders pull in as I followed him around the

desk to the wall, feeling dozens of empty eye sockets and glass eyeballs on me. Any way you looked at it, displaying the prey of a guy who'd gone insane and massacred half a dozen people was both incredibly tacky and unbelievably macabre.

"The state requires that I sign a few documents relating to finalizing my guardianship," Simon explained, sitting himself behind the desk. He was way too small for the giant thing and still looked like a little kid playing with his dad's stuff. "I just wanted to make sure I had all your details correct."

He wrote with a fountain pen on a stack of forms while I rattled off my social security number and our last address in Omaha. A clanging sound came from the kitchen, and Mrs. MacLeod bellowed. "Simon! Telephone for you!"

Simon winced, heaving a sigh. "Once in a great while, I miss the days when my mother reigned supreme and insisted that the help didn't holler at you from other rooms." He pushed back from the desk. "Wait here, I won't be a minute."

He was gone a lot more than a minute, and I got bored and started wandering around the office, touching all the taxidermy. It was creepy, like touching too-realistic stuffed animals, and I thought I'd really screwed myself when I touched a snowy owl mounted on the wall and its head halfway came off.

"Crap," I whispered, trying to push the piece of foam back

onto the rest of the body. I stopped when I saw a spring-loaded latch inside the owl where its foam core should be. I twisted the head all the way to the left.

One of the panels of wallpaper whispered back and into the wall, leaving a small open passage behind the desk.

"No way," I whispered, peering into the small gap. I expected something spooky, dripping with moss and moisture, or sticky with salt like the cave at the beach, but instead a set of stone steps led down into the darkness, and the brick wall was clean and free of any sinister lichens or drawings of demon goats or 666 diagrams.

I grabbed one of the ever-present flashlights that were all over the house from the top of Simon's desk, snapped it on, and stepped onto the top stair. I didn't even wonder if I should be doing this—I was definitely investigating any hidden passages I stumbled across.

The steps went down a long way, deeper than a basement, into a long room held up by arched brick columns. I saw the shadow of huge granite blocks above. I was looking up at the bones of the manor house, and I shivered at the faint sound of water droplets echoing from somewhere in the dark.

My light picked up the edge of a circular stone well. It was too perfect to be natural, circular and wider than a hot tub, and I saw faded chisel marks on the stone: BLOOD-GOOD 1726. Great. Creepy-ass Connor was probably the last person to come down here.

I dipped my hand into the gently lapping water just below the lip of the cistern. It shocked me, so cold it almost burned at the tips of my fingers. It was the kind of cold things only get when they come from some place so deep and dark nobody has ever laid eyes on it.

"Ouch," I muttered, flexing my fingers to get the blood flowing again.

I stepped around the cistern and looked into the beam of my flashlight. It illuminated a flat slab of the same flaky white stone the entire island was made out of under the thin coating of trees and sand. This one had flat black markings carved into it, rough ragged lines that looked like scars more than anything.

I fidgeted. This place made me feel like I had ants crawling all over me, a sensation that I couldn't shake off.

"Ivy!" Simon's voice echoed off the ceiling, made me jump a foot.

"Down here!" I called, and watched the bobbing light of Simon's electric lantern as it came down the steps.

"Ivy, for the love of Pete," he said. "This is not safe. There are quarry holes down here that go fifteen feet deep. Come upstairs this instant."

"I'm sorry," I said, pointing to the rock. "I was just looking at this."

"The altar rock," Simon said. "The first inhabitants of the island used it to worship, to mourn, and to celebrate.

Connor built the house over it, hateful sort of man that he was. Superstitious idiots would probably say he thought he'd draw some kind of power from it."

"Yeah, this place is giving off a real Amityville vibe," I said.

Simon snorted a laugh. "Come upstairs. All that's really down here is that cistern, and the water in it is terribly tainted. You'll be seeing colors and hearing voices in no time if you ingest it. Who knows, maybe that's what made Connor go batty."

"You sure that isn't what messed up Mom and my grandmother?" I asked. He shook his head.

"Connor's son dug a new well, and so far so good."

He turned to go back up the stairs, and then glanced back. "Ivy," he said hesitantly. "The tunnels connected to this cellar run clear under the island. Any map that may have existed is long gone, but one could still find their way with enough time." He raised the lantern so it dazzled my eyes. "I need to know: Did you see Neil Ramsey the night he died? Did he find the route to this cellar and come inside the manor? If he tried to hurt you, Ivy, I'd understand. I wouldn't be angry."

He stepped toward me. I took a corresponding giant step back. Suddenly he wasn't my nerdy uncle. He was a guy I barely knew, and we were alone in a place where nobody would hear anything, no matter if I whispered or screamed.

My pulse was vibrating so hard it felt like someone was squeezing my throat shut. He knew. He must have found the shirt somehow. *He'd followed me into the woods and seen . . . what?*

"I don't know anything," I whispered. Fortunately it was dark, because I was way beyond controlling my microexpressions or keeping eye contact to sell the lie.

"Ivy, it's very important that if you start to have any . . . urges you tell me immediately," Simon said. "If you did something, even if it was an accident . . ."

"I didn't kill Neil Ramsey, okay?" I shouted. My voice rolled back to me through the narrow space. "I've never been down here, and I didn't hurt anyone."

I felt sick and dizzy, like all my lies might choke me. I *didn't* know that I hadn't done something. If my brain was as defective as all the other killers and freaks in my family tree . . .

I turned, whether it was to run or just curl in on myself I wasn't sure, but my foot caught a rock and I pitched forward, over the edge of the cistern.

The cold water felt like being hit by a car. My lungs seized up, and for a long second I sank, unable to move. Then survival instinct took over, and my legs started kicking of their own volition. My head broke the surface, and I choked and screamed, a big mouthful of the water making its way down my throat. It tasted heavy and earthy, almost medicinal, and it burned a little on the way down.

Simon was yelling—I couldn't tell what, from the water sloshing and my blood roaring in my ears. His hand grabbed my collar and yanked me from the water. I landed on the dirt floor, coughing and shaking.

"Ivy." Simon's voice was getting farther away. "Ivy!"

I tried to crawl toward him. The rock under my hand gave the slightest of vibrations in response, and I started to feel prickles of electricity working their way through my fingers and up my arms. The vibration spread, the rock rumbling like a heavy truck had passed by, and I heard a faint hiss growing from behind me. My eyes slowly adjusted, and I realized there was a small bit of light coming in from somewhere above me, just barely enough for me to make out shapes. A pale cloud rose from the cistern, and I felt hot steam. The water—the frozen water—was boiling, hissing and sloshing over the sides of the pool that held it.

The shaking increased, and I felt the same kind of breathless feeling, that sensation of being perpetually perched at the top of a roller coaster, rush through me. I tried to reach for Simon, but when I did, he wasn't where he'd been standing, the strobing light from above showing I was alone. "Simon?" I called. "Simon!"

Rock screamed on rock in response, and I heard something collapse off in the dark. Panic did start then—what if

I was trapped down here?

The water hissing and churning drowned out everything, even my own heartbeat, and all at once I wasn't at the top of the coaster—I was plunging over, free-falling as something gripped me just like it had when I'd dreamed I was in another body. I was only a passenger inside the vessel of my body, and I felt a scream building inside me.

Stop! I shouted internally. *This has to stop!* All at once, like the ride had crashed back to earth, the shaking ceased. I still felt floaty and disconnected, but this was different from the dream—I was still a passenger, but at least I could steer. I hoped I wasn't dead. I'd died enough for one lifetime.

I made myself stand up and felt my way along the rock wall. I'd seen light—that much I was sure of, and light meant a way out. Doyle had said the tunnels all ended at the beach, where the bootleggers would transfer their cargo to small boats bound for the mainland.

My knuckles scraped along the rough granite, leaving my blood behind, and I kept stumbling on the uneven ground, but I managed to stay up. I wouldn't say my thought process was anything approaching clear, but I managed to put one foot in front of the other until I stepped from the rocky passage into a dim, chilly cavern. The light I'd glimpsed was coming in from a crack high above, and I could only hear wind, not waves. I must be farther inland, somewhere deep underground. I slumped to my knees when I realized there was no way out, no way to reach that light. The walls were smooth, like the inside of a genie's bottle, the chimney tapering until it truncated in a crack barely big enough to reach my fingers through.

I smooshed my knuckles into my face, trying to massage some feeling back into it, and when my vision cleared a little I saw the faint light from above gleaming off something small and gold in the corner of the cavern.

I crawled over to it slowly. Moving at all still felt like I was inside a particularly shitty carnival ride, and my head throbbed like someone's jacked-up bass. The gold thing was a ring—one of the big chunky ones guys loved to show off, even if they'd graduated from high school twenty-odd years ago and were now selling tractors in Topeka. I reached out for it, the metal stinging my fingers with cold, but when I picked it up something skinny and white came with it, and clattered out of my grip against the rock.

I shoved the ring in my pocket and scratched at the gravel, hoping what I was seeing wasn't real, just like the boiling water or the sounds, or me missing the fact Simon had vanished, but the skeletal hand practically grabbed mine as I freed it from the ground.

That wasn't the end either—attached to the hand was an arm bone, still encased in some kind of disintegrating plastic jacket. I dropped it, gravel biting into my palms as I scrambled backward, until my wrist twisted and I landed almost face-to-face with a human skull.

In my panic, all I really saw was the dry, stretched flesh clinging to the cheekbones like cheap leather clings to an old suitcase, and the straw-soft pale hair sticking to the scalp. The skull rested against a rock, like the dead person had just lain down for a nap, and on the flat surface above it, in a dip carved by the lava that had left these tunnels, sat a small gray figure, faceless and made of a material just as rotted as the corpse's clothes. Some sort of little doll, a grotesque parody of the dead person who'd ended up just below it.

I ran, falling like I was drunk, back through the passage. My lungs wouldn't draw enough air to really scream, or I would have been yelling until my vocal cords gave out.

Half running, I tripped over a corner of that damn altar stone Simon had been so excited about and landed on my face. Things went blurry and black, like when you chase a Valium with a mouthful of cheap drugstore vodka, and I blacked out for a second.

Wakefulness crashed over me like a bucket of cold water. I started into a sitting position and vomited, managing to mostly avoid Simon's shoes and my own legs.

"Ivy?" Simon gripped my shoulder, holding my hair out

of my face and running a hand across my cheek. "Are you all right?"

I shoved him away. "How could you leave me alone down here?"

Simon stumbled onto his butt on the rock, eyes widening behind his glasses. "Ivy, I've been looking for you for an hour! I never left the cellar!" He stood, brushing off his pants. "I came down here to tell you the cellar isn't safe and you took off running like a bat out of hell. I've been practically having a stroke yelling for you down every tunnel in this place."

"NO!" I yelled. "You left me," I rasped. My throat burned from throwing up and the screaming beforehand. "You left me down here with a *dead fucking body!*"

"Ivy," he said, offering me a tissue, "you hit your head. I have been trying to find you, and I did not leave you—you ran from me in a panic. Calm down before you really hurt yourself."

I snatched the tissue and wiped off my face, glaring up at him. My muscles ached from the fall, from running through the dark, stumbling blind. I'd be lucky if I didn't get hypothermia, given how I was soaked through with water . . .

Except a touch told me my jeans and shirt were bone-dry. Underwear and bra too. I was dry right down to my socks. The only dampness was a sheen of panic sweat coating my face and sticking hair to my neck.

"I'm so sorry," I muttered. Simon held out his hand, and I let him pull me up. I was shaky, but I made myself stand on my own. I don't know if I was falling back on my tough act because I was freaking out, or because I didn't want Simon to know just how off the rails I'd gone.

"I'm sorry to ask, Ivy, but . . . are you taking any drugs?" he said. "I won't be angry, I just . . ."

Now not only my head but my entire body ached, and I sat down hard on the edge of the old altar rock. "I'm not," I sighed. "Even back in Nebraska I never did much more than smoke a little pot or steal pills from whoever Mom was seeing that week."

Rather than tsking or acting like he was disappointed in me, Simon lowered his head. "I was half hoping you'd say something you ingested could be causing this," he murmured. "Ivy, you really frightened me. And what's this about dead bodies?"

"It's . . ." The memory of that cavern was so real, the feeling of the smooth, cool finger bone rolling between mine vivid as the pain in my shin from where I'd tripped. And fallen into the water, which hadn't happened at all.

"Simon, did you . . . did you warn me about the well water?" I said carefully. His brows drew together.

"Other than saying don't drown in it?" he said.

I waved the comment off, my heart sinking. "Never mind."

Everything I'd seen when I was blacked out before *seemed* real.

My mind wasn't the go-to source for reliability right now, anyway. When I looked to where the gap in the wall had been, the light leading to the cavern, there was nothing except smooth rock. Whatever had caused this, I wasn't in any shape to keep exploring a bunch of caves, so I let Simon help me up.

"Come on," Simon said, taking me by the hand like I was five. "Let's get you cleaned up. I may have to call Julia and take you to the emergency room if you've hit your head badly."

I faced Simon as he shut the hidden door to the tunnels and brushed off his hands. "I want to know everything. All the signs, how long I might have if I'm sick. I want to go to a real hospital and get a brain scan or something."

Simon looked reluctant, but then he nodded. "There are a lot of other things that could be causing this, Ivy. A lot of explanations for the things you thought you saw in the basement that made you run from me."

"Whatever," I said. "I just want to figure out if this is my fault or not." I scuttled upstairs and shut my door, propping the chair from my desk under it. I didn't think, I just moved. Instincts ingrained since I was a little girl kicked in, and I slumped down on the floor next to the chair, my heart pounding. It's not an easy thing to admit you're sick. Everyone pretty much goes through life assuming they're fine, until they're not. And even when you hear the word *schizophrenia* or *Parkinson's* or *cancer,* you want to deny it. Bullshit psychics and healers would go out of business if you didn't.

I wondered what I'd hear when I saw a doctor or a shrink.

I wondered if it would make me remember anything about Neil Ramsey, the lighthouse, the "dream" where I'd cut my foot. I couldn't remember, but clearly that didn't mean much. I was for sure losing time. I was running around caves, hallucinating skeletons. Who said I wasn't capable of anything when the black curtain came down over my memory?

I made myself get off the floor after a few minutes. I was sixteen, not five, and way too much crap had already happened today for me to spend the rest of it hugging my knees and shaking.

I showered and shoved the clothes that I'd been wearing to the bottom of my laundry bag. They smelled overpoweringly musty and dank from the cellar. I couldn't feel that I'd even lightly tapped my head, never mind bruised it after examining myself in the mirror for cuts. I must have keeled over in a faint down in the basement. I was a fainter now. Awesome.

Flopping on my bed, I took out the small book I'd found

in my mother's room and riffled the pages again. Her hand-writing was spidery and dense, like trying to read through a thicket of pricker bushes. She had serial killer handwriting, and didn't really believe in spaces.

Doyle would know what to do, I realized. I rolled off the bed and slid into my boots and my jacket.

The sun was almost down by the time I left the man-sion. The rosebushes were mostly naked, just a few brown leaves and dead flowers clinging to their branches. They rat-tled in the wind, trying to snag my jacket and my hair as I walked to the forest. By the time I got back to the stream the moon was up. Flashes lit the clouds spotlight white for a few seconds at a time before it got dark again, blotting out everything but the indistinct skeletons of the pines.

An eerie wolf howl cut through the woods on the wind, and I sank deeper inside my coat. Obviously, there were no wolves in Maine. Especially not on a tiny island. I was just letting myself get wigged out, substituting the things I was rightfully upset over with stupid crap like wolves and mon-sters. The me of six months ago, before all this started, would have laughed her butt off at me skulking through the woods, afraid of shadows.

Doyle's house was mostly dark, but I knocked on the back door anyway. After what had happened, having a run-in with Doyle's father suddenly scared me a lot less.

The porch light flicked on, and a guy who looked a lot like Doyle, just bigger and meaner, opened the door. "Yeah?" he grumbled.

"Um," I said. He was huge—like club-bouncer huge. Pro-wrestler huge. I tried not to stare.

"Doyle!" the guy bellowed. "The Bloodgood girl is on our porch, bothering me!"

"Oh, you can go back to eating protein bars and injecting hormones into your butt cheeks," I told him with way more bite than was probably prudent, given how 'roided out he looked. "I can show myself in."

"You got a problem?" the giant demanded. Fortunately Doyle came thundering down the stairs into the back hall before I could tell this guy what exactly my problem was, and probably end up swallowing a few of my smaller teeth for my trouble. I could only feel sad and scared and off-balance for so long before I just started wanting to lash out at anyone near me. It was one of my less charming traits, but there you go. I hadn't exactly had an awesome role model for anger management with Mom.

"You're a dick, Blake," Doyle grumbled, taking me by the wrist and pulling me inside and down the hall. We were in his room before I could blink, and he slammed the door. "Are you crazy?" he demanded. "You know how jumpy my family is right now. The last thing they want is one of the

Bloodgoods at their door. You're just lucky Dad is on the mainland."

"Do *you* want me to leave?" I asked. The floor creaked outside the door, and Doyle growled.

"Go away, Blake!" he shouted. He pushed a pile of laundry off his bed and gestured. "Sorry. I don't clean much. Or ever."

"I'm still getting used to the idea of a room where all the furniture isn't bolted to the walls," I said. "My standards are insanely low."

Doyle flopped back on the ratty patchwork quilt and grinned up at me. "Lucky, lucky me, then."

I didn't join him, choosing a seat in a ratty easy chair in the corner. Girlfriend, boundaries, et cetera. "This is okay, right?" I said. "Valerie won't be pissed I'm in your room?"

"Valerie doesn't have any say over who I hang out with," Doyle said. "Plus, I'm being honest, it's not like we're gonna get married. She's heading to college in a few years, and I'm staying right here. It's fun while it lasts, but she made it pretty clear it's temporary."

I pulled my knees up to my chest, feeling kind of crappy for how happy Doyle's words made me. I did have a little bit of a thing for him, and just because I'd never act on it while he was with someone else didn't erase it. But for right now he was off-limits, and I wasn't exactly in a flirting mood anyway.

Doyle sat up, bouncing a little on the creaky bed. "So what are you doing here, anyway?"

I got to my feet and started looking through the stuff on Doyle's dresser. Suddenly I didn't know what to say. "It just got kind of intense at home."

Doyle stopped bouncing and tilted his head. "Must have been a little bit more than intense if you'd risk coming over here. Not that I'm mad you did. If nothing else, you have more balls than most of my family. Or yours, for that matter. They all act like they'll be burned at the stake if they're caught on the wrong side of the island."

"It's a lot harder than I thought being here," I said. "My mom's house. Her room. Her stuff. Seeing what she was like before is . . . it's weird. And my fucking uncle—he has the nerve to tell me that, oh yeah, we're all sick in the head apparently, and we tend to die prematurely and take anyone close down with us. Bonus, no modern medication works and no doctor is even entirely sure what's wrong with us."

I slumped back down on the easy chair. "I know nothing is set in stone, but I'm scared. I haven't admitted that since I was, like, eight years old, but I don't want to hurt anyone. And I don't want to lose my mind like my mother apparently did. I don't want to spend half my adult life in a psych ward. I just want to move to California and just . . . live an entirely normal life. That part's lame, I guess, but I . . ."

"Not lame," Doyle broke in. "Where in California?"

"San Francisco," I said.

Doyle reached up to a wall of photos, postcards, old ticket stubs, and similar items littering the wall above his bed and handed me a dog-eared postcard showing an expanse of desert and blue-gray mountains rising into an indescribably clear sky. I recognized it without looking at the caption on the back as New Mexico.

"Farmington," he said. "That's where my mom ended up after the divorce. Sometimes when this island feels really small I look at that and pretend I can go out there after high school."

"Can't you?" I said.

Doyle shook his head.

"Dad would cut me off, and I don't exactly have scholarship grades. We're not Bloodgood rich, but all my cousins get college paid for, cars, living expenses. I can't just show up on my mom's doorstep with no college plans and no job skills. Dad made sure she got absolutely nothing when she left him. I don't want to be a burden."

Much as I hated touching people, I kind of wanted to hug Doyle. He looked so deflated, the usual spark burned out in his eyes. "Farmington is nice," was all I could offer. "I think you'd be really happy there."

"Yeah," Doyle sighed. "Basically, anywhere is better than Darkhaven. But you didn't come over here to listen to me bitch and moan. Tell me what's going on with you."

I pulled the notebook out of my pocket. "I found my mother's . . . diary, I guess? I don't know. It's literally the only thing I have that might tell me why she ran away. My uncle just keeps saying there were problems, and she left." I tapped the book against my leg, suddenly irritated. "I don't know why it's such a big secret. *She* sure as hell never tried to protect me from anything. I mean . . ." I tossed the diary on the cot. "It's clear as day she was already nuts, and she was like what, seventeen?

Doyle picked up the book and paged through it, scanning the pages of scrawl in the five different colors of ink. "Why don't we ask her friend?"

"What?" I grabbed the diary back. "My mother did not have friends. She had people who tolerated her until they realized she was a kleptomaniac con artist."

Doyle leaned down and ran his finger along a line of scribbles. "Mary Anne. Says right there." I leaned over his shoulder as he read it aloud, envious of his ability to decipher Mom's scrawl.

Went with Mary Anne to the lobster bake. She brought her dad's schnapps. My dad won't stop asking me what Mom said last time I visited her in the latest glorified prison ward he had her locked in. I just want to float away, feel like I did when I was warm and dizzy and standing with my toes in the ocean on the mainland. You can't go into the water out here on the island. You'll drown.

"Even if this Mary Anne exists, I bet she's long gone," I said. "This was, what, nearly eighteen years ago?"

Doyle took the diary and flipped rapidly. "Mary Anne's dad, the one with the super-sad liquor cabinet, lives in Camden," he said. "That's not too far. We should go."

I raised one eyebrow. "Are you serious? In case you didn't notice, we're stuck on an island and my uncle's weird little minion is the only one with a boat I have access to."

"She's not the only one," Doyle said. "Meet me tomorrow morning around six and we'll take my dad's cabin cruiser."

"Won't your dad be pissed you stole his boat to go look for a teenage alcoholic who may or may not have been friends with my mom?" I said.

"Oh yeah, he'll kick my ass," Doyle said. "But it'll be worth it. I don't like seeing you this worried."

"Yeah, let's go." I locked eyes with him. "I could pretend I'm not worried, but I am, and I need to know, and I really don't want to go alone." I made myself stop talking. Now I was just spilling all my fears and feelings to anyone who'd listen. I needed to get it together.

"So we'll go together," Doyle said. "Six a.m. There's an old dock on the other side of the lighthouse that nobody uses. I'll pick you up."

I almost thought he was more nuts for suggesting I wake up at 6:00 a.m. than we go track down Mom's friend, but I nodded. "Okay."

"And if you feel the urge to kill, let me know, so I can get a head start running," he called as I opened his bedroom door and stepped into the hall.

"I hate you," I said. Doyle grinned.

"I'm adorable and you know it."

"Now who's delusional?" I said, and shut the door.

Chapter

17

The old dock where Doyle told me to meet him jutted out into the water at a crooked angle, like a broken bone. It must have been there for decades, the boards slowly rotting until I could see the black water lapping through the gaps. It felt like walking into an enormous mouth that only had a few ragged teeth left.

I stood on the very edge, my toes over the water, and after a minute a motorboat nosed around the point by the lighthouse and drifted in, Doyle at the helm. He helped me in and revved the motor. "Doughnut?" He pointed at a half-crushed box plastered with powdered sugar. I wrinkled my nose.

"It is way too early for supermarket pastry."

"Yeah, if I were really smooth, I'd probably have some croissants and a thermos of hot chocolate, and be like, wearing a scarf," Doyle said. "And I'd find a way to work a Jane Austen quote or two into our conversation."

"And brush the droplets of spray from my lips," I said as the boat skipped a wave and a welter of salt mist hit me in the face.

"Good one," Doyle said. "Remind me to pick your brain for tips some time."

"That doesn't actually work," I said. "If some creep lured me onto his boat, I'd throw him overboard and it'd be spring before somebody found the body," I said.

Doyle shoved half a doughnut in his mouth. "Fortunately I'm a jerk who scares off women before I have any chance of luring them anywhere." He pointed the boat toward the mainland. The cabin was all wood and shiny metal, and the hull was so varnished I could see the ocean reflected in it.

"So how many James Bond boats does your dad have anyway?" I said. Doyle snorted.

"It's his thing. He has boats and cars and motorcycles, because what you need on a tiny island is twenty different ways to drive in a circle."

"How are we supposed to find this Mary Anne woman, anyway?" I said after another bone-crunching jolt over a wave. Doyle huffed.

"You always ask this many questions?"

"Only when I'm trying to fill an awkward silence," I said.

Doyle pushed the throttle up, and the boat started to bounce across the surface of the ocean in earnest. I took the hint and sat down. I'd read more of the diary the night before, and I hadn't slept much. Most of what Mom wrote was just babbling or inane "dear diary" type stuff, and scouring through her handwriting for any mention of Mary Anne had left me with a headache that felt like an icepick to the eye.

* * *

Simon doesn't go to visit Mom like I do. He only goes to spy. He tells Father everything, when we're forced to visit him and his new wife on the mainland. I tell him nothing. I guess that fits. Mary Anne thinks Father is just worried about Mom's condition, but I know better. He's not worried. He's waiting. Waiting to see if Mom will snap out of it or end up like everyone else in that damp, smelly hospital he calls an "institute," like that somehow makes it smell less like pee and bleach and takes away the hopeless look in Mom's eyes after they give her a shot of tranquilizer. He's waiting to see if she'll finally give in to the dark thing that's lurking inside all of us that are Bloodgoods by birth. He never forgave Mom taking Simon and me in the divorce, and taking back her own family name, giving it to us so the Bloodgoods live on and his family tree dies with him. He started calling her crazy way before she actually started acting that way. Joke's on him. I've seen Mom's will. He gets nothing. Figure I'll save that news for when he makes us visit him at Christmas. Bloodgoods know how to stick together, if nothing else.

I didn't know for sure why my grandmother had been institutionalized, but I could guess. Mom was devoted to her, though. There were more entries about her trips to visit than everything else combined.

All I'd found that could possibly help me track down Mary Anne were a few lines toward the end of the writing, just before the barren expanse of blank pages that concealed anything else I might have learned about her.

> *Mary Anne won't meet me. She's always busy, like because she has a job she's now better than me. As if she'll ever do anything with herself. She'll be stuck at the Crow's Nest until she finds some guy to shack up with. I just have to go. I feel the tide pulling me. Go go go. Run until I can't stop. Run until I drop. Until I die. I'd rather die than be here one second longer.*

We tied up at the Ramseys' slip in Darkhaven, and Doyle led me to a beat-up Jeep wagon in the parking lot of the marina. "Camden's about forty minutes from here," he said. "You want to drive? It's my car, so if you dent it, you'll just have to deal with me, not my dad."

I shook my head. "I don't have a license."

Doyle grimaced. "You and I can practice if you want. I helped Valerie pass her road test."

"I can drive," I said. "Just not legally."

"Like so many good things in life," Doyle said. The Jeep took a few tries to turn over, but soon we were on the twisting coast highway, passing tiny antiques shops, lopsided barns, and restaurants with giant lobster statues waving us in from their parking lots.

"You know, whatever we find," Doyle said after a few miles, "I won't tell anyone. Not Valerie, not anyone in my family. Certainly not your uncle."

I leaned my forehead against the cold window glass. "I trust you, Doyle. Much as I trust anyone."

He sighed. "I get the sense that isn't very much."

"You're not wrong," I said quietly.

"I get it," he said. "People who should protect you don't, and the ones you should trust aren't worthy of it. Believe me, Ivy. I get it more than you know."

I sat up and looked over at him, but he was staring at the road. I felt really shitty—I was dealing with a lot of stuff right now, to be sure, but that didn't mean I had to be self-absorbed when it came to my friends.

"You want to talk about it?" I said, knowing the answer.

"No," he said, and that was it until we started seeing signs for Camden.

I told Doyle about the Crow's Nest, and he handed me his phone to look up the place. "It's a bookstore," I said, showing him the search page as we slowed down at the Camden town line. A Maine State Police car sat to one side, the trooper glaring at everyone who passed. I reflexively sank down in my seat.

"You got warrants?" Doyle smiled as I shrunk away from the window.

"Cops usually meant us having to pick up and move before one of them called CPS," I said. "I'm not their biggest fan."

The trooper didn't pull out after us, though, and we crept along behind tourists with out-of-state plates and locals in rattletrap pickups until we spotted the bookstore and parked.

The Crow's Nest was tucked into a small building with a sagging roof, covered in gray shingles and those spiny climbing roses that seemed to be everywhere in Maine. A small brass bell jangled when I stepped inside.

This was not the kind of bookstore you found in a romantic comedy, where you ran into your crush in the philosophy aisle and pretended to be smart by grabbing some esoteric book in French, or the sort where you could curl up for hours, wear cute vintage glasses, and be that quirky girl everyone teased except for the new boy in town, who was of course also hot and super into you for your brain, not your stunning looks. This place was more the kind of bookstore you'd go to if you needed a handy one-stop tome for casting spells and summoning the devil.

Shelves ran all the way to the ceiling, and across the rafters ancient bundles of dusty herbs hung. I think they were meant to combat the smell of mildew and rotten paper, but they'd given up a long time ago. Every table was piled high with books—books that nobody would ever want to read, or had, by the look, even opened. A thick layer of dust sat on everything, and I felt my throat start to tickle.

The counter was made of rickety plywood, also stacked all around with books, newspapers, and magazines so old people in the ads were still wearing suits and smoking. A guy my age leaned against it, reading a dog-eared copy of *Snow Crash.* He looked about as musty as the rest of the shop—his hair was stiff and black, shaved around the ears to show off a collection of studs and rings. He had two more in his lip, and alternating black and white nails. He was wrapped up in a black hoodie and a striped purple-and-black scarf, like Tim Burton's geeky kid brother.

He looked up from his book, gave me a once-over, and let out a long sigh. "I doubt I can help you."

"Funny, I was about to say the same thing," I muttered. Somewhere behind me, a stack of magazines collapsed, sliding to the floor with a slithering rush.

"If you need school books, try Amazon," said the kid, seemingly oblivious to the poltergeist-like movement of his clutter piles. "We only do used and rare here."

More like moldy and ancient, but whatever. "I'm actually looking for a woman who used to work here. Mary Anne?"

The kid sucked on his lip ring for a second, rolling his eyes. "She's not an *employee*," he explained, as if I'd asked him how pants worked. "She's the *owner*."

"Fine," I said. "Do you know where she lives?"

He scrutinized me again. "Does she owe you money?"

"Does she owe a lot of people money?" I asked.

"No. Business is slow, but fortunately we've got this stash of Nazi gold in the office safe," he said.

"She and my mom were friends a long time ago," I said. "I just wanted to ask her something."

"Oh em gee," said the kid, coming to life like one of the vampires he was impersonating at the first whiff of scandal. "Are you, like, searching for your real identity? Did Mary Anne get pregnant and your mom raised the baby?" He grinned at me, showing a bumper crop of adult braces and dispelling my suspicion he was just being an asshole. Small-town Maine was really boring. If I was trapped working at the Crow's Nest, I'd get excited if we got a pizza delivered. I shrugged. "Yeah, something like that."

The guy scribbled an address on the back of a paper bag and slid it to me. "You have to come back and tell me what happened," he said. "It is *so boring* here I literally think I will die most days before my shift ends."

"You got it," I said, hurrying back toward the door with the intention to never see him again.

"Don't ask," I said to Doyle when I got back in the car.

We drove through downtown, more gray buildings with

more discreet little signs, and up a winding hill of Victorian homes into an older, shabbier neighborhood that dead-ended at a cottage that was even more ramshackle than the bookstore.

I opened my door. Doyle started to stay put, but I tilted my head. "You mind? I didn't expect to actually meet her, and now I'm not sure I want to do it alone."

He got out without a word and followed me up the overgrown walk. The house was practically hidden from the road by a thicket of bushes and thorns, and the windows were covered from the inside by newspapers. The screen door was hanging by one hinge, and I gingerly pushed it aside before I knocked.

I was about to turn around when Doyle perked up. "Someone's in there," he said. "I can hear them moving around."

I knocked again, harder. "Hello?" I called. "I'm Myra Bloodgood's daughter, Ivy. Can I talk to you?"

It wasn't my best cold open ever, but now that I was standing here, most of my con skills deserted me. What was I supposed to say?

A lot of locks clicked, and then the door opened a crack. "Go away."

"Are you Mary Anne?" I said. I held up the diary. "I found your name in this. Mom—Myra—talked about you a lot." A tiny lie, but hopefully that would get me in the door.

The eye at the crack was wide and bloodshot, and I wondered why it hadn't occurred to me that Mary Anne might be as looped as Mom. Like attracting like and all that. "Where is Myra?" she said. Her accent was precise and clipped, definitely not from around here.

"She's dead," I said. The door slammed, and Doyle sighed.

"Want me to try? I can lay on the charm, or something."

I listened, heard half a dozen deadbolts rattling, and held up a hand. "Wait a second."

The door flew open again, slamming against the wall like a rifle shot. Mary Anne stared at me, at Doyle. She was wearing one of those dresses that looks like a blanket, and her hair drifted around her head in loose waves. "Who the hell is he?" she said, pointing at Doyle.

"My friend," I said. "He doesn't bite."

Doyle grinned in response, showing his blindingly white teeth. I elbowed him in the ribs. "Knock it off," I hissed.

Mary Anne stared at both of us, eyes narrowed. "Myra is really dead?"

"Really," I promised. "We aren't here to bother you or cause trouble. I just wanted to ask you something." This was my wheelhouse—lying to nice, average people and talking them into doing things they wouldn't normally do. Although looking at her stained clothes, bag lady hair, and the slice of hoarder mess I could see behind her, I judged Mary Anne was probably several city blocks away from average.

Mary Anne sighed. "Poor Myra. Rest in peace." She went back to glaring at us, then slowly let go of her death grip on the door. "I guess you can come in."

The house was at least as crowded as the bookstore. A sour odor blended with the kind of cheap, cloying incense my mother had always loved. Doyle wrinkled his nose as Mary Anne shoved a pile of books and pillows off the sofa. "Sit," she said. "You want some tea?"

I nodded, even though I was fairly sure anything that came out of her kitchen would probably poison me.

Doyle leaned over when she stomped away into the cramped little kitchen. "This is not what I was expecting."

"This is exactly what I was expecting," I muttered. Mary Anne shouted, making me jump.

"So what did you want to talk to me about, Amy?"

"It's Ivy," I said. I got up, looking around the room. It was cramped, covered in tapestry prints and scarves on all the furniture and lamps. My feet sank into at least three layers of Persian carpet along with a decade's worth of newspapers.

"Whatever," Mary Anne said, slamming a kettle onto an old wood-fired stove and poking at the embers under the burner. "What did you want to know?"

"Can you just . . ." I swallowed, my throat tight from more than the dust in the air. *Just get a grip, Ivy,* I commanded. "I don't know much about Mom before I was born. You were her best friend, I thought maybe you could just tell me a little bit about her." So I chickened out on the real question. I was working up to it, I told myself. First a little color about Mom as a teenager, then I'd start interrogating Mary Anne about my paternity.

"Not much to tell," Mary Anne grunted, wiping her hands on a filthy towel. "My family came here from Bosnia. We were refugees. I was the new girl, no English, no friends. Your mama was kind to me. Even started calling me my English name, Mary Anne, so the others would stop picking on me."

"That's it?" I narrowed my eyes.

"What more you want?" Mary Anne replied, glaring at me in return.

"Look, I know my grandmother died in a mental hospital," I said. "I know my mother was struggling with a lot. I just want to know why she left Darkhaven." I cleared my throat and tried to smile. "Anything you can tell me would be really helpful." *Come on, Ivy*, I chided myself. *Suck it up and ask what you really want to ask.*

Wanted to ask, sure. Wanted to know, maybe not so much. While my father was still a blank space, he could be anyone, maybe even somebody who wasn't totally horrible. Once I'd asked, I'd opened the door to certainty, and any grifter could tell you that the certain truth was a dangerous thing to have in your grasp.

Mary Anne cut her gaze at Doyle, who had picked up a rotund stone figure from one of the overcrowded window-sills and was turning it in his hands. "Put that down!" she snapped. "I may tolerate *zla krv* in my house, but I do not have to tolerate rudeness."

I glanced between her and Doyle. "Sorry," he said. "Didn't realize your, uh, rock was so important."

"Why are you dragging yourself through the gutter?" Mary Anne snapped. "An innocent boy going around with a girl of tainted blood."

So much for any more questions. "Hey, lady," I said. "You don't want to tell me anything, just say so. I don't need to be lectured, and I'm full up on crazy." I waved off the chipped mug she handed at me. "Thanks anyway."

"Wait!" she hollered desperately as I started to walk out. "Your mama, she died . . . she was murdered? You know who the killer is, or no?"

I turned back on her. Suddenly I felt monumentally stupid for reacting so strongly. She was just a lonely hoarder, stuck in her smelly little house, and I was an idiot to think finding out anything new about Mom would make the past two weeks easier to deal with.

Mary Anne watched me, mug gripped so hard her knuckles were white.

"She killed herself," I said, making sure to enunciate each

syllable. It was still weird to say it out loud to a stranger. It was surprisingly easy. "Nobody hurt her. Nobody killed her. She was weak, and she took the easy way out. That what you wanted to know?"

Doyle put his hand on my shoulder, and I shoved it off. Mary Anne's face twitched, like I'd reached across the distance and slapped her.

"No . . . ," she whispered. Her eyes went wide, and it was like she was seeing me for the first time. "You did not come here for Myra," she breathed. "You come here for your father." She put a hand to her mouth, fingers shaking. "The darkness around you . . . Myra told me then, and I didn't believe her. . . ."

"Okay, that's enough," Doyle said. "Come on, Ivy, we're really leaving now."

"You!" Mary Anne shrieked. The mug dropped from her hand and shattered as she pointed a finger at Doyle. "You run while you can, boy. Myra knew the sickness, knew it was in her bloodline. Knew it would come for her!" She let out a sound like a wounded animal and crumpled to the floor, shaking.

Doyle guided me firmly to the door. "She doesn't know anything," he muttered. "Let's just go, okay?"

"Oh yes," Mary Anne spat from the floor. Her eyes were alive and gleaming like twin oil slicks, and she pointed a finger with a ragged, bloody nail at me. "Go with him. Your mother knew, and I should have listened. Your coming to be, it drove her past the edge. She should have killed you the moment you drew breath."

Rage boiled up into my words before I could stop it, and I turned around, starting for Mary Anne. "What did you say?" Doyle caught the sleeve of my jacket, hard enough to rock me back on my heels.

"Don't, Ivy," he murmured in my ear. "We don't need the police coming over here."

"You think you know anything about me?" I shouted at Mary Anne. "You don't know shit! You have no idea what it was like to put up with her all those years. The drinking and the fights and her beating on me whenever she was fed up with her own crappy life!"

I picked up one of her stupid rocks and threw it to the ground. Something under the layers of newspaper and junk on the floor shattered, and Mary Anne screamed.

"I'm not bad!" I also screamed, outpacing her. "I'm just trying to deal with this shit as normally as possible, which is more than she ever did! I am *not* like her!"

It was like I couldn't stop myself, like the few times I'd let myself get really drunk at some barn party back in the Midwest. I picked up another rock, poised it over a cluster of glass figurines on a table near the door. "Say something else about me!" I shouted. "I dare you!" I didn't care that I was scaring Mary Anne. I was glad. She was going to taunt me and call me names? I was going to break all her dusty crap.

"No," Mary Anne was wailing. "No, no, no . . . not me. I'm no threat to you. That's why he let me live. I'm no threat to either of you."

Just like that, when she spoke, the surge of adrenaline that had led me to lose my shit on this poor old crazy woman thudded to a stop. I realized that I was having a total melt-down for reasons that had nothing to do with Mary Anne. I dropped the rock, and it thudded on the carpet.

"Who?" I said, feeling my heart thudding like I'd just finished a cross-country race. "Who let you live?"

Mary Anne pulled her knees to her chest. She looked like a little girl who was scared of the dark. "No . . . I can't . . ."

"WHO?" I thundered. Even Doyle jumped at that. I glanced over and saw that his brow was furrowed and his eyes were wide and almost all pupil. Great. Not only had I lost my temper on a pathetic woman who probably needed a heavy dose of lithium even more than Mom had, I'd done it in front of the one tolerable person I'd met since I came to Darkhaven.

"I'm sorry," I said softly. "I'm really sorry, okay? Please tell me who said that."

Mary Anne let out a small sob. "The devil," she whispered, staring up at me, her whole body quivering. "Your father."

Chapter

18

D oyle drove us down to a parking lot at the public beach, and we sat in the car for a long time, watching the waves roll in and out without speaking.

"You wanna talk about it?" Doyle said finally. He leaned over and flipped the passenger heating vent toward me, gesturing for me to put my hands on it as warm air billowed out. I felt a sharp tingle in my palms and realized the beds of my nails were blue.

"Not really," I said. Doyle looked back at the ocean.

"I'm sorry that wasn't what you were looking for," he said. "I know how it is when you go looking for something you think will help you understand, and it all goes wrong."

"I just feel stupid," I muttered. "Stupid for thinking anything Mom was involved in wouldn't just be a massive ball of screwed up." I hesitated. "And *really* stupid that you saw me lose my shit like that."

"Don't," Doyle said. "As far as berserker rages go, you can't hold a candle to my brothers and cousins after about twenty beers." He shifted, leaning back against the seat and staring at the ocean, letting out a sigh that mingled with the blasts of lukewarm air from the heater.

"It's not even that," I muttered. "I don't know why I thought finding out anything about my father would do the least bit of good." I sighed. "And I didn't find out anything new, other than he's apparently the devil and I'm the devil's kid."

"That old bat was way far gone," Doyle said. "People like her love to yell about the devil."

I was glad he was looking out at the ocean and didn't see me flinch. Flippant remarks about crazy people were hitting close to home these days.

"I'm sorry I wasted your day," I said. "Let's just go home and forget I was ever this stupid, okay?"

Doyle rubbed a hand over his face, then turned to look at me, arm on the back of the seat. "Look, I don't tell people this, but about a year ago I ran away and went to live with my mom's extended family up in Canada. Ass-end of the Yukon, all survivalist and shit. I thought if I left, I could get away from all the small-town politics and all of my dad's crap." He rubbed a hand over the back of his neck. "It sucked. They were these überconservative, insular rednecks who treated me like shit because my mother had left the family and married an Irish Catholic. Then divorced him and moved to a blue state. Between the ultraright screeds and having to field-dress more deer than any one group of people should be able to eat in ten years, I had to admit I screwed up and came home. Then my dad was pissed at me too."

I knew it was just the shock and the general awfulness of the day talking, but I started to giggle.

"What?" Doyle demanded.

"The Yukon," I snickered. "Doyle, you're half Canadian."

"Yeah, so?" he grumbled. "Not the good kind."

"Hey, so, I'm the school bad boy, eh? So sorry about your mom, eh?" I said, trying to bite back laughter.

Doyle grunted, but then he smiled. "And you Hulk out when you get mad."

I felt like shit again. Mary Anne's words wouldn't leave me alone. *The devil. Your father.*

Doyle turned on the radio while we drove back to the marina, and I was glad we didn't have to talk anymore. I thought I'd be relieved to know anything concrete about Mom. Instead, Mary Anne had left me with ten thousand new questions.

You didn't start referring to the father of your friend's unborn child as the devil unless something seriously messed up had happened between them, so bad that Scary Anne back there clearly thought there was some dimension of actual supernatural evil to the man. I didn't believe in God, so the devil was also a nonstarter for me, but knowing Mom's taste in guys, the chances were good that my father was a grade A scumbag at the very least. Was he doing something so bad—stalking her, beating her, threatening my safety—that she'd *had* to run away?

I dismissed that idea. Mom may have taken stupid risks

and picked shitty men, but it would have taken more than an evil ex-boyfriend to drive her out of her home. It was just like I'd always thought—she'd left because she wanted to. That was the only reason she did anything.

"Thanks," I said to Doyle when we were on the boat, cruising out of the harbor and toward the island. The sun was going down, and a thin line of orange ate away the horizon, burning through the cloud layer. "I'm sorry it was such a bust."

He shrugged and then reached inside his jacket. "This might help make up for it."

I looked down at the leather-bound book in his hands. It was oversized, like a Bible, hand-stitched with thick, rough thread. I took it and turned the pages. Every one was full of scrawled, blurry handwriting and detailed pen drawings, lines so dense that they soaked through the paper and blotted out the text on the other side.

"What the heck is this?" I said.

"It's a journal," Doyle said. "Entries start around 1998. I saw it on Mary Anne's side table when you started throwing stuff, so I grabbed it."

"Doyle . . . ," I started, then tucked the book inside my own jacket. "Thank you." I wasn't about to lecture him for stealing—more impressed he'd been so cool and light-fingered.

"I figured it at least might tell you something about your mom," he said. "Or what they were up to right before she ran off."

"This means a lot," I said. Doyle grinned.

"I don't usually have to resort to burglary to impress girls, but whatever works."

"First of all, that'd be petty theft at most," I said. "Second of all, you have a girlfriend, and if this were a date, it would be pretty fucked-up."

"I told you, Valerie and I aren't anything serious," he said. "I just don't want to break up with her right before the Halloween dance. That would be a dick move."

I felt a flare of heat just under my heart and tried to keep my face neutral. "Yeah, that would be. Cheating your significant other out of a dumb couple's costume is just the worst."

"Look who's jealous," Doyle purred. I hated the way I knew I should tell him to knock it off, stop trying to play his flirt game with me, but I didn't want to. I liked that he was interested in me. I liked that my crazy didn't faze him, just pulled him in closer, like metal to a magnet.

"I'm not jealous," I said. "I don't have a jealous bone in my body. I'm just that awesome."

"And who's your date to the dance?" Doyle said. "Betty?"

"Oh, *stop*," I said. "She's not that bad."

Doyle winced. "Okay, if you say so." The island loomed

large in the windscreen of the boat, and he turned to take us around the point and back toward the old dock at the manor. "Good luck," he said as he cut the throttle and glided up to the dock. "Call me and let me know you survived the walk home, okay?"

I nodded, hopping onto the dock with his help. He didn't let go of my hand, and I stayed suspended for a moment, with him looking up at me. His eyes were slightly luminous in the impending dark, and he gave my fingers a warm squeeze before he let me go. "See you later, Ivy."

I watched until the boat disappeared around the cliffs by the lighthouse, then turned and climbed the stairs back to the manor house. The book was a heavy weight inside my jacket, even heavier than my thoughts.

Nobody noticed that I'd been gone all day, which would have irritated me if I wasn't so relieved. It was like Simon and Mrs. MacLeod only noticed me if they wanted something or I was in their way. I didn't think Simon had a job—certainly not one where he left the house—but I had seen a lot of letters and packets laying around his office from brokerage firms and a money manager, so I figured he spent his days being nerdy with numbers, minding the Bloodgood fortune. I'd never been rich, but I'd helped rip off enough actually wealthy people to know managing old family money could be a full-time job.

I heard a vacuum whining somewhere upstairs, which I hoped meant I was free of Mrs. MacLeod for the evening. I microwaved some leftover sludge in the fridge with my name scrawled on the Tupperware, which turned out to be beef stew, and ate it while I looked through the stolen diary. Mary Anne's handwriting was even tinier and more inscrutable than Mom's, and to top it off, the book was in what I assumed was Bosnian. Certainly nothing I could read. There was bad art too, scattered among the crazed spider-track handwriting. The largest drawing showed two figures standing face-to-face, one dark and one light, with lines of text between them in an alphabet I didn't recognize.

If I'd had a computer, I could have translated the writing, or tried to at least, but the only laptop was in Mrs. MacLeod's room, and I didn't even want to try to think of a lie elaborate enough to cover why I needed to use her internet connection to translate pages from a journal I stole from a stranger.

My mother had had a similar book for a while, probably a sequel to the diary I'd found in her room, but she lost it somewhere along the way. I'd always thought it was a leftover from one of the few times she'd tried to be a street artist, selling paintings and drawings of fairies and elves and demons—things that weren't real. This book of Mary Anne's was almost too real, dripping with the sort of thick insanity you usually only saw in exhibits at a murder trial.

I fell asleep fast after supper, which surprised me, and managed to not only not dream but to sleep through my alarm. Mrs. MacLeod pounding on my door snapped me awake.

"Breakfast has gone!" she shouted when I grumbled I was awake. "Get dressed or you'll miss the boat, and I will not be writing you an excuse note."

"What's *your* excuse?" I muttered, putting on the same clothes from yesterday and stumbling downstairs. The book was in my backpack, hidden inside a folder. I wasn't taking any chances on Mrs. MacLeod finding it and ratting me out to Simon.

"And did we sleep well?" Mrs. MacLeod sneered as I crossed the foyer.

I didn't even bother responding as I walked down the steps and across the drive. Mrs. MacLeod shouted something else, but it might as well have been "Blah blah blah, I'm a mean old witch" for all I cared.

I decided to hide the book in my locker until I could get some time to translate it, but just as I was stacking my econ worksheets on top of it, someone snatched it out of my hands.

"Wow!" Betty exclaimed. "Is this what you were doing

on Saturday? I love estate sales. You should have called! I'm awesome at thrifting!"

I was way too tired to decipher her babbling, so I just blinked. "Excuse me?"

"You went to a vintage store, silly!" Betty exclaimed. "This thing is awesome. Is it like an antique?"

"I . . ." I shook my head. "No, Betty. It's just a . . . family heirloom. I was going to go plug it into Google later and see what the writing says." I couldn't quite meet her eyes. Betty was annoying and in serious need of some chill, but it wasn't like me to be an asshole because I was so wrapped up in my own crap. Considering she was one of two humans who'd been nice to me since I got to Darkhaven, I definitely needed to pull my head out.

"I'm sorry," I said. "I will call next time."

"It's okay, Ivy," she said. "I know you will."

"Yes," I said, glad not to have to lie for once. "Anyway. Google. Translating. Fun."

"I'll do it!" she chirped. "It's Russian. My grandmother spoke it. My mom's grandmother. Before my mom died she wanted us to learn, and I still practice just in case."

I didn't want to ponder *in case of what.* "You really don't mind?"

"No!" she trilled. "Speaking Russian with Gram was one of my favorite things to do back home. Our old home, not the mobile home we live in now. That one wasn't on wheels."

When I didn't immediately hand over the journal she wilted a little. "I mean, I know it's probably private and all. And everyone knows I can't keep my mouth shut. I did a search on the internet about disorders that make you talk a lot, but I don't think I have those, I think I just like to talk. I used to mostly talk to my parents, but now my dad has two jobs and he's way too tired at night."

I thought back to Doyle telling me I was going to have to trust somebody here in Darkhaven. He'd been talking about himself, but I held the book out to Betty. "I know you won't tell anyone about this. There's nothing in here that I don't want you to see. It's just a . . . storybook . . . that somebody illustrated."

Betty's smile powered back on like a Christmas tree. "I'll meet you after your practice, in the library!" she practically shouted. Everyone in the hall turned to look at her, and she blushed and shuffled away.

I tried to stay away from Valerie while we ran laps, but Mr. Armitage paired us up for a relay race. She looked at me with her head tilted. "How's Doyle?"

I bit my lip. That was a loaded question if ever there was one.

"He texted me and said he had the flu," she said. "I know you live near him. Is he going to be in school tomorrow?"

Doyle had missed classes? That was news to me. I looked over my shoulder, back to where he usually waited for the last bus when I had practice. The parking lot was empty.

"I have no idea," I said truthfully. "I haven't seen him since the weekend."

Mr. Armitage blew his whistle into my ear before Valerie could say anything else. "Rejoin us on planet Earth, Ivy!" he shouted. "Let's get this show on the road."

I had a terrible practice. I was slow, stumbling, and couldn't manage to clear out my brain and just run like I usually could. I avoided everyone afterward and found Betty in the library. She was hunched over the book, a spare pencil shoved through her bun, and she shrieked when I touched her shoulder.

"Shhh!" the librarian hissed.

"Sorry!" we both hissed back.

"I'm almost done," Betty said. "Give me ten more minutes, and I'll have it worked out." She traced her finger across the mirror-image drawing. "Not just one person wrote this. The first couple of pages are old. Like, gaslights and gramophones old."

"Most stuff in my house is old," I said. I sat down at a computer and logged on. I had decided one thing on the track—I was going to find out what happened to make my mother leave Darkhaven. Abusive boyfriend, my grandmother's suicide, some sort of criminal trouble—not totally out of the question, knowing Mom—whatever it was, people didn't just drop their entire life when they were pregnant and alone and run off to the other side of the country for no reason. Mom was a black box on that score, just like she'd been about everything, so I was going to have to be smarter than her.

I typed in *Bloodgood* + *Darkhaven* and got a bunch of news articles about the manor house and Simon giving to charity. Mom used to say that computerized records made things almost too easy—it was amazing what was public information if you searched a county's archives. Property assessments, court documents . . . everything a phony psychic needed to milk every last cent out of her marks.

Knox County's website wasn't stellar as far as those things went, but I searched arrests, civil cases, births, and deaths, and after a moment I had a screen full of birth notifications and obituaries for Bloodgoods, going as far back as the 1820s. Nobody had been arrested recently—in fact, no Bloodgoods had made the news in a serious way since my great-grandfather had murdered the members of the Ramsey family. SIX SLAIN—ONLY SON LEFT ALIVE, the headline blared when I clicked through to the local paper's online archive. Other than the press surrounding the murders and the inquiry—my great-grandfather had killed himself right after he'd finished with Doyle's family—it was just marriage, birth, death for the last seventy-five years. To look at it from this angle, our family was positively boring.

I went back to the birth records. I found Simon and

Mom, two years apart. I wasn't there—I had no idea where I'd actually been born. Probably in the back of some kind of mass transit, like a crappy country song. I also found a tiny obit for my grandmother, practically a cut-and-paste job. *Simone Ellen Bloodgood died Saturday of natural causes as an inmate of Mid-Coast Psychiatric Institute.* I raised an eyebrow. Suicides were "natural causes" now? I guess if you had as much money as Simon you could whitewash anything unpleasant right out of the public record.

"Got it!" Betty exclaimed, scaring the hell out of me and getting us another murderous glare from the librarian. She spun the book around to that creepy drawing of the facing figures again. "It says 'The Children of Cain shall walk upon the earth as men, though they are not men, and you may know them by the darkness of their brow, and the malice of their presence. They will wither land and boil sea, and all men will tremble before them.'"

I didn't answer. I was transfixed by the next line on the screen, and Betty leaned across the table. "Ivy? Are you okay? I didn't make you mad, did I? I have no idea what this means but it's spooky. I don't think whoever wrote this was totally sane. This drawing is kind of creeping me out, honestly—"

"Betty, shut up!" I snapped. She drew back, her mouth shutting, and bowed her head. "Sorry!" I whisper-shouted. "I'm sorry. Really." I looked back at the county records for my grandmother. The obituary in the paper was plain, but the actual official birth record for Simone Bloodgood simply read *Born 1934.* There was no death date. Fingers shaking, I clicked over to death records and typed her name in. 0 *RESULTS* blinked up on the screen. It could be a mistake, but I doubted it—and if she'd died in 2002 like Simon stated, her death certificate would definitely be in the computerized records.

"I need to go," I told Betty, grabbing the book. "Thank you, and I'm sorry again. I'm not mad at you."

The book of Mary Anne's wasn't what I should have been focusing on. Rather than being excited I'd uncovered someone babbling about monsters that looked like men, I should have looked at what was right in front of me. If I'd done that, I might have realized days ago that my grandmother was still alive.

I spent the entire boat ride home deciding whether to tell Simon what I'd found. We hadn't really talked since I'd had my episode in the cellar and asked him to make me a doctor's appointment. Confronting him with this wasn't going to make him anything but pissed off at my snooping. I didn't know my grandmother, and I had no idea what her relationship was with Simon. For all I knew, *he* didn't know she was alive and hadn't been lying to me at all. Mental patients who'd been institutionalized for decades didn't usually have the wherewithal to fake their own deaths, but who knew what she was capable of?

She could be dead, and an overworked county employee could have never filed a death certificate. She could be in witness protection for all I knew. It didn't *have* to mean Simon was hiding anything. It didn't have to mean he'd been lying to me.

But it could.

I called Doyle the second I got in the door. His phone rang and rang, and nobody picked up, not even a machine. I huffed as I hung up. Now that I was theoretically rich, I really needed to get a cell phone.

I decided to go down to the beach, just to move and get out of the stuffy air and the press of my own thoughts. I stopped by the lighthouse before I descended the steps, looking up at the glassy, cracked panes staring out sightlessly at the sea. Had it really only been five days ago that Doyle had saved my life up there? Only five days since I'd spun completely out of control?

Something white tucked into the rusted lighthouse door caught my eye. It fluttered, and the plastic bag protecting it from the salt spray ripped as I pulled it free.

The graveyard at 9. Light a candle in the mausoleum if you're there.

I shoved the note deep inside my coat pocket. After the nightmares I'd had, the last thing I wanted to do was spend any more time near dead people, but if Doyle needed me, then it was sort of the least I could do.

After a long walk around the grounds I ate dinner, by myself again. I hoped that Mrs. MacLeod's supply of awful, bland stews wouldn't run out before spring came because they were about the only food in the fridge on any given day.

I heard Mrs. MacLeod's laptop going strong, canned yelling and shooting from some Netflix show drifting into the hall. Simon's office and his room were dark. Wherever he was, it wasn't here, and that was the best possible place he could be as far as I was concerned.

I grabbed my coat and a flashlight from the hooks by the kitchen door and headed for the graveyard.

It wasn't just the dreams that made the graveyard the last place I wanted to be—the temperature went through the floor on the island as soon as the sun went down, and wind snatched my hair out of its braid, cutting through my jacket until my hands shook so hard I could barely hold my flashlight.

I avoided looking at the spot where my mother was buried. I didn't need to see the cement block where a headstone would sit once one had been carved, the still-fresh earth frozen in stubbly humps of dead grass and shovel marks.

The Bloodgood family mausoleum was downright ornate, for a graveyard no one but the rest of the family would ever see. The iron mesh in the door was twisted into a rose motif that mimicked the real ones gathered around the foundation. The inside was tiny, just a stone bench, recessed spots for five coffins, and a cross carved in relief high on the wall.

I found a waterproof box of matches, a moldy Bible, and a water-stained map of the cemetery plots under the little altar, and lit one of the mostly melted, yellowed candle stumps hanging out in the indentations on top. I turned off my flashlight and waited, until I got twitchy not being able to see who was coming up the hill. Rule number one of a successful life on the lam: always be able to see them coming before they see you. I went out and sat on the steps, shivering until I saw a dark-haired figure approaching in the moonlight.

Doyle stepped through the gate, its rusty hinges screeching like some kind of night creature. "I heard you had the flu," I called, but I felt the smile drop off my face as he got closer. Doyle had gotten the crap beaten out of him. His lip was split and swollen, and there was a cut on his cheekbone, angry and red like it had been inflicted by a rusty nail. His left eye had a crescent moon of blue-black riding under it.

"Doyle . . ." I trailed off. He hunched his shoulders and waved me off.

"Don't worry about it."

Before I could stop myself, I reached up to touch the cut on his cheek. He hissed and bared his teeth.

"What happened?" I said.

He shrugged, kicking a hole in the grass with his boot. "Dad got pissed that I took out his boat without asking."

I could have climbed up on the lighthouse all over again, and this time actually thrown myself off. I knew all too well the burning that churns deep in your stomach when somebody has smacked the crap out of you and you still have to look other people in the eye. Doyle had gotten hurt trying to help me. His dad was a bastard, and it was my fault Doyle had gotten the brunt of it. I gently rested my palm against his cheek again, and he didn't pull away. "Does it hurt?"

He grunted. "I really don't want to talk about it."

I started to say something dumb, like he didn't deserve it, people who hit their kids because they couldn't hit what they were really mad at were scumbags, but I stopped myself. Doyle knew all that. *I* knew all of it. It hadn't stopped Mr. Ramsey, and it sure as hell hadn't stopped my mother.

I dropped my hand down and knotted my fingers with his. "I'm sorry."

"I'm not," he snapped. "It's not like he can hit that hard. He's an old man."

I'd seen Doyle's dad, and while he wasn't a teenager, he was built more like an aging pro wrestler than your average middle-aged dad body. "I'm glad you came," I said. "Truth, I had a bad shock today, and I can't tell anyone about it. Plus, you helped me, and now your face is bloody, and I feel like I'm going to be sick."

Doyle brushed my damp hair off my forehead. "I want to be the person you call, Ivy. No matter what happens after."

"My grandmother is alive," I blurted. "I mean, I'm pretty sure, I think Simon . . ." I dropped my head and inhaled, really not wanting to say the next words. "I think Simon might have known she didn't die and lied about it."

"No *might* about it," Doyle growled, and then flinched when I dropped his hand. "I told you the guy was shady, Ivy. I warned you. You can't believe what he tells you."

"I could live without your gloating," I said. "Simon hasn't done anything except welcome me and treat me well. Forgive me if I don't instantly suspect every single person in my immediate vicinity is up to no good." I had, just a few short months ago. But a lot had changed since then. I felt a heavy knot in my stomach. I'd actually gotten a little used to trusting that not everyone was out to screw me, which made this potential betrayal sting even more.

Maybe Simon wasn't lying. Maybe Doyle was just biased and I was just panicking.

But there was uncertainty now, tainting the trust I'd extended to him, and it made me feel sick. If I didn't at least wonder about Simon's level of honesty, I'd be gullible, and that was the one thing I'd never, ever been.

"He's fine now," Doyle grumbled. "But it wasn't always like that. My dad has known Simon since Simon was a little kid. And Dad is a bastard, but he's not a liar. He said that

Simon used to scare him. Dad said he was a bad seed."

The thought of my rail-skinny, five-foot-ten and balding uncle scaring somebody with both the temperament and size of Mr. Ramsey did give me a pause. I *had* seen Simon lose it that one time. That had sure as hell been scary when it was happening.

Then again, Mr. Ramsey was a dick who beat his kid, so why should I take his word for anything?

"Betty translated some pages from Mary Anne's book," I said, deciding the safest thing to do until I had this straight in my own head was change the subject. Doyle I trusted, but I didn't trust his family, and if he let it slip there was trouble between Simon and me, I was genuinely terrified of what they might do if they suspected anything about the bloody shirt, what I might have done to Neil Ramsey, my mental illness, any of it. This situation was the kind that ended with bodies buried in shallow graves and true-crime shows covering the story for years.

"She can be annoying in a whole second language? God help us," Doyle said.

I shot him a glare. "Betty's not nearly as annoying as half the bumpkins in that school, and you know it." I sighed. "Anyway, the journal is all just ranting about children of Cain and some tent-preacher crap about demons in the guise of men, so that was a totally useless crime you committed, sorry to say."

"Wait." Doyle frowned. "Children of Cain isn't crap."

I felt a cold tendril of unease worm its way up my throat. I could already tell this was going to be something I didn't want to hear. "Oh?"

"Well, not in the same way the Bloodgood gold and Bigfoot are crap, anyway," he said.

"The cave full of gold," I said. "Right. I think that'll be mine on my eighteenth birthday. And my very own pet Bigfoot too."

"Jealous!" Doyle said, hissing in pain when he smiled. "My family rented some land to the Children in the eighties, I think. They were some kinda hippie commune, and all they did was drop acid and howl at the moon. My dad got into it with a couple of the guys once. 'Course, my dad gets into it with everyone eventually."

"They were here," I said, feeling my mouth open and cold air worm its way down my throat. "Here on the island."

"Yeah." Doyle shrugged. "I mean, back then, everyone who was cool was in some kinda cult, right? They believed some real weird shit. My brothers and I went up there to the old campsite once when I was like thirteen with a Ouija board and some whiskey, but we didn't conjure up anything except a hangover."

"Your family let a cult move onto the island?" I said, feeling my eyebrows trying to crawl up into my hair.

"Listen, for real, they were just stoners who read a few

too many tarot cards," Doyle said.

"What did they believe in?" I said. "How many of them were there?" My mind and my heart were both racing. If a cult had taken up residence on the island, a member of said cult would be a strong candidate for "the devil" Mary Anne had been ranting about.

"I don't know," Doyle said. "It all happened way before I was born and my dad and uncles were also pretty stoned for most of the eighties and nineties, so they don't exactly have a lot of detailed memories. All I know is they were a real thing—real enough to pay rent for the land to my dad."

"Did they live here a long time?" I said.

Doyle shrugged. "No clue. They left all their stuff, though, when they went. My dad and my uncles still talk about the radio and the guitars they snagged. Plus one guy had this real sweet leather jacket that got my uncle Matt a 'freight train's worth of tail.' That's a quote, by the way. Uncle Matt is a dickhead."

I felt a swell of nausea at the memory of my dream. It had seemed so real, but it wasn't. Doyle was telling ghost stories, and I was falling for it. "The story in the book you stole was a lot older than Led Zeppelin and LSD," I said. "Like, gaslights and carriages. I'm thinking your dumb-ass cult was just copying something way before their time."

"There is another story about the Children of Cain that goes around my family this time of year. Halloween and all.

They used to tell me when I was a kid to try to scare me into going home when we'd sneak onto this side of the island," Doyle said. He looked out at the ocean and then back at me. "We should sit down."

We leaned against the granite wall, feeling salt spray hit our faces. I pressed myself into Doyle's side, feeling his warmth through my jacket, liking the way his voice vibrated through my whole body. "Neil was actually the one who enjoyed trying to scare the piss out of me with this story," he said. "It goes that Cain killed his brother on purpose as a blood sacrifice to the beasts of the wild, so that he could hold dominion over them. And that Cain also drank that blood and became something that wasn't entirely human. Something that he passed on to his bloodline, which in turn bent the force of their will in unnatural ways." Doyle let out a small shiver. "Made people lose their minds, murder, steal free will."

"They sound cuddly," I said.

"Cain became something that was totally against nature," Doyle said. "Half demon, half man. He had more relation to the things that dwelled in hell than someone who was flesh and bone anymore. He had many wives and he spread his descendants far and wide, all of them the same beast in their heart. Connor Bloodgood was one of them. Evil powers, murderous rituals, whole nine yards." He snorted. "Cute story, right?"

I turned to look at him. "Your cousin told you all that as a kid?" Maybe I was just a little sensitive to the whole "totally against nature, unnatural freak" angle of the story right now. I never thought I'd be looking forward to a brain scan, but right now that appointment couldn't come fast enough.

"It's just a story," Doyle said. "It's crap. But it does explain why the IRL cult morons came out here." After I stayed quiet he said, "I'm sure if your dad was one of those cult people he wasn't *that* bad."

"You don't have to try to make me feel better," I said. "My mother has—had—shitty and prolific taste in men. Nothing would shock me in the dad department. But if they were around in the eighties, I'm safe. They were long gone by the time Mom got knocked up."

The moon was starting to crest the sky as we sat there, and Doyle kept looking back at the road that would take him to his side of the island.

"It's okay," I said. "Go home. I don't want to get you in more trouble."

We stood, brushing off the sand and grit from our jeans, and I got on my toes and brushed my lips across the cut on Doyle's cheek before I could stop myself. His skin was so warm, and he smelled so good, I just wanted to sink against him and stay that way until I'd gotten my fill of being close to him. Instead, I dropped back and waved awkwardly as he gave me a crooked smile and loped through the tombstones and down the hill. The screeching gate was the last sound I heard before everything went quiet again.

I blew out the candle and shut up the mausoleum, flicking the flashlight back on. The beam burned through the misty night air and hit my mother's grave.

The light dropped from my fingers into the dirt at the sight of what had happened. Instead of fresh earth and spiny rosebushes, a berm of brush had been erected, like someone setting up for a bonfire. At the top of the pile, just an outline in the beam of my flashlight, was a smaller pile, crude figures stitched out of burlap, their eyes black thread crosses, mouths smeared with some kind of dark, shiny liquid. The same as the strange little fetish doll I'd seen in my cellar nightmare—or whatever—when I'd found the cavern of bones, except there were a dozen of them, bigger and more detailed. One, sitting on top, had a wisp of copper-red yarn stitched to its scalp, and was wrapped in a scrap of black fabric. Not wanting to look closer but unable to stop myself, I bent down, scrabbling for the flashlight, and focused it on the little burlap figure. It wasn't yarn, I realized, my stomach rolling over. It was a strand of my hair. The black fabric wasn't actually black—it was stained, and each of the dozen or more was wrapped in an individual piece. The fabric was stiff, soaked with the dark substance, and I pressed a hand into my mouth so hard my teeth dented my palm. Each doll was decorated with a piece of my bloody tank top, the one I'd been stopped from digging up and destroying. Each doll's mouth was smeared with fresher blood.

All of the dolls were me.

I whipped around at the sound of a branch cracking in the forest, the scream that had been building dying in my throat. "Doyle?" I whispered, my voice a terror-muted squeak. The flashlight started to flicker, and I smacked it frantically against my palm, but it flared one last time and went out.

Another crack, two in succession, like firecrackers. Or footsteps.

I wanted to run so badly I felt myself vibrate like a plucked string. But I made myself go forward instead, reaching into the thorny branches on top of my mother's grave and grabbing at one of the crude little dolls until it pulled free, ripping along the seams. Clutching it in my hand, I turned and let myself run, hitting my shin hard on the cemetery gate. It screeched as I ran, and I was almost to the bottom of the hill when I heard it again, the cry and groan of rusted hinges.

Somebody *was* following me.

I clearly couldn't get ahead of them—whoever they were, they were coming up faster than even my seven-minute mile could beat. I took a hard right turn into the far edge of the hedge maze on the mansion grounds, pushing myself into the spiny, naked branches and trying to still my raspy breathing. I normally wouldn't be panting after barely a half mile, but panic had knocked the wind out of me.

I waited there, for so many thudding heartbeats I lost count. I had just about convinced myself I had to take whatever cash I could find in the manor and get to the mainland. I could buy a bus ticket and be someplace like Chicago in under forty-eight hours. I could steal the cash for a fake passport, go to Canada, and disappear, just like all those times Mom drilled me on an exit plan for if things went *really* wrong. She'd known a guy for everything—fake ID, jobs across the border. If I cut my hair and started wearing different clothes, I could pass for eighteen easy. Maybe twenty if I really classed it up.

I'd have to forget about San Francisco and my plans. But nobody from Darkhaven would ever find me. Especially not whoever was chasing me through a graveyard in the dark. But none of this would matter if I didn't get away from them, so I plunged into the maze, hoping that I'd make it through to the other side.

I stumbled out of the hedges on the gravel path leading back up the gentle slope to the manor house, and almost smacked face-first into a figure dressed all in black.

I screamed and lashed out, but whoever it was caught my wrist. "Calm yourself, young lady," Doyle's father growled.

"What is *wrong* with you?" I yelled, yanking my hand away from him.

"I could ask you the same question," he said. He glared at me, his face a blank black mask in the dark. Just the shine of his eyes was visible, and I shivered.

"I was going home, because I live here," I said. "Last time I checked, you don't, so . . ."

He sighed sharply. "I had business with your uncle, but I might as well just tell you directly—you stay away from my son. My whole family is off-limits to you as of right now."

My breathing was finally under control, and I snapped my head up to glare right back at him when he said that. "Who the hell do you think you are?"

He mirrored my outraged look. "Who *I* am? You're nothing but trailer trash who washed up on shore and you have the nerve to talk back to me?" He shook his head, turning to walk away. "Unbelievable."

"I may be trailer trash," I said loudly, above the wind rattling the hedge maze. "But at least I don't have to hit my son to feel like a man."

Liam's shoulders clenched together like I'd shot him with a dart. He turned slowly, advancing on me. I stood my ground, even though I could feel every inch of me quivering from the rise and crest of adrenaline triggered when I fled the cemetery. "What happens in my home is none of your damn business, Ivy Bloodgood, and if you want to stay healthy, you'll keep it that way."

"You don't scare me," I hissed, even as I moved up on my toes, ready to run. The kind of guy who'd threaten me without a thought was definitely the kind I didn't want to be out here alone with.

"Then you're even dumber than you look," Liam said, his voice no longer angry, just low and hateful, like a rabid dog growling. "You know that sooner or later I'll find out what happened to my nephew. *I* know you either had something to do with it or you know who did." He was close enough to bump chests with me, and he looked down, almost blocking out the light from the moon and the manor's porch lamps. "You should be plenty scared of me, little girl, because I don't stop once I've got somebody in my sights."

I started talking without thinking, in some kind of weird survival reflex. "You know what I think? I think that you've lived on this island across the water from a shitty little town for so long you think you're God. But I'm not from here, and I'm not impressed by you. Maybe the Darkhaven cops don't care what you do, but somebody, somewhere will. You keep harassing me and see what happens. You have a lot of boats and cars and fancy guns for a guy with no job, Liam, so I bet the state police would be interested in what you do with your time. Maybe the IRS and the DEA too." I swallowed, throat desert-dry. I had no intention of telling anyone about what the Ramseys were doing—I didn't hate Liam enough to risk bringing somebody more competent than local cops to look into Neil's death. As far as I knew, everyone had, like Simon, put it down to a vendetta or a jealous husband, like Doyle thought, but if the state police or the Feds got involved that could change real fast.

But Liam didn't know that. And I must have struck a nerve, because he lunged at me, hand up, before I could get away. Somebody grabbed me by the elbow and hauled me back, so hard I tripped and fell in the dry grass by the path. Liam's blow whiffed harmlessly through the air, so much force behind it he stumbled a little. "You little bitch!" he hollered.

"That is enough!" Simon shouted. Liam started for me again, and Simon put his body between us. "I mean it," he said, so low I almost couldn't hear him. Liam's barrel chest was heaving, his face blotched with red rage spots visible even in the low light. He stayed where he was, though, and didn't make a move at Simon.

"I see her on my property again, she'll get a lot more than

a slap," he muttered, then turned and stormed away down the path.

Simon came and helped me up. "Are you all right?" he asked.

I nodded, accepting his hand.

"Good," he said. "That brings me to my next question: What the hell were you thinking?"

That was a good question. Threatening a man like Liam Ramsey was literally one of the dumbest impulses I'd ever had. I stayed quiet. I was just embarrassed, honestly. Spend a few weeks without grifting and scamming people and I was losing the ability to sweet-talk my way out of bad situations. Soon I'd be a normal person who mostly told the truth. That was a terrifying thought.

"Ivy," Simon said quietly, guiding me back toward the house. "You can never do something like that again, understand?"

I nodded numbly. The adrenaline had worn off, all my muscles ached, my butt hurt where I'd hit the ground, and I still had to deal with knowing my grandmother was alive and Simon had lied to me for some reason.

"Good," he said. "Go get cleaned up and get some rest. I'll make you a cup of tea."

"I'm good," I said quickly. Bitter horrible herbs were not going to help this sick feeling. "I just want to sleep."

"You won't sleep like this," Simon said. "Take a few moments to relax before bed. I'll make it herbal, so you won't wake up."

"Simon," I said, clasping my hands in front of me. "I get that tea and snacks and stuff are your way of letting me know you care for me, and I appreciate that, I really do, but free advice?"

He inclined his head, looking surprised but not mad. I normally wouldn't have been this open with anyone, but I figured after our little family drama at Mom's burial I could at least talk to him like he wasn't a moron.

"I'm a teenage girl," I said. "And sometimes we just want our parental figures to stay out of our business and let us be."

Simon didn't get mad; he actually gave a small chuckle. "Fair enough, Ivy. You sleep well."

"You too," I said. "Good night, Uncle Simon."

I went up to my room, stripped out of my damp clothes, and put on sweats, and a T-shirt. I felt in my jacket pocket for the doll. It was gone.

I cursed, throwing my jacket to the ground. It must have fallen out of my pocket when I was running. And I couldn't go back out now. Not with Liam Ramsey prowling around.

If I'd even really seen what I thought I'd seen, or picked

up anything at all. I had the terrible, pricking idea that if I did go back out there, I'd see nothing but the same old temporary headstone and frozen earth. No funeral pyre, no dolls.

I got in bed, pulled the covers over my head, and tried to block out the never-ending wind.

I tried that for about an hour and couldn't sleep, so I flipped my light back on and dug around in my backpack, under my homework and my mother's tarot cards, to find one of the crappy vampire books. I also pulled out my track team schedule. I'd made the decision without even realizing it, pretty much as soon as I'd found those county records. There was an away meet in Portland in two weeks. We'd be gone overnight, and I'd have plenty of time to drive to the hospital where my grandmother had last been committed.

That way I'd know for sure whether Simon was lying to me, and if he was, whether it was motivated by good intentions or the more usual reasons why people lied. Then I could figure out what to do, if I got to stay here or if I had to pack up and get the hell out all over again.

I didn't sleep much and woke up around dawn to the faraway honk of the ferry going between the mainland and the nearby populated islands. I sleepwalked through school, avoiding Doyle and everyone else, and told Mrs. MacLeod

I wasn't feeling well when she tried to press some kind of meat loaf on me for dinner.

Two weeks seemed like a year. I didn't sleep again that night, and dawn didn't bring me any relief.

Chapter

19

Simon and Mrs. MacLeod left for the mainland early to buy groceries and do errands, and Simon knocked on my door to invite me along, but I played sick. Trusting normal souls they were, they believed me and left me in bed. Mrs. MacLeod even told me I could use her laptop to watch a movie—she'd pulled out and hidden her mobile hotspot card, of course, though; couldn't make it easy on me even once. She brought me a little silver packet of cold medicine and a bottle of water along with the laptop. I wasn't used to anyone caring I was sick. Mom's usual response was to sigh heavily, drop a bottle of cough syrup on the bed next to me, and then cover her nose and mouth whenever I so much as breathed in her direction.

After I heard the Jeep pull away from the gravel drive, I got up and got started on my real reason for staying home—for the first time, I knew where both Simon and Mrs. MacLeod were and when they'd be back. I had a good eight hours to explore the house on my own, with no interruptions. There might be something about my grandmother dying in Simon's papers that would set my mind at ease.

Maybe even information about my father.

I ended up back in my mother's room first. I went through her drawers again, the few winter coats hanging inside the wardrobe, a worn-out pair of combat boots with a hole over the big toe.

I got a lot of cobwebs in my hair and dust up my nose for my trouble, but nothing about my grandmother or my mother or who my father might be. I flopped back on her bed, the springs groaning under me, and stared up at the water-stained ceiling. The sun blinked on outside the window as a cloud blew away, and I tracked a void in the stains high on the wall next to the wardrobe. I sat up, looking at the massive, ugly piece of furniture. It was definitely big enough to lead to Narnia. There were gouges under the lion feet too—somebody had moved it from the spot where it had clearly rested since it was put in the room, judging by the condition of the wall.

I jumped up and grabbed a corner of the wardrobe. It was even heavier than it looked, and I braced myself and used my feet to shove it away from the wall. A trickle of plaster dust sifted to the floor, and I saw the edge of a crude hole hacked into the wall, wallpaper and horsehair fringing the edge. It was tucked between two wall beams, leading to a void about as deep as my forearm.

I could barely reach, and the wardrobe wasn't budging any more, but I stuck my hand into the opening, praying I wasn't going to touch anything gross. Something crinkled, and I yanked out a plastic bag taped around a small stack of papers. The tape was mummified, and I ripped the bag open.

The papers inside had mostly crumbled, their edges brown and burned. The whole thing smelled faintly of lighter fluid. I sifted through the ashes. Only two bits of paper had survived mostly intact—one a thick official-looking sheet stamped with the state of Maine seal and one a photograph, mostly bubbled away, one corner burned off entirely, but still clear enough to make out the image of a blond boy, six or seven years old, in horn-rimmed glasses, a tie and jacket. It was posed, the smile fake and awkward, but I'd recognize Simon's pale eyes and widow's peak anywhere.

I set the photo aside and looked at the other sheet, which was a birth certificate. The first name of the baby had BEN-JAMIN typed crookedly above the line, but the rest had been burned away.

I set the birth certificate next to the photo, wondering what they meant. If my mother had hidden these, it could be nothing—who knew what significance she'd given Simon's old school picture and a random birth certificate? I would have thought it possibly meant I had a brother, except the certificate was clearly way older than my seventeen years—it was typed, rather than printed out, and the ink from the typewriter ribbon was faded.

I shoved the wardrobe back into place and took the photo

and the birth certificate to my room, hiding them in my school bag, deep inside my econ textbook. Mrs. MacLeod had already searched my bags, and I felt reasonably sure she'd pass over my book bag if she snooped again. More secrets, more questions. I should have known nothing good would come from more snooping around. I needed to see my grandmother. Then maybe I could actually unravel the knot of secrets that had snarled me up when I'd come here, before it choked me for good.

Doyle avoided me all week, until Friday afternoon when I was waiting for the bus. His bruises had gone down, and just a faint purple crescent under his eye indicated he'd ever been hit. "I'm sorry about my dad," he said, after standing beside me silently for a minute.

"Don't apologize for him," I said. "I'm sorry I got you in trouble."

"If it wasn't you, it'd be something else," Doyle said. "He's an angry bastard." He surprised me by taking my cheek gently in his palm. "I'm sorry if he scared you."

I shrugged. "I've seen scarier." I moved away, feeling myself flush a bit. "You probably shouldn't be petting my cheek where Valerie can see."

"We broke up," Doyle said.

I stared at him, waiting for more, but he just kicked at the ground with one toe. I didn't know how to respond to that, so I pretended to be really interested in the flagpole until the bus pulled up. I did want to take things further with Doyle, but not like this, as his rebound after Valerie. If we dated and broke up, we couldn't be friends anymore, at least not in the same way, and I really needed a friend in this place, more and more every day.

"Ivy!"

I felt like I jumped a foot when Betty grabbed my shoulder. "Don't do that!" I said, brushing her off. "I hate being touched without any warning."

"So they changed the schedule and the movie this week is *Harold and Maude*," she burbled. "It's a little weird but it was one of my mom's favorites, and if you wanted to go you could spend the night. My dad said it was okay, and it's obviously okay with me because I'm asking. We could make popcorn and watch TV if you stayed over. We don't have HBO or anything because there's too much explicit content—that's what my dad calls anything that's R-rated, but we could watch old comedies. Like *Bewitched*. I love Samantha, I was her for Halloween four years in a row—"

"I'd like that," I cut her off. I didn't know how spending a weekend with Betty and her family would turn out, but it had to be better than being alone in the manor house. And whatever the food situation, I bet it wouldn't include stew.

"*Really?*" Betty's face lit up. I felt like a real jerk—Betty was weird and socially stunted, but she was genuine, and that was a pretty rare trait in people in general, and high school girls in particular. I didn't get the feeling around Betty I needed to lie and trick her to make myself seem acceptable.

I wasn't forgetting about my mission to find and meet my grandmother, just putting it on hold for a weekend, I reasoned. Besides, I'd need an excuse that let me leave Darkhaven alone for a day or two. I didn't want Simon to know what I was doing. Not yet.

"Really," I said. "If you can pick me up at the dock tomorrow, I think going to a movie would be fun." Even if it was a movie about creepy age-difference romances and assisted suicide.

"I'll be there!" she promised. "Well, me and my dad. He only has the one truck, so he'll have to take us around, but usually he doesn't mind as long as you don't mess with the radio or get mud on stuff."

"See you tomorrow," I said as the bus pulled up and I climbed on. I waved to Doyle as we drove away, but he pretended he didn't see me. I sighed and shut my eyes. I was going to have a lot of damage control to do there. I needed Doyle, I admitted. He was the only other person on Darkhaven I trusted.

"Are you sure?" Simon frowned at me over his glasses when I went into his office to tell him I'd be gone overnight. He had a laptop I hadn't seen before open on his desk, and was doing something with a bunch of financial spreadsheets. I saw one of the little hotspot antennas sitting on his desk next to a taxidermy rabbit, and pointed at it.

"Can I get one of those?"

Simon blinked at the subject change but then nodded. "Of course. You probably need a computer for school. I'll order you one, and a smartphone."

Wow, that was easy. I should have started asking for stuff the second I stepped off the boat. I probably could have worked my way up to a car by now.

"Ivy," Simon said. "Are you really certain you want to spend time with this Betty person?"

"I spend time with her at school every day," I said. I was surprised Simon was pushing back at this. I'd figured anyone I hung out with who wasn't Doyle would get an automatic pass from my uncle.

"Some residents of Darkhaven, the town—especially those who are, shall we say, socioeconomically disadvantaged—harbor resentment toward the Bloodgoods," he said. "They feel the town's fortunes waned with ours, starting when my grandfather committed mass murder."

"So Doyle isn't okay because we're in some weird feud with his family, and Betty isn't okay because she's too poor?" I said sharply. "Who *exactly* would you approve of as my friend, Simon?"

Simon sucked in a breath, and at least had the courtesy to look embarrassed. "That is not what I meant. I don't appreciate having my words twisted."

I spread my hands. "Then what?"

"I'm trying to protect you," he said. "From how nasty people in a small town can be."

"I've done a pretty good job of protecting myself so far," I said. "So, thank you, but I'm fine." My real thought was that Simon, who stayed in his manor house and only ever socialized with his equally reclusive housekeeper, hadn't exactly taken up the mantle on improving my family's bad reputation with the townies.

"Very well," Simon grumped. "But you be home by noon on Sunday. I don't want you exhausted and missing school."

I waved to show him I'd heard as I walked out. He was starting to get better at sounding like a parent, which sucked. I kind of liked the whole easygoing, confused-nerd thing we'd started with.

But I could go, and that was what mattered. I actually felt kind of light for the first time in months. It had been a week since I'd hallucinated or had a blackout, I was going to do something normal with a friend—it was almost like I *was* normal. Or could at least fake it for a weekend.

Chapter
20

Betty and I had fun at the movie, at least I thought so. It was a tiny theater, the seats smelled like decades of dust and creaked when I moved. I laughed in all the right places, although watching Betty react to the movie was more fun than the actual film, which I'd seen before with PJ, in between us watching his Dario Argento collection for the twentieth time. After, Betty's father picked us up out front, Betty and I squeezing into the front seat of his pickup.

Mr. Tyler was silent as we drove, a tall, skinny guy with a couple of days' beard, dressed in dirty work clothes. I wondered where Betty got her chattiness from, considering aside from saying hello her father literally hadn't spoken. I started when he did speak as we pulled into the flat gravel parking space next to the Tylers' trailer. "So, Ivy," he said. "Where are you living?"

"I . . ." I considered lying, but Betty would just rat me out. "I live on Darkhaven Island," I said. "Simon Bloodgood is my uncle."

Mr. Tyler stared at me more closely as he unlocked the door and let us inside. The trailer looked like a dingy time capsule, everything that had been inside it in 1960-whatever when it was built still in place. "You're Myra's daughter?" he said. It was my turn to stare. Suddenly the avocado wallpaper and the plastic furniture were the least interesting thing in my vicinity.

"You know—knew my mother?" I corrected myself.

"Yup," he said. "We've spent some time away, but I grew up right here in Darkhaven. Just down the road."

"Daaaad," Betty sighed, opening the fridge and taking out the kind of soda that has all the caffeine and sugar left out. "Ivy doesn't want to hear about that."

"No!" I said quickly. "I do. I don't know much about my mom's life here."

"Myra was a good girl," he said, surprising the heck out of me. "I mean, we were all trouble back then. Me, her, our whole group of friends. Your uncle was the only straight arrow in the bunch. But I'm glad to see Myra straightened out and had a family. You look like her."

I tried to smile, feeling my throat tighten up. "Thanks," I managed. I didn't know what else to say. It wasn't my job to burst his bubble about Mom.

Betty handed me a soda and tugged on my arm. "Come on, Ivy," she said. "Dad let me put the TV in my room because you're company. We can watch *Cheers* and *Bewitched* and . . ."

"Elizabeth, she's barely gotten her coat off," her father said, laughing a little. "Why don't I make you two some popcorn and you can settle in?"

Not for the first time since I got here, I realized I hadn't judged somebody correctly. I saw Betty's dad and assumed he was basically the same as Mom and most of the people I knew back in Nebraska—blue collar because they had to be, mostly focused on getting enough cash to get wasted and not have to work for a few weeks. The Tylers clearly weren't that. They were nice people, normal people, a functional family from what I could see. Poor, sure, but Mr. Tyler clearly worked his ass off making this trailer livable—it was the cleanest, neatest mobile home I'd ever been inside. There were no overflowing ashtrays, no empties in the kitchen sink, and no clutter anywhere. It reminded me of the tidy main cabin of a ship.

Betty's "room" was a tiny space behind a plywood partition and a folding door, but it was cozy and decorated with fluffy pink everything. "This is nice," I said, trying to find a place for my stuff amid all the sequins and satin.

"I made all of it," she said. "The curtains and the duvet and everything."

"Wow," I said, meaning it. "I can't sew or anything. It's cool you can."

"I learned because we don't have any money," she said, still smiling as she turned on the ancient tube TV with a remote the size of a sandwich. "If I want to look nice, I have to buy things at the thrift store or make them. I got tired of being teased where we lived before, so I taught myself to sew, and sometimes I go to the swap meet and sell stuff I find to help out Dad with bills. He works construction and he's gone all the time, so I have to make sure to buy groceries, and if a bill comes when he's not here, I pay it."

I sat on the edge of her bed as she flipped channels, the TV fizzing. "That sounds rough," I said.

Betty cut a sharp glance at me, the first I'd ever seen her give. "I don't want your pity," she said. "I know I'm poor. It's a fact of life, and it is what it is."

I held up my hands. "I'm sorry," I said. "Obviously you have it handled." I thought about telling her about my life before Darkhaven, but I didn't want to come across like I was one-upping her. I'd always hated that game when I'd been the one with the thrift-store clothes who lived in a trailer.

We watched *Cheers* in the longest silence I'd ever had around Betty. Finally the microwave beeped in the main room and Mr. Tyler knocked at the partition. "Popcorn, girls."

"Come in," Betty said, muting the TV. Her dad handed over a bowl of popcorn and then looked at me.

"Do you need anything, Ivy?"

I smiled my best parent-pleasing smile. "I'm fine, thank you. You've been a very good host."

"It's the Christian thing to do," he said. "Besides, Betty speaks very highly of you." He started to leave, and then turned back. "If I can ask, since you're in my home—do you have a personal relationship with Jesus?"

I felt my embarrassment at my prejudgment and my gaffe with Betty ease a little. There was always one weird quirk to even the most normal-seeming people. I guess all the talk about Mr. Tyler and his fundie leanings wasn't totally off base.

"I'm good," I told him. "Jesus and I are tight." I glanced at Betty, crossing my fingers she wouldn't rat me out.

"Good," Mr. Tyler said, seeming more relaxed. "No later than midnight, girls. Sleep well."

Betty didn't last until midnight, falling asleep and snoring lightly. I curled up on my side of her bed after I shut off the TV, watching branches weave shadows on the trailer's ceiling as moonlight streamed in. I usually never had trouble sleeping in strange places, and tonight was no different.

I bolted awake some time later. Betty's clock, which was shaped like a pink plastic heart, glowed on her nightstand, reading after 2:00 a.m. I blinked, trying to figure out what had woken me. Wind whined around the trailer's curved walls, shaking it down to its foundation. The shadows on the ceiling twisted violently, seeming alive.

All except one. The shape was an indeterminate height and gender, but it was definitely a person, near enough to the Tylers' window that their shadow had crept inside.

I breathed in, out, slow, trying to ground myself, digging my fingers into the edge of Betty's cheap mattress so I could feel something real. I guessed I'd spoken too soon about the hallucinations. I couldn't let on what was going on, and I didn't know what would come next, so I stayed frozen, watching as the shadow got longer.

The person was moving, closer.

"It's not real," I whispered out loud. "It's not there. Make yourself not see it."

I kept up the mantra, and it kept moving, until a crack from the other room made me squeeze the mattress so tightly I bent back a fingernail. I knew the sound of an air pistol anywhere.

"Hey!" Mr. Tyler bellowed from outside. "I see you! You come around here again and you'll get more than a pellet in the backside!"

Betty jumped beside me, waking up. "Dad?" she called. I heard the outer screen door of the trailer bang, the inner door slam, and a bunch of locks clicking.

"It's all right!" Mr. Tyler called back. "He's gone."

He opened the door to the bedroom, still holding the camo-painted airsoft pistol. "You girls okay?" he said. Betty rolled her eyes.

"Put the gun away, Dad. What is going on out there?"

"Prowler," Mr. Tyler said. "Probably those damn kids from the other side of the park, excuse my language."

I wasn't so sure. The shadow had been out there for a while. That wasn't kid behavior. That was stalker behavior. I had the bad, bad feeling that whoever they were, they weren't out there because of the Tylers.

"You actually saw him?" I said. "The person?"

"Saw the back of him," Betty's dad grunted. "Just track pants and a hoodie. He's lucky I didn't see his face, or I'd be out there running him down."

I exhaled long and slow. It had been real. I was still in the clear.

Of course, now I had to handle the fact there had been somebody out there watching me, in all likelihood. I wondered if one of Liam Ramsey's creepy clan was keeping tabs on me.

"Are you all right, Ivy?" Mr. Tyler asked. Betty also laid a hand on my arm. "You don't have to be scared. I've got plenty more guns that don't just shoot pellets, and I'm a light sleeper."

"I'm not scared," I said. That was the first non–white lie I'd told the Tylers—had to be some kind of record.

Mr. Tyler nodded and backed out of the room, and Betty flopped down, turning the light out. It took me a long time to fall back to sleep—until it was light out, and the shadows were gone.

Betty asked me again at breakfast if I was all right—I wasn't hiding my jumpiness very well. It had been nice to get off the island for a while, but now I wanted to go home. I turned down Mr. Tyler's offer to go to church with them and told him I'd be ready to go whenever he was. Betty looked down, pushing her cereal around in her bowl.

"I'm sorry," I said. "I just didn't sleep very well last night even before the prowler. I was doing more research into that Children of Cain thing you helped me translate from the old journal and it kind of freaked me out." That was better than letting on I was pretty sure somebody was following me around, creeping on me when I was asleep.

Mr. Tyler turned sharply from the mirror over the kitchen sink, where he was tying his ratty tie at the collar of his church shirt. "Did you say 'Children of Cain?'"

I nodded hesitantly, worried I was about to earn a Bible lecture or possibly just be thrown out of the trailer.

Mr. Tyler frowned. "What's your interest?"

"It's research," Betty said quickly. "For our independent study. Local history."

"You know about the group in the eighties," Mr. Tyler said, not a question.

"A little," I said.

"I assume your project is focused on the disappearances," Mr. Tyler said. I raised an eyebrow.

"Disappearances. Right. You know, newspaper stories we found are vague. Anything an actual local knows would be really helpful."

Betty cut me a look, a small grin on her face. I was just

lucky she thought my ability to spin bullshit on demand was cool, and not a sign of sociopathy.

"Four of the five people in the commune disappeared from Darkhaven Island in 1985 and were never found," Mr. Tyler said. "I was just a kid when it happened, but my father was involved. He was chief of police."

I felt a small ball of nerves form in my stomach. Another island secret Simon hadn't told me about. Maybe it was just an honest omission, but those were starting to add up to something deliberate.

"Could I talk to your dad?" I asked. "It would be helpful."

"He's dead," Betty piped up. "He had cancer. And a stroke. And he smoked all the time."

"The only one still around is the guy who made it off the island," Mr. Tyler said. "And I wouldn't go looking for him if I were you." He picked up his jacket from the back of their sofa and indicated the door. "Let's get you to the dock, Ivy. Unless you've changed your mind about attending service."

I declined politely, again, and got my stuff. At the dock, Betty got out of the truck with me. "I'm sorry everything at my home is so crappy," she said. "I know after this you probably won't talk to me anymore, so I have to say it now before—"

"Betty," I said. "My mood has nothing to do with staying at your trailer."

Her expression perked up. "Really?"

"Really," I said. "I had a nice time. I'll see you tomorrow at school."

"Okay!" she said. Her father honked, and she started for the truck but turned around and ran back to me. "If you really do want to know about those commune people, you should ask Bob Brant. He's my cousin. My aunt is my dad's sister, so she got married and they have a different last name, but he totally knows all about all of Grandpa's old cases."

"Officer Brant?" I said, holding up my hand to stem Betty's verbal tidal wave. She stopped and took a breath.

"Yes. His first name is Robert but he goes by Bob. Never Bobby."

"We've met," I said.

Mr. Tyler honked again, and Betty waved at me. "I have to go. Good luck, Ivy!"

I looked down the dock at the empty slip where Julia's boat was usually tied up. I looked back across the street toward the main cluster of Darkhaven buildings, including the police station and the courthouse.

I knew what I was going to do even as I jogged across the street and started up the sidewalk. I'd made the decision to find answers, even if I didn't like them. And it was clear to me there was something dark about my family's island, something that gathered tragedy to it like a magnet. Thirty years ago four people had vanished without a trace. My great-grandfather had massacred the Ramseys. My mother had gone mad there. And now Neil Ramsey was dead, and near as I could tell, somebody was following me, on Darkhaven and now the mainland.

Maybe I was fooling myself that I could use one to make sense of the other, but I'd tried lying my entire life, and it had gotten me here. I needed to know what was true about my uncle, my family, and the island. Then I could figure out what to do next.

The cop at the front desk glanced up when I opened the door. The police station was tucked into an annex of the courthouse, and the waiting room was tiny, barely bigger than a walk-in closet. A window of cloudy bulletproof glass separated us. "Can I help you, sweetie?" she asked through the little speaker grill.

I tried to smile and tamp down my instinctive reaction to cops, which was hostility tinged with a desire to run. This was definitely the first time one had called me "sweetie" and meant it.

"I'm looking for Officer Brant," I said. She shook her head.

"He's working nights this month, hon. He'll be on at seven."

Hon. That was also a first. I must have showed the strain of keeping a pleasant look on my face because she sighed, giving me a pitying stare.

"Is this about the school outreach program?"

I nodded, hoping it was the right answer. She reached for a card, scribbling on the back of it. "He said if anyone from his at-risk group came around to give them his home address. Are you all right? Do you feel safe right now?"

I accepted the card she slid through the slot at the bottom of the glass. "I'm not in crisis," I said, borrowing a phrase from one of the many ER shrinks who'd seen my mom. "I just really need to talk to him."

Brant lived in a tiny wooden house on a street of almost identical houses—everything about the street screamed quaint, from the pocket-sized lawns to the wind chime hanging on Brant's porch, swaying in the cold breeze trickling off the harbor.

I rang the bell, and when that didn't work I started knocking. After a few rounds of my fist on the weathered wood of the door, Brant opened it, staring out at me with bleary eyes. "Ivy?" he said, surprise waking him up. He was wearing pajamas and a faded Darkhaven High tee.

"I'm sorry," I said. "This is going to seem really weird, but I need to ask you about a case your grandfather worked."

"Come in," he said, stepping aside. His house had that obsessive neatness that only a certain type of young single guy possesses. Everything in its place, nothing decorative, muted colors, almost as generic as a motel room. A gun safe in the corner of the living room was the only off note.

"Want some coffee?" Brant asked.

I shook my head. Keyed up as I felt, caffeine was the last thing I needed.

"So what's up?" Brant said, pressing buttons on a silver machine that whirred and dispensed espresso. The smell of the grounds filled the air.

"I'm really sorry to come here like this . . . ," I started.

Brant held up a hand, wincing as he sipped the jet-black coffee. "It's my job to help you out. You and anyone else in Darkhaven who needs it. You said it was about an old case?"

"The Children of Cain," I said. "The four people who went missing in 1985."

Brant sat opposite me on his sofa. "Let me guess," he said with a laugh. "Betty?"

"She said you knew your grandfather's cases," I said.

Brant nodded. "I got all his case files when he died. I became a cop because of that, really. More than to follow in his footsteps. He was pretty much every bad thing you can imagine about a small-town chief. But some of the stuff in those files is dark. I figured I owed it to the town to try to do better."

"Somebody died on the island recently," I said. "And I just . . . I . . ."

"Neil Ramsey's death was ruled accidental, Ivy," Brant said. "You have nothing to worry about. And if anything happened to those hippies, my grandfather never proved it.

It was a lot easier to disappear in the days before computer-ized records."

"I'm not worried," I lied.

Brant gave an approving nod. "Good. Stay away from the Ramseys, and you'll be fine. They're the real problem on that island. They've been on the wrong side of the cops since way before my grandfather's time. That Doyle kid who goes to school with you and Betty is the only one without an arrest sheet."

"There are a lot of stories," I said. "About the island, about my family. The cult thing too."

"Look," Brant said. "I can give you the case file if you really want it, but I'm afraid it'll be boring compared to the stories. There's witness statements, and some background on the people who went missing, and that's about it. There weren't many people to interview—just the Ramseys, and your grandparents."

"My grandmother?" I felt my head go up. Brant nodded, getting up and going to a bookshelf stacked with old card-board file boxes. He ran his hand across the labels, pulling out one labeled DARKHAVEN ISLAND '85 and blowing dust off it.

"Ivy," he said, handing it over. "Take it from me—people in small towns love to gossip, and they're cruel a lot of the time. Whatever people are saying about your family, all that's there is a lot of tragedy. You don't have anything to be ashamed of."

"My great-grandfather did hack up six people with a hatchet," I said.

Brant checked his watch. "That's not your fault, though. I'm going to go for a run. Feel free to stay here and read that file."

I sat back, opening the box but waiting until Brant came back from his room in shorts and a hoodie and headed out the door to start reading.

He had been right—the case file was slim. The statements took up the bulk of it, and I read through the Ramseys', which basically amounted to eight versions of "we didn't see nothin'" and hesitated before flipping to the first page of my grandmother's. It had been retyped, but I could imagine her posh elocution, the kind that nowadays only exists in old movies, dripping off every carefully chosen word.

```
I did not know the campground residents
well, but never noticed any untoward activ-
ity. I take daily walks on the advice of my
doctor and they would always be sociable
and friendly when I passed their campsite.
One of them even carved a rattle for my
daughter, Myra, and often asked after her.
```

> They were a quiet and courteous group, and
> I never saw anyone else at their camp.

I thought back—in the summer of 1985 my mother would have been a little under a year old. It was weird to think about her as a baby. Simon wouldn't even have been born yet.

> I hadn't been to the campsite in several
> weeks when Mr. Ross appeared at the manor,
> asking to use our phone. My condition had
> deteriorated again, and I was on strict bed
> rest. Mr. Ross appeared upset but coherent,
> and while we waited for the police to arrive
> from the mainland he expressed his sympa-
> thies for my illness and even apologized
> for inconveniencing me.

I dug through the box, and found the name in the main file—Peter Ross. The one person left at the campsite. His witness statement was just an empty folder, with a note clipped inside—*Interview File #22565.*

I went through the rest of the box but there was nothing else. I went back to Brant's bookcases, until I found another box marked 1985 that was full of half-mildewed crime-scene photos and reel-to-reel audiotapes. Even for the eighties, the technology was ancient. Darkhaven was lagging behind the times way back when, too, just like the island and the manor. I pulled the reels with the right file number and shoved them into my jacket pocket, then replaced the box, careful to line up the edge exactly with the dust line on the shelf.

I was back on the sofa with the paper files when Brant banged the door open, damp from the fog outside. "I've got a boat," he said, taking a bottle of water from his fridge. "I'll run you home—my shift doesn't start until seven p.m."

"Thanks," I said. "I really appreciate all your help."

"I appreciate you spending time with Betty," he said. "That poor kid needs a friend."

I felt the tiniest bit of guilt for stealing the tapes from Brant, but only the tiniest bit. "It's no problem," I said. "I'm not exactly winning any popularity contests myself. I get it."

Brant changed and drove us back to the marina in his civilian car. His boat was smaller and way less fancy than Doyle's, but it got the job done, and we were back at the dock on Darkhaven just as the sky was starting to get pinky-orange from the impending sunset. It was getting dark earlier and earlier—soon we'd have barely eight hours of daylight.

"Ivy, you really can't put too much stock in what people say about your family," he said. "They're just stories.

Strip away the ghosts and all you have are people. People are flawed, but they're not evil, and if anyone tells you that you are, they're wrong."

"Thanks," I said, climbing out of the boat. "I'll keep that in mind."

I watched the boat leave and climbed up the hill to the manor. Brant was a nice guy and obviously thought I was a little bit of a lost soul in need of guidance, but he didn't know me. I wasn't worried about what other people whispered about my family. I cared about what the members of my family were telling me—or weren't.

The manor house was always dark, even when it was still daylight, and I missed that there was someone standing just inside the door, and screamed when Simon shouted at me.

"Where the hell have you been?!"

Simon looked angrier than I'd ever seen him. "I said be home by noon!" he yelled. "It's practically sunset, Ivy!"

"I'm sorry," I said, holding up my hands. "I just decided to spend a little more time with Betty, and we lost track of time."

Simon grabbed me by the upper arms, squeezing to the point where it hurt. "I was *worried*, Ivy! You can't just ignore my rules!"

"I'm sorry," I said again, quieter. This was not the Simon I'd come to expect. I didn't know what to do—I couldn't get away from him, and I couldn't make him less angry.

"You *can't* do that to me! It isn't okay for you to just do whatever you want. I tell you to be home at a certain time for a reason!" Simon shouted. I flinched away, and he finally let me go.

"I think you should go upstairs," he said. "I'll have Veronica bring you dinner."

"Okay," I whispered. I felt tears blooming just behind my eyes, and I wasn't entirely sure why. It wasn't like I'd never gotten screamed at before.

"Ivy," he said as I reached the kitchen door. I turned, and he pulled a plastic bag off the coat hook by the door, taking out a thin white box and tossing it on the table. "I went to the mainland yesterday and did some shopping. I'm going to be in New York this week, meeting with the manager of the Bloodgood trust, and I'd appreciate it if you keep that on so I can reach you."

I picked up the smartphone box without a word and practically ran up to my room. I shut the door behind me and felt my heart pounding against my ribs.

Maybe Simon really was just worried about me, but I'd seen the same look in his eyes when he'd lost his temper at Mrs. MacLeod. He hadn't been worried because I hadn't checked in. He'd been pissed off at being defied.

If I was going to keep sneaking around on Simon, I was going to have to come up with an ironclad cover story.

I curled up on my side facing the wall. I was still shaking.

I'd gotten used to laid-back, soft-spoken Simon. His rage had more than surprised me; it had actually scared me. I didn't like being scared. It made me feel like a helpless little kid again.

I jumped when Mrs. MacLeod knocked, and swiped at the tears on my cheeks before I opened the door. She came in without a word, holding a tray with a bowl and a sandwich on it.

"Thank you," I said, sitting up and trying to smooth down my hair and look like I hadn't been crying. Mrs. MacLeod grunted as she set down the tray and then squinted at me.

"He means well," she said at last.

I sighed, really not in the mood to hear Simon apologia. "Seeing as I'm stuck in here until school tomorrow, could I just eat my dinner?" I said.

Mrs. MacLeod surprised me by putting a hand awkwardly on my shoulder. "You're lucky," she said. "He's willing to be patient with you. He'll forgive and forget. Don't push his kindness too far, miss. Take it from one who's known him since he was a boy. Forgiveness isn't in his blood."

She left, and I stared after her, suddenly not all that hungry. Still, chicken soup and a PB&J was probably the most normal food I'd been served since I got here, so I took advantage and ate.

I tried doing homework and sleeping, but it was a nonstarter. I was still up when the sky started getting light, and

I heard the Jeep grumble away, taking Simon to the boat. I was going to get up and go for a walk, but I felt the tape reels I'd taken from Brant in my pocket when I reached for my jacket.

A house this ancient and stuffed with junk had to have a reel-to-reel player somewhere. I took the tapes and went hunting in the library, I found a player with a bunch of other obsolete technology stacked on a shelf below the grim family photos that adorned every free space of wallpaper.

I plugged the player in and perched the old-school padded headphones over my ears. I threaded a tape, glad I'd paid attention when PJ went on about all his old sound systems and the reel-to-reel demos he collected of unknown punk bands. Static hissed for a few seconds, and then a gravelly voice with a thick Maine accent spoke.

"Chief Tyler interviewing Peter Ross, July 27, 1985."

There was a sound of chairs scraping, breathing, the clicks and buzzes of the tape. It was in bad shape, wrinkled and dusty, and crackled as it fed through the player.

"Peter, tell me what happened," said the chief. I heard a shuddering intake of breath, and then a young voice spoke. It surprised me how young—he didn't sound any older than guys I went to school with.

"I woke up and my brother and Steve and our buddies Fred and Lance were just gone," he said. "I already told all this to the other officer."

"Tell me," the chief said. "Because, frankly, a lot of what you said isn't making sense."

"Their sleeping bags were empty," Peter said. "There was blood. Blood on the grass, blood on their sleeping bags. Their packs were gone."

"See, this is where we run into a problem." The chief sighed. "We've had men out to that island, dogs, we even got the state police to fly over with their helicopter." The tape clicked. "There's nothing there, Peter. No blood. No sign anyone but you had been there."

"They wouldn't just disappear," Peter muttered. "Not my brother. He wouldn't leave me."

"Son," Chief Tyler said. "You five come up here from the city, you stay a summer, you don't cause trouble, that's fine. But I know what kind of people you are, and I'm not surprised your friends packed up and left. Telling stories won't change that."

"I saw the blood," Peter insisted. "I know something happened. Ask Mrs. Bloodgood! She saw us. We talked, a lot."

"You and Mrs. Bloodgood," Tyler said. "What's going on there? Lonely woman, all on her own, husband always off in New York."

Peter's voice was much steadier and harder when he answered. "Nothing like that happened. She's all alone with a new baby, she had a complicated pregnancy, and she didn't have anyone to talk to. I gave her a recipe for some herbal tea my grandmother and my mom used when they had babies, and I let her talk to me about how she couldn't have any more kids and how it made her feel. That's *all*. You want to insinuate, that's your problem, man."

"So you woke up, and your friends were gone," Tyler said, abruptly changing tones.

Peter sighed. "I *told* you. I woke up; they were gone. There was blood everywhere."

"And you didn't see or hear anything before? You slept like a baby?"

"We heard plenty while we were camped out there," Peter said. "All kinds of weird noises in the night. People stealing shit from our camp. I just figured it was those redneck pot farmers on the other side of the island."

"Those folks aren't your concern," Tyler said. "We haven't found any evidence of lawbreaking. We haven't found anything. And unless you're going to be honest, and have more to back you up than some hysterical housewife doped up on painkillers sitting in that big house, then I'm either gonna close this case, or I'm gonna arrest *you*."

"You don't understand," Peter said, his voice cracking. "There's something out there. Something on that island making us—"

There was a sharp crack, and I jumped. The tape snapped,

broken end flapping, and the rest of the reel crumpled up in the machine, chewed to shreds.

I sat back, not sure what to think. Who knew what drugs that Peter kid was on, who knew what he'd seen? I couldn't deny what was on the tape, though. My grandmother had been his friend. Close enough to talk about her health, my mom's birth.

About the fact she wasn't having any more children.

What did that make my uncle? Maybe it was all bullshit, maybe Peter was a serial killer and my grandmother had just been oversharing because she was lonely and all by herself with a young child.

I went to the kitchen to make some coffee, only to discover that the jar of instant was empty. I opened the fridge to find a bottle of juice with a Post-it stuck on the front that read *IVY*, next to one of those packaged granola-and-yogurt breakfasts. It was better than nothing. After a sleepless night, my mouth was sandy and dry, and I gulped the juice. I was going to get ready for school when I smelled the smoke.

It wasn't a bad smell, just sharp, and I followed it back to the library, where I saw the small blond girl I'd seen before standing in front of a roaring fire in the library's head-tall fireplace. The walls around her were empty, the squares where the photos had been darker against the evergreen-colored wallpaper. She stared blankly into the flames, tossing another handful of photos in, the black-and-white images crumpling and flashing different colors as the chemicals burned off the paper, erasing the faces.

"Hey!" I said as she tossed in a formal portrait of my mom and Simon, taken in front of the doors of the manor.

She turned to me. I took a step back and tripped over my own feet. Her dress was white and covered in blood, so much that it soaked the fabric and dripped onto the thick Persian rug.

"Look what you made me do, Ivy," she whispered, guttural and low, like nails scraping across wood. She advanced another step, as the thick gray smoke began to billow, filling the room. "Look what you made me do!"

I jolted awake, falling off the library sofa and slamming my elbow hard on the wooden table. The reel-to-reel machine tumbled to the floor, the ruined tape flapping.

It was full daylight, the photos were on the wall, and the fireplace was cold and unlit, a layer of ash and dust telling me it hadn't been used in years.

"Well, your uncle is off to the airport," Mrs. MacLeod said, bustling in. "Are you . . ." She took in my face and the machine lying on the floor. "Christ almighty, Ivy. You can't just go around breaking Simon's things."

"I tripped," I said. "I'm sorry." I did the thing where I just told myself none of it mattered—not that I'd had another nightmare, or hallucination, or whatever, and that meant I wasn't getting any better. Not that I'd been listening to a stolen piece of police evidence. Not that I was starting to wonder if anything Simon had told me was the whole truth.

All that mattered was I had tripped, I was sorry, and otherwise I was fine.

Mrs. MacLeod grumbled. "At least he hasn't used this thing in ages."

I helped her pick up the reels and the headphones, trying to put the scattered pieces of the player back together. "You've known my uncle a long time, right?"

"Since he and Myra were small," she said. "Ten and eight. And before you ask, yes, he was always as particular about his things as he is now."

That wasn't what I'd been asking, but whatever. I spotted the photo I'd watched burn in my dream hanging on the wall with the others, and looked at it more closely. Simon and my mom were wearing tennis outfits, posed with their rackets, even though Simon's arm was in a cast and my mother looked like she'd rather be anywhere else.

"Fourteen and sixteen," Mrs. MacLeod said. "Simon was nationally ranked until he broke his arm. Poor thing had to have three pins put in. He was so disappointed. His mother bought him that tape machine to take the sting out of having to stay in and recover all summer. He collected old recordings, could never listen to them until she hunted down that player. She did spoil him so."

"Was that before or after she got sent to a mental

institution?" I said. I wasn't in the mood to hear Mrs. MacLeod's happy-time stories of days gone by.

"Between visits," she snapped back. "Get dressed. You'll miss the boat for school."

I did as she said, wanting to be off the island. I had charged the phone Simon had given me, and I played with it on the boat ride over, setting it up and putting in Doyle's number. I had to take advantage of the freedom of my uncle being in New York. I had to visit my grandmother and figure out what was going on there, ask her about Peter Ross and all of it.

Then I'd know. I'd be back in control, the one who knew what was really going on. Then I could decide what to do, and maybe stop having this sick feeling in my stomach that had nothing to do with the rolling of the boat taking me to the mainland.

Chapter
21

I found Doyle in the parking lot before school started. He looked relieved I was still talking to him. "How was your Betty adventure?" he said when I waved.

"Way more full of Jesus and prowlers than I'd like," I said, and left it at that. "Listen, I've got a track meet this weekend. After, I'm going to meet my grandmother."

Doyle's forehead wrinkled. "You want some company?"

My skin warmed at his words. I'd been hoping he'd offer, even though I knew we'd both get into a world of hurt—literally—if Simon or Doyle's father found out. I couldn't imagine doing this without him.

I smiled up at him. "If you're not over my family drama yet," I said.

"I can't think of anything I'd rather do this weekend than go visit your dead grandma," Doyle said.

"Spoken like a true gentleman," I said. He laughed.

"Never that. But ferrying you around is a good reason to not be at home, and I'll take all of those I can get."

"Happy to help," I said. The bell rang, and I let him walk me inside. I just had to get through one more week, I told myself. Then I'd know.

Doyle picked me up in his rust-bucket Jeep that weekend after the meet—which we lost, but I was so keyed up I could barely sit still, even after running three events and listening to Armitage's speech about why we all sucked.

Valerie caught up with me as I was walking to Doyle's car. "We're gonna drown our sorrows in coffee and chocolate—you want a lift?"

I froze, not sure what to do. I had started to genuinely like Valerie, but I needed Doyle with me to see my grandmother. He was the only one I trusted with whatever I was going to find at the psych hospital.

She followed my gaze toward Doyle. "Oh."

"Valerie," I started. "It's not—"

"You know what?" she said, putting up a hand to stop me. "It's cool. I'm not into jealousy and girls hating on other girls. All I'm gonna say is you could do a lot better than Doyle. He's never gonna leave Darkhaven, and you seem like you've got bigger plans."

If only she knew. I exhaled, and tried the truth, which was unusual for me. "I'm not dating him," I said. "He's helping me with a family problem. I . . ." I forced myself to keep talking, be sincere, even though the urge to lie, to placate, to say the thing that would bend the other person into doing what I wanted was so strong I could taste it. "I do like him, Valerie. But I like you too, and I want to keep being friends. I haven't had a lot of female friends. Okay, any, really. If my hanging out with Doyle will make things weird, please tell me."

"Pfft," she said. "Go on, your knight in rusty armor awaits."

"It's really not like that," I said.

She patted me on the arm. "You're a bad liar, Ivy. Look, am I thrilled? No. But I'm not surprised either. You're his type. Way more than I am."

"Meaning what?" I said, hesitating.

"Damaged," she said. "Vulnerable. In need of a white knight. I was just having fun with him. He couldn't rescue me, so I wasn't fun for him. I've got my shit together."

I thought about telling Valerie that she might have all that, but she sucked at reading people. But I bit back my impulse to say something cutting and awful. She was angry, she had a right to be, and I just needed to give her space. "Okay, Valerie," was all I said. "You have a good weekend."

I crossed the lot and got into Doyle's car. He looked at me as he started the engine. "I won't ask what that was about. Where are we going?"

"Mid-Coast Psychiatric," I said, reading the address off the screen on my phone. I propped it on the dash so Doyle could follow the little blue arrow on the screen.

"Glad you're not Amish anymore," he said. "But you know that thing won't work on the island."

"Simon got it for me because I stayed out longer than I said I would and he flipped his shit," I said.

"I'm having a hard time picturing that," Doyle said.

"Much as he sorta creeps me out, he's pretty quiet."

"I wish I still had a hard time picturing it," I muttered.

We drove, the silence less than awkward but more than pleasant, until the hospital came into view. It wasn't at all what I was expecting—not that I'd spent a lot of time in psych wards that weren't state-run, where patients actually paid to be treated rather than being locked up there by the county sheriff after they tried to stab their boyfriend with a linoleum knife. To give Mom credit for one thing, I at least knew how to bullshit my way past the front desk and the doctors at most of these places.

Doyle looked out the windshield at the modern glass-front main building, orbited by several pleasant dormitories that looked like upscale country hotels. Patients in scrubs or civilian pajamas were walking on the lawn between build-ings, some sitting in a circle on the grass in heavy sweaters and bathrobes taking advantage of the last of the warm fall days before it got really cold, chatting with a nice-looking female shrink. It was about as far from the bleach-scented, Thorazine-tinged nightmares my mother had been locked in as you could get.

"You need me to come in?" he said. I shook my head.

"I'll be fine."

He sat back, looking relieved. "Good. Hospitals give me the creeps."

"So you're fine living on the creepy island and chatting

me up about curses, but one hint of a white coat and you're over it?" I said.

Doyle grunted. "Some people are bothered by normal shit that bothers people," he said.

I patted his shoulder. "Don't worry. I won't let them give you any shots." He didn't laugh, so I slid out of the Jeep and crossed the damp pavement to the entrance by myself.

The door swished in front of me, and an orderly wearing a jacket and tie approached when I stepped into the lobby. Fountains, classical music—if my grandmother was here, this place had to cost a small fortune. Maybe that was why the manor house on Darkhaven was falling apart and we ate practically nothing but meat loaf.

"Can I help you find something?" the orderly said, and it took me a second to realize he was being genuine, not snotty.

"Uh . . . I'm here to see about visiting my grandmother," I said. "Her name is Simone Bloodgood."

The orderly raised an eyebrow and then gestured me over to a desk. "I'll need to see some ID, Miss . . . ?"

"Also Bloodgood," I said, handing over my student ID. He scanned it through a little reader, tapped a few keys, and then nodded.

"You'll have to forgive the procedures. I didn't know Simone had any family besides her son, so we don't have a visitor list set up for her."

I felt my stomach flip hard, like I was still on the deck of the boat that first morning I'd come to the island. She was alive. Not "I'm so sorry, your grandmother died years ago." Not "We have no record of that name."

She was here; she was alive enough to have visitors.

That was that. Simon had lied to me.

"I lived a long way away up until a month ago," I said, when I realized I'd been quiet a heartbeat too long. "I'm just now meeting most of my extended family."

He nodded as he typed again, then picked up his handheld radio and muttered into it. "It's day-room time right now," he said. "Someone will be here to escort you in just a minute."

He'd barely finished talking when a nurse in pink scrubs came out of the locked ward, all smiles, and took me by the elbow. "So nice to hear Simone has some family," she said. "We're all very fond of her."

"Is she . . . ," I said, trying to tamp down the reflexive nervousness at being in a mental institution. It might be nicer than most of the homes I'd had, and there might not be screams and straitjackets, but I didn't miss the two layers of security doors we had to walk through to get to the day room, the thick metal mesh over all the large windows, and the panic buttons by every door. A locked ward was a locked ward, no matter how you dressed it up.

"What's wrong with her?" I tried again, as the nurse

indicated a small table against the wall in the hall outside the day room.

"Your grandmother is a paranoid schizophrenic, and unfortunately in the last few years she's also been showing signs of dementia," the nurse said. "She's not violent, though. You don't have to be nervous about seeing her."

"Trust me, this is not my first rodeo," I said, and to prove it I emptied my pockets and bag onto the table, letting the nurse see I didn't have contraband or anything the patients could use to hurt me or themselves.

"Take as long as you like, but don't be offended if she doesn't know you," the nurse said. "Does she? Know of you?"

"Yes," I lied as she waved her key card at the sensor and the day-room door swung open. I felt my vision spiraling down to a tunnel from nerves and took a deep breath to calm myself. "We're family."

The nurse pointed me across the day room to a pair of easy chairs by the window. I felt like I might throw up. If I'd managed to eat anything after the meet, I definitely would have heaved into one of the plants decorating the day room. I didn't know if I was livid at Simon's lie or just nervous about talking to Simone.

Maybe Simon had a reason to lie. Hard-core mental illness wasn't pretty. Maybe this was just his effed-up attempt to protect me.

But I'd never been that good at giving people the benefit

of the doubt. People lied because they were selfish, because they got something out of it.

I stopped just short of the chairs. A woman sat in the one closest to the window, head nodding in time with something only she could hear, as her hands worked a puzzle spread out on a tray in front of her. The box lid had a picture of three napping kittens.

I had to keep moving, sit down across from this woman who was supposed to be dead, and try to think of some way to get her to talk to me. I was sure Mom had never sent baby pictures, school photos, good report cards—not that I had many worth bragging about. For all this poor woman knew, I was some con artist out to take her for everything she had.

And until recently she wouldn't even have been far off the mark.

I still sat, trying not to stare as she looked up. Even though her face was sunken and one cheek muscle trembled slightly, her eyes and her nose and her whole face were like a version of Mom's, if she hadn't done what she did and had lived to be as old as Simone.

"Hello," she said pleasantly. "Are you the young woman from the library?"

"No," I said. I didn't know what else to say—leading with the whole long-lost granddaughter thing seemed like it might be coming on too strong.

She pursed her lips, looking disappointed. "The library

sends volunteers to read to me sometimes. My eyes are starting to go. Cataracts." Her cheek jumped again, more violently. I had the crazy urge to reach out and smooth it down, like a parent would do to a child.

"I can read to you," I offered, pointing to a book sitting on the arm of her chair.

"Oh, thank you, Myra. I do love listening to you read."

I bit my lip, trying not to react. She thought I was Mom. I reached for the book, rough cloth cover scratching my fingertips. Maybe this was for the best. "You're welcome, Mom," I said.

She blinked at me as she locked another puzzle piece into place. "Myra, you come visit me so seldom. Why do you stay away?"

"I don't like these places," I said, giving an actual Mom answer.

Simone snorted. "And you think I do? You think I belong here? I know you won't talk about it, but I don't belong here, Myra. Not locked up with these people. My sickness isn't the same."

"I'm sorry," I said. "It's not up to me."

"You let him take everything," she snapped. "You were supposed to be smarter than that, Myra. You let me sign those papers, and you did nothing."

"Who?" I asked. She pursed her lips disapprovingly.

"I don't know what kind of silly game this is, Myra, but a

woman pregnant with a child of her own should behave like an adult, not a spoiled girl," she grumbled. "I may be the one in the crazy house, but you aren't far behind me if you're already starting to forget things."

I looked down at the cover of the book. *Rebecca.* Of freaking course. "I guess I've got the Bloodgood sickness," I ventured, wondering if she'd take the bait.

"Don't be ridiculous," she grumbled. "Sickness, there's no sickness besides bad brain chemistry and too much time alone on that damn island. Now either read or get the hell out, Myra. I get enough nutty talk from the people in here."

I sighed, thinking that Mom had come by her shitty temper honestly, and opened the book to the marked page. I started reading. *"If only there could be an invention," I said impulsively, "that bottled up a memory, like scent. And it never faded, and it never got stale. And then, when one wanted it, the bottle could be uncorked, and it would be like living the moment all over again."*

I jumped when Simone's hand clamped on my knee, her leaning into me, staring like she'd just seen a ghost. "You're not Myra," she rasped. "Who are you?"

I shut the book carefully.

"I'm Ivy," I said. "Myra's daughter."

She looked at me and it was like somebody had pulled back the curtains in a dark room—suddenly she was as mentally sharp as I was, all the fog and helplessness gone from her face.

"I'm sorry I didn't come sooner," I said. "I was under the impression that you were . . . um . . ."

"Ivy," she rasped, pulling me into a violent hug. For a skinny old woman she was strong as a steel cable. "I am so sorry," she whispered in my ear. "It's the damn drugs—starts with the muscles twitching, then your mind goes soft, and pretty soon you're like a rotted-out beam, just mold and dust that crumbles if you touch it."

An orderly was watching us, and I gently extricated myself from her grip.

"Where's Myra?" my grandmother said, her face lighting. "Is she here? Did she finally come back for me?"

"No," I said softly. "No, I . . ." I took a deep breath. "My mom is dead, Simone. I came back to Darkhaven because of that. I didn't know I had a grandmother still living until two weeks ago."

Simone sank back in her chair. She didn't move, but tears worked their way down her face. "Poor girl," she said. "She was always a butterfly's wing. Beautiful. Fragile." She blinked the tears away and sat up straight. "You live here, you said? On Darkhaven?"

"Yes," I said. "With Simon."

Before I could ask her why the hell Simon would claim she was dead all this time, she lunged at me, and this time it wasn't friendly. She grabbed my wrist, pulling my hand close to hers, her nails digging half-moons out of my skin. "Leave," she rasped. "Leave and never go back."

"Hey! Simone, let's calm down," the orderly called, starting for us. I turned back to my grandmother, who was holding on to me like I was a lifeboat.

"Why?" I said. "Why do I need to leave?"

"Before the devil finds you!" my grandmother said, starting to shake all over, her muscle twitches practically contorting her face. "Bloodgoods always die badly," she cried as the orderly tried to pry us apart. "We tried! We took Benjamin in, we made him one of us, we even changed his name so he'd feel like family, but nothing worked! The devil found him, and he's got his eye on you now!"

She let out an enraged howl as the orderly flipped the cap off a syringe and plunged it into her upper arm.

I flopped back in my chair, shaking, until the friendly nurse from before touched me, and I jumped.

"I'm so sorry," she said. "It's probably better if you give her a week or so before you come back."

"She was . . ." I swallowed and got hold of myself, standing up. My wrist was bruised and covered in bloody nail marks. "For a minute there she was lucid. We were talking."

"Dementia comes and goes," the nurse said. "She's best this time of day. The delusions, though, those are harder to control. Even with antipsychotics, your grandmother is very ill."

"I'm sorry," I said as she let me out the locked door. "I didn't mean to upset her."

"Don't blame yourself, sweetie." She patted me on the arm. "I just hope this won't keep you from visiting again."

I could still hear Simone screaming from the hallway. Suddenly I had to get out of this plush, overly clean and bright parody of a hospital before I vomited all over their tasteful carpet. I speed-walked as far as the lobby and broke into a run across the parking lot, jumping back in the Jeep and startling Doyle.

"Ivy," he said. "What happened?"

"Drive," I said, pressing my hands over my face, trying to get control. I did not want to break down in front of Doyle, not now. Not before I'd had time to process what Simone had said.

Doyle stayed quiet for about ten miles before he pulled over at a chain coffee place, disappearing inside and returning with a bottle of water and a bag of doughnuts. "Here," he said. "Hydrate. Eat some sugar."

The doughnuts tasted sickly sweet, but I forced one down, and after a few swigs of water I did start to feel better. "Thanks," I said quietly.

"I take it you didn't get what you wanted," he said.

"She's really far gone," I said, but I didn't elaborate. I *had* learned something. Not anything I wanted to hear, but that didn't make it less true. I understood the photo and the birth certificate now. Why Peter Ross had been convinced my grandmother couldn't have any more kids after my mom. Not why the certificate and photo had been hidden after someone tried to burn them, but why they existed in the first place, how *Simon* existed after my grandmother had been so sick giving birth to my mother she'd had to stay in bed for almost a year.

Simon was Benjamin. My uncle was adopted. And for some reason, my grandmother was convinced the devil—or whoever Mary Anne and my grandmother used the word to represent—was coming for us both.

The rest of the weekend felt like a year, and I still felt like I was underwater when I went back to school on Monday. Valerie confronted me at lunch. "Did somebody you love die or something? You look like you haven't slept in a month and you're about to cry."

"Just my mom," I said. "And love is debatable."

Valerie flinched, and I reminded myself that Valerie was normal, and normal people felt bad when you said you hated your dead mother. "Sorry," I muttered.

Valerie let the silence stretch until she pointed at my open backpack. "Tarot cards!" she said. "Cool."

I shrugged. "They're bullshit."

"Then why do you have them?" She reached over and took the cloth-wrapped deck, turning a few over. "Wow, these are really old, huh?"

"Yeah," I said, setting down my fork. My lasagna wasn't getting any less inedible. "How can you tell?"

"I'm into this stuff," she said. "I know it's a little weird, but it's fun too."

I took the cards back from Valerie, laying out a simple five-card reading. I'd been playing with them ever since I went back to the island, thinking about my mom, and all the stuff she'd said to me that hadn't made any sense at the time. About the fact when I got home from school that afternoon Simon would be back from New York and I had no clue in hell how I was going to act, what I was going to say.

Plus, the doctor had left a message on the house phone confirming my psych appointment later in the week. I'd seen what my actual chances were in the genetic lottery when I'd met my grandmother. Who knew if it was really schizophrenia, or just a label the shrinks had slapped on whatever was wrong with all three of us—her, my mom, and me.

I could ignore that for now, as I flipped the cards down on the sticky cafeteria table. In my old life, Valerie would have been a prime mark—rich, young, and credulous. Just the way Mom liked them.

Maybe it was spite at her memory, maybe just a desire to prove I was nothing like her now more than ever, but I decided to do the decent thing for Valerie.

"I didn't know you liked new age stuff," I said.

"Maybe because you don't let anyone know anything about you and you close yourself off from them just as much," Valerie said, cocking one ginger eyebrow.

"Okay, smart-ass," I said, flipping over the cards in succession. "Here's how tarot readers work. They start vague—like 'I see here a relationship just ended.'"

"Yeah, Doyle," Valerie said. "Duh."

"And this has left you wondering what's next, in more than love. You're worried about a big decision."

"College," said Valerie. "Again, duh."

"A female figure in your life is pushing you one way, but you feel like another path is your true calling," I said. Valerie raised a hand.

"Okay, whoa. *That* is freaky. My mother is totally pressuring me to apply to a bunch of state schools, and what I really want is to move to New York."

I swept the cards back into a pile and tapped them. "That layout didn't say any of that."

Valerie frowned. "Then what the hell, Ivy? You were so spot-on."

"Cold reading," I said. "You're almost college age but your biggest concern is your ex-boyfriend, not college or family problems, so it's a good bet you come from a relatively stable home. You're wearing expensive clothes and carrying a bag that costs more than a used car, so your parents are probably professionals and overachievers who push you. The rest is just watching your face and steering the conversation in whichever direction is right."

Valerie sighed. "Anyone ever tell you you're a fun-killer, Ivy?"

"Hey," I said, "the more people I can save from being defrauded by people like my mother, the better."

Valerie pushed back her chair as the bell rang, and I shoved the cards into my backpack. "You never did explain why you're so grumpy today."

I sighed as we walked to world literature. "I found out my uncle was adopted."

"Does it matter? That he was adopted?" Valerie said.

I shrugged. "I guess not. It's just a really big thing nobody ever told me."

"Maybe he doesn't know," Valerie said. "He's what, like in his thirties? A lot of adoptions in the eighties were closed, and the prevailing parenting wisdom was to keep it secret from the kids."

I stared at her for a beat too long, and she flipped a hand. "My mom is in family law," she said. "You weren't wrong about the pushy overachiever thing, by the way. Because of her I know wayyyy more about adoption law than any non-lawyer should."

"Simon isn't exactly the type of person I can just ask," I

said. "And I guess . . . I just want to know why he kept that from me. I kinda feel like I can't trust him now." Ironic, I knew, but something about the enormity of Simon's two lies sat in my stomach like a boulder. They weren't small lies like mine. They had shifted the earth under me, and I'd felt off-balance ever since I'd walked out of the psych hospital.

"If you really want to know, your best bet is to find the local branch of social services that handled the adoption," Valerie said. "If it's a closed adoption, that'll be a dead end, but if not, it's way quicker than requesting records from the state."

"I have his original birth certificate," I said, not exactly sure why I'd let that slip. "Well, what's left of it."

"Perfect," Valerie said. "If you know the town he was born in, that helps narrow it way down."

"Ladies!" Mr. Armitage snapped from the front of the room. "If it's not too much to ask, could you attempt to let me educate you for the next forty-five minutes?"

I turned my eyes to the front, but all I could think about was maybe, finally, getting some answers.

Chapter

22

I'd been worrying all day about how Simon and I would interact when he was back from New York, but after all my fretting he barely spoke to me. We ate supper in near silence beyond a few pleasantries about New York and how school had been. Simon was clearing the plates when he finally said something more than five words long. "Do you want me to come with you to the doctor on Friday?"

I looked up, surprised. I'd kind of figured he would—he was my legal guardian and all, and it was a big deal. "I don't know. Do you . . . want to?"

"I don't think anyone *wants* to spend time with a psychiatrist poking around, but if I must," he said. I actually felt hurt. Never mind the lies and the weirdness after he'd screamed at me, wasn't he supposed to engage in the stuff a normal adult would do with their teenager?

"I think you have to," I said, standing up and putting my plate in the soapy water in the sink basin. "There's probably forms to sign and stuff. And you know our family medical history. If there's anything else that's genetic?" I waited to see if I picked up anything from his expression, but he was bland as ever.

"I'll pick you up after school then," he said.

"Yeah, okay," I said. I started for the stairs. "I have homework."

"Very well," he said, picking up a sponge and turning on the water. The pipes groaned under our feet and the tap shot out gobbets of rust. "Damn thing," Simon cursed as it spattered his shirt.

"And I have a late practice tomorrow," I said. "Regional qualifiers are coming up. I know you're mad at me about last time, but I thought I should stay with Valerie tomorrow to save Julia a late trip."

"Fine," Simon said. "Call me after practice and the next morning, and you are not allowed to go out anywhere. This friend of yours has parents?"

"I assume so," I said.

"I'll expect their contact information as well," Simon said.

"Fine," I said, and headed upstairs. Suddenly I didn't feel guilty at all about what I was going to do.

The rest of the night and the next day passed agonizingly slowly—all I could think about was what I'd find when I went after Simon's birth records. I had more awful night-mares. By the time school let out I was struggling to keep my eyes open.

Valerie and I drove to the northeast of Portland, and after working our way through three levels of managers at the social services office, determined that my uncle *might* have been adopted from an orphanage near the hospital listed on his birth certificate.

I was sure Valerie would want to give up, but she just started her car and punched the orphanage address into her GPS. "We really don't have to . . . ," I started.

"Are you kidding me? I've spent the last five weekends running and doing SAT prep. This is the most fun I've had in months," she said. So I guessed we were definitely just not talking about the bitchy stuff she'd spouted in the parking lot right after she and Doyle broke up. Fine by me—I didn't like holding grudges. They just complicated everything.

I felt hopeful right up until we got to the orphanage and found it mostly boarded up. It was an ugly industrial building that looked more like a factory than a place where kids had ever lived. One corner of the parking lot was still full of cars, though, and the door was open. From inside, I heard the whine of power tools.

Valerie and I stepped in, plastic draped everywhere wafting in the draft from the door. The power tools cut off, and a guy in a plaid shirt and dusty jeans appeared from around a corner. "You can't be back here," he said. "If you're looking for the records archive, go around to the front and ring the bell."

We followed the overgrown, cracked concrete path to the front of the building, rang the bell, got buzzed in, and after a few judicious lies on my part, the clerk in charge of the records archive now housed in the orphanage let us have the run of the records room for our fake genealogy project.

I went right for the boxes from 1986, the year I'd seen on Simon's birth certificate. Valerie pretended to look through the older records our made-up project was based on in case the clerk came back, but judging from the sound of a Patriots game coming from speakers in the office, I doubted we'd be disturbed.

It took a couple of hours—there were a lot of children born in 1986. I found a certificate for a live birth from the same date as Simon, but the info wasn't the same. The next certificate was the jackpot. A copy of Benjamin's full certificate, attached to a yellowed, typed adoption form that had been mimeographed. The ink had bled and run together, so I could barely make out the chicken scratch, but I managed to parse a few lines.

> Benjamin Jones has completed his trial placement with the Bloodgood family and formal adoption proceedings have begun.

"Got it," I said to Valerie, shoving the entire file inside my jacket. "Let's get out of here."

"Thank God," she said. "I'm never going to stop sneezing."

We got back in the car and were driving when I opened

the file and read the rest of the social worker's notes. I froze, feeling all the blood in me rush to my feet.

"Ivy?" Valerie said, glancing at me as she drove. "You look pale. What's wrong?"

I stared at the scribbled sentence, reading it over and over to be sure I wasn't imagining it.

Benjamin Jones has completed his trial placement with the Bloodgood family and formal adoption proceedings have begun. His twin brother, Brian Jones, remains at the North Portland care facility.

Valerie pulled into a coffee shop and made me come inside and get a drink. I sat at one of the little tables, staring at the line over and over. "Why would they adopt one kid and not the other?" I said.

Valerie shrugged. "They split siblings up a lot more back then," she said. "Nobody cared about how messed-up that makes you."

I shook my head. "I can't believe this," I said. "I have another uncle out there somewhere. Well, adopted uncle."

"Really sucks for him," Valerie said, sucking on her frozen drink. "Your uncle got adopted into one of the richest families in Maine, and Brian got to stay in a crappy orphanage."

I tried to drink my coffee, but it turned my stomach. I didn't feel better now that I knew the truth about Simon. I felt worse.

"He has to know about this," I said, tapping the page. "Simon. It says here he was adopted when he was four years old. You remember that if you're four."

"Ivy, not to be a total devil's advocate, but he might have his reasons," Valerie said. "Look, if you go back to when they got placed in state custody, it says they were found abandoned outside a gas station in Portland. That's not a happy beginning."

"It's not that he didn't spill all his secrets," I said. "It's that he acted like he didn't have any. There's something weird about letting me think I'm his biological niece, you have to admit."

"Yeah, it's super weird," Valerie agreed. "But maybe talk to him before you go nuclear?"

"I wish I knew if my mom knew," I said. "She'd know, right? She'd have been five or six."

Who knew what my mother knew, or believed, or had talked herself into believing. For all I knew my grandmother had told Mom that Simon had been kidnapped like the Lindberg baby and just turned up again.

"You can ask the social worker," Valerie said. "Can't hurt to have all the facts when you ask Simon about this."

"I'm sure they're long gone," I said, but I still pulled out my phone and punched the name of the social worker who'd signed off on the adoption into Facebook. In thirty seconds I had her page, and another few screens of searches got me an address and phone number. Valerie tilted her head at me.

"Go on, Sherlock. You shall know the truth and the truth shall make you free, or whatever."

I called as we walked back to the car, standing and watching cars swish by on Interstate 95. I felt a lot more comfortable in wayside places like this one than places like Darkhaven. If things went bad, I could always go a few exits down the road and try again.

"Hello?" The voice was creaky with age, and sounded suspicious.

"Hi," I said perkily. "Is this Sharon Swenson?"

"Yes," the voice said hesitantly.

"The Sharon Swenson who worked for family services in 1990?" I said.

"Who is this?" she snapped. I heard the click of a lighter on the other end of the phone and the crackle of a cigarette.

"I'm hoping you can help me," I said. "I'm looking for information about a child you worked with—Brian Jones? He's my uncle." Only a half lie. Legally, we were related: Benjamin and Brian were both my uncles.

There was a long silence on the other end of the line. Only an exhalation that I assumed was smoke let me know the call was still connected. "Hello?" I said finally.

"If Brian Jones is your uncle, you need to get away from him. Get away and stay away," Sharon said.

"Why?" I said. She practically shouted, and I held the phone away from my ear.

"Brian Jones is not a person you want in your life! That's all I'm going to say. Don't call here again." The phone beeped three times, and the call went dead.

Valerie looked at me expectantly as I got in the car. "Well?"

"Dead end," I said. "I think I just want to go home."

I thought about what the social worker had said the entire ride back to Darkhaven and the island, getting more and more worked up as I did. This actually helped the argument that Simon had a good reason for not telling me about any of this. If his brother was as bad as the social worker implied, maybe Simon had totally cut ties. Maybe he felt like he was protecting me. But that still didn't explain the lie about my grandmother, or reveal if he'd lied about anything else.

I hit the door open so it banged against the kitchen wall. I was shaking, not sure what to think or do. I wanted to scream for Simon, but I had enough sense to realize that confronting him now wouldn't get me what I wanted. I needed to calm down, to think, form a plan.

I needed to talk to *someone*, though, or I was going to have a complete mental breakdown. I picked up the kitchen phone and punched in Doyle's number. He picked up on the third ring. "Hello? Ivy?"

"Ivy."

I just about jumped out of my skin when Simon's voice rolled over Doyle's in my ear. He came over and depressed the disconnect switch on the phone, taking the receiver out of my hands. "I was worried," he said. "I called your friend Valerie's house, and her mother said the two of you never came home after school let out. I've been trying to call you."

"We just went shopping before I took the boat back," I said, amazed at how calm I sounded. My heart was still thudding, but I'd fallen back on the persona I used to keep marks interested, keep Mom from going nuts on me, keep everyone at arm's length. "I must have already been in the dead zone when you were calling me." My lying felt like armor in this moment, as I smiled pleasantly at my uncle.

"If you were shopping, then where are your bags?" he said. Crap. Never tell a lie you need props for. That was a rookie mistake.

"Okay," I said. Maybe there was a way I could salvage this and get the truth at the same time. "Valerie drove me to Mid-Coast Psychiatric. To visit Simone."

I waited. Only one tick of the ancient kitchen clock went by, but in that second I saw a flicker behind Simon's glasses, the short circuit of genuine surprise and anger. Then it was gone, and he was the same dorky guy with a bad sweater vest he'd always been. "I really wish you had told me before you did that," he said. "I would have warned you not to go."

"Why did you lie to me?" I said. "Sure, she's sick but it's not like she's the first family member I've visited in a psych ward."

"It was a mistake to keep you in the dark," Simon said instantly. "I was trying to spare you the pain. You never knew her when she was in her right mind, and I didn't want that . . . thing . . . to be the only memory you had of her."

I had always thought Simon was a bad liar, but I was starting to see how wrong I'd been. Simon was a great liar. This whole absentminded professor thing had been the lie, and the flash I'd seen when he'd realized I'd found out about my grandmother was the real him.

"I am sorry, Ivy," he said, regretful pinch to his mouth. "I know that must have been traumatic for you."

"Yeah, it sucked," I agreed. He bustled over to the big six-burner stove and lit the gas under the kettle, taking down two cups.

"I'll make us some tea."

Suddenly, I felt exhausted. I didn't know what Simon's deal was, but I knew I didn't want to spend another second pretending we were all okay with each other. "I'm good," I said. "I have homework to do."

"If you change your mind, I'll leave the kettle hot," he said.

"You should have told me," I said before I went upstairs. He looked at me blandly, scooping a spoonful of tea from the tin on the counter into the little silver ball that went in the hot water.

"Ivy, there are many things you think you're ready for and you're not. Your mother was the same way at your age. That tough shell you show hides the fact that underneath there's a part of you that's a scared little girl."

"How the hell would you know?" I said quietly. "She left you. You had no idea what she was like."

"She left Darkhaven, but she did not leave me," he snapped, jabbing a finger at me. "I knew her better than anyone, and I know you too. That bothers you because that's how you've survived, not letting anyone see your true face. I understand, Ivy. I sympathize. But you do not have that option with me."

He took a step toward me, eyes flat behind his glasses. "I know who you are. You and I are going to have to learn to live with each other."

I realized it had been a long time since I'd taken a breath. I turned and went upstairs, running all the way to my room, and shut my door. I waited. I'd learned the rhythms of the house by now—Mrs. MacLeod cleaned up from dinner and retreated to her room to watch crappy detective shows into the early morning. Simon went to his room a little while after her. I waited, flipped my mother's tarot cards aimlessly, thought about what a bad idea this was.

So Simon had lied. It was a big lie, but maybe he really was just trying to shield me from what had happened to my grandmother—remembering her saucer-sized eyes, twitching face, and voice like a seagull screaming sent a shiver through me even now. If that was going to happen to me, maybe he really was being kind.

But I'd lived with Mom too long to believe that anyone, never mind a family member of mine, would have my best interest at heart. Keeping the fact he was adopted private, maybe. Posting fake obituaries and lying to me about my grandmother? That was a lie with intent behind it. And that friendly mask had been slipping further and further. Every time I did something he didn't like I felt a little more uneasy being in the same room as Simon. I had the sense something was going to happen, like when black clouds piled up on the horizon back in the Midwest. That flat look in his eyes was the tornado warning, and when the storm hit I wasn't sure what damage it would do.

I got up and slipped out my door, my feet silent in my socks even on the rickety wood floor. I didn't know Simon's intent, but if I was stuck here until I was eighteen, I needed to find out. I needed to know if I was safe, if I could still trust my instincts, or if I really was losing my mind.

If Simon wasn't Mom's biological brother, that would explain why the "curse" had passed him by. Why they looked nothing alike. But not why he'd pretend otherwise.

I didn't love the idea of being in his office with the creepy animal skeletons in the middle of the night, but it was that or have another conversation full of veiled hostility and god-awful tea, so I used my phone as a flashlight and tried the door of his office. Locked. That had never happened before. I guess after the scene in the kitchen he didn't trust me anymore.

At least I was way better at burglary than the average girl. All the locks in the house were old-school and used skeleton keys, the easiest thing in the world to pick. A quick trip back to my room for a nail file and the curved hook that clipped my school ID to my backpack, and I was in business. Thirty seconds of wiggling and the door opened.

I discovered pretty quickly there was nothing in most of the desk that would point toward Simon being up to anything other than being a rich guy with a lot of rich-guy hobbies like wine and golf. The upper-left drawer was locked, and I went to work on it with my tools.

There was standard lock-and-key stuff in the drawer—a checkbook, a few years of tax returns, some credit cards that normally I would have snatched just on principle, a file folder of financial statements from the trust manager in New York. I wasn't out to grift my uncle, so I ignored them, digging to the bottom of the pile of paper. My fingers brushed against hard plastic, and I pulled out a small case with a snap latch. I flipped it open and stared. It was like the kits diabetics used, except the bottle of clear liquid inside was unlabeled and was more like one of those vials you could buy to mix up perfume at home than a medical thing. There was a small clear packet of whitish-gray powder as well, tucked behind the syringes.

Drugs? Bullshit alternative medicine? Whatever it was, it had been hidden, and that meant Simon had a reason to lock it up. He didn't act like any addict I'd known, and I couldn't decide if the other possibilities were better or worse.

A board creaked over my head, and I scrabbled in the desk drawer, pulling out an extra packet of needles, each in a paper wrapper. I stripped one, jammed the business end into the red rubber circle on top of the bottle, filled it with the liquid, popped the cap back on and shoved it deep into the pocket of my hoodie. I put the case back where I'd found it, shut the drawer and gave the nail file a twist, relocking it.

It was definitely footsteps I'd heard, coming my way overhead. I waited, frozen, not sure what I'd do if Simon came down here. Despite being crammed full of dead animals, the office didn't offer much of a place to hide. There was the passageway, but after what had happened last time, I'd rather have him catch me than go back down into that cavern.

After another long set of breaths, the ancient pipes groaned as an upstairs toilet flushed, and then I heard the footsteps retreat toward the master bedroom. I exhaled, wrapping my fist around the syringe and keeping it there until I was safely back in my room.

Simon wouldn't notice anything missing, unless he kept track of the needles, and I rolled it in my palm, staring at it in the lamplight.

The fluid was a little bit cloudy, a few shades off from white. I uncapped the needle and squeezed out a droplet from the tip, sniffing it. An acrid, earthy odor drifted to my nose—something that smelled not medicinal but more like a folk remedy, the stuff some of Mom's friends peddled in addition to their psychic scams. I put the cap back on the needle, but I couldn't stop trying to remember where I'd smelled that before.

I didn't sleep at all that night, listening to the house breathe. How had I never noticed before how loud it was, popping and creaking, glass panes rattling in the wind, doors slamming as Mrs. MacLeod got up before sunrise to make another one of her hideous breakfasts.

I stumbled into the kitchen yawning, syringe still in my pocket. Only Mrs. MacLeod was there, and she slammed a mug of coffee in front of me. "You look like death warmed over," she said.

I looked at the coffee, tan and steaming, milk thoroughly stirred. I didn't reach for it. I hadn't seen her pour it, and after what I'd found, I didn't know what was going on. The stuff in Simon's desk wasn't for him or Mrs. MacLeod, so it had to be meant for me.

"Too fine for coffee, now," Mrs. MacLeod grumbled. "I've never seen the likes of you."

"Just gotta go," I said. "I don't want to be late."

I met Doyle after school and pulled him aside. "Is there somewhere we can go this afternoon? On the island? Not that cave," I added, when he started to talk.

"There's a hunting blind my brothers use sometimes," he said. "We can meet there. Is everything okay?"

I touched the syringe in my pocket. "I don't know."

"There's no way this is good," Doyle said, holding the syringe up to the light. We were sitting inside a hollowed-out tree, enormous and ancient, with slits cut to watch for animals in the open field in front of us. "You're positive nobody is diabetic or allergic to bees or something?" he said.

"Insulin doesn't come in blank bottles and isn't kept locked in drawers," I said. "And if you're allergic you have one of those pens, not this thing."

"Well," Doyle said. "Maybe it's nothing bad."

"Doyle," I said. "I've been blacking out. I thought it was my family's sickness, but maybe it's this. What if somebody has been drugging me?"

He pulled a bottle of water from the pack he'd brought

and unscrewed the top. "Only one way to find out." He popped the cap off the syringe and discharged about half of it into the water, lifting it to his lips.

"Doyle!" I cried. "No! What if it's something really bad? It could kill you."

"If they've been drugging you, you're not dead yet," he said, taking a huge swig before I could stop him. I hit his arm hard.

"Why did you do that?" I demanded. Doyle stared at me.

"Ivy, if someone is drugging you, you need to know. And I want to know, because I feel like I might have to kick somebody's ass."

"You are so dumb sometimes, I swear," I said. "I'm not a little lost girl. I don't need your protection."

Doyle shrugged. "But you could use my help, so I'm helping. If I get dosed, eventually I'll come down, and then we'll know."

"And if something worse happens?" I said. Doyle didn't answer me. His chin sunk down against his chest and his breathing smoothed out, like he was asleep. I poked him. "Doyle!"

"Ivy," he said, raising his face and grinning at me.

"You scared me!" I said.

"Ivy, has anyone ever told you how beautiful you are?" he said. "Not just that you're hot, because you are, but because you care about people. You pretend you don't, but you do.

You have a light in you." He reached for me, touching something in the air next to my face. "I can see it. . . ."

"Okay," I said. Obviously whatever had been in that syringe had made Doyle seriously loopy.

"You coming here is what made me think I might actually get out," Doyle said. "My family's into all kinds of shady shit. I'm the youngest, and they think I don't know but I do. Like stealing the stuff from those campers who vanished back in the day. Tip of the iceberg."

"It's okay," I said. "Really. Let's just get you home."

"Right out there," Doyle said, breaking free of me as we climbed out of the blind and running into the meadow, arms spread. "Come on, Ivy!" he shouted. "Let's commune with nature!"

I started to follow him to get him back to the trail, so I could take him home, but there was a cracking sound and Doyle dropped out of sight. I raced over to the spot and saw a jagged hole in a circle of rotten boards hidden in the tall dead grass of the meadow. "Oh crap," I muttered, pulling out my phone and shining the flashlight down into the hole. "Doyle?" I called.

"I think I broke my foot," he said cheerily from the bottom of the hole. "But you know what? I know everything will be okay, because you're here. I've never felt that with anyone."

"Just be quiet," I said. The rest of the boards seemed

solid, and I got down on my stomach and looked down into the opening. Doyle waved at me, pupils totally dilated, and then stared off into the shadows. "Hey," he said. "There's a little tunnel down here. . . ."

"Doyle, wait!" I hissed. "Do not go wandering around down there on a broken foot!"

The boards creaked, and I lowered myself down before they gave way and I also ended up with something broken. Doyle smiled at me, pointing into the corner. "Ivy, look. We can all be together here. It's going to be so beautiful."

"What are you talking about?" I said, following Doyle's finger.

Just as before, the sunlight picked up the glint of the gold signet ring embedded in the dark gray pebbles that made up the cavern floor. And just as before, I slapped a hand over my mouth to muffle a scream when I realized I was sharing the tiny space with at least one human skeleton.

Chapter
23

Like in my dream, I did what any sane human would do when trapped with a dead body—I tried to get the hell out of there. But Doyle was in no shape to move, and the narrow passage just led into darkness.

I slid down to the gravel, folding my legs up to my chest. I was trapped here.

My cell phone dug into my side, and I pulled it from my pocket, but I didn't have any bars on the island, never mind underground. The screen blinked with a low-battery warning, and I turned it off. I could see all right, at least. I just didn't want to see what was in front of me.

There were three bodies, in reality. Unlike my dream they lay in one corner, skeletal limbs akimbo, wrapped in the faded remains of denim and nylon and even a ragged Ked. I saw, horribly enough, a grinning skull looking back at me from a T-shirt one of the skeletons had been wearing when they weren't so skeletal. The skull had a crown made of roses and some swirly colors floating behind it. A Grateful Dead tee.

Aside from the irony, I thought back to what Doyle had said about the Children of Cain, the cult that had come to the island in the eighties and then simply disappeared.

I guess now their disappearance wasn't so mysterious.

Breathing the dry, salty air flowing from the crack in the

rocks, I heard something I hadn't in my dream. Water. Not the bass roar of the ocean but the lazy ripple of a stream. The stream that separated the island between the Bloodgoods and the Ramseys.

"Doyle," I said. "I want you to stay here. Okay? Don't move. I'm going to get help."

"You save me," he said. "You were always meant to."

I approached the darkest part of the cavern, hearing the trickle get louder, and echo, like part of the stream was underground. If it was, it had to come out somewhere, and I could follow it.

I went back to the shallow-buried skeletons. Behind them was a pile of old camping odds and ends, anything with initials, personal markings—anything that cops could identify as belonging to a pack of missing campers, basically. The Ramseys had been smart about what they stole.

Doyle's father was a creeper, but I doubted he was a cold-blooded killer. He was the type to explode on impulse, not carefully hide several bodies. He was definitely a thief, but I didn't think he'd killed the campers—just robbed their corpses.

Moving gingerly to avoid stepping on bones, I went through the pile of camping stuff. Everything was half-eaten with dry rot, metal bits just rust, but I found an old-style candle lantern painted with the name *Ross* near the bottom of the pile and a tin of waterproof matches. I went through almost all of them before I found one that actually struck, but the candle sputtered and caught, and the soft glow illuminated all the dark corners I hadn't seen in my dream.

Not a dream, I corrected myself. I'd been here before. Had to have been. When my uncle dosed me.

How had I not noticed it? All those nightmares I'd been having, and the stuff I'd thought was a dream, until I found tangible things like the bloody shirt . . .

The tea. The bitter, disgusting tea I kept taking out of politeness.

"Doyle," I said. "I'll be back soon. I promise."

"Watch out for the dark," he said, squeezing my hand. "Being alone in the darkness is frightening. Don't let it extinguish that light. . . ."

I squeezed his hand in return and climbed through the second passage, between human-sized boulders at the back of the cavern.

Sure, the detached part of my brain was wondering *why* Simon was drugging me, but I figured I could chew that over once I got out of here. If the "sickness" I'd experienced was induced by whatever was in that syringe, had Mom and my grandmother also gotten dosed? It had to be something natural, something Simon had easy access to, that wasn't detectable in a tox screen unless you were looking for it.

Clearly it didn't make everyone see horrible stuff—Doyle had turned into a chatty oversharer. Just my luck it made me see stuff straight out of PJ's weird Japanese horror movies and my own worst nightmares. That was probably the Bloodgood genes, I admitted. Dosed or not, we did have a strong streak of mental problems, and who knew how that interacted with whatever was in the syringe?

Focus, I told myself. One thing at a time. Get out of these tunnels alive, then get help for Doyle, then I could confront my uncle.

I saw a low opening leading to a damp passage cut into the rock, and bent over to peer into it. I could see the flash and dance of the stream at the end of the tunnel and could feel fresh air on my face that smelled like the damp, slightly musty odor of dead pine needles and earth.

Something snapped when I put my foot down, and I moved the lantern to see another set of bones, these ones much more brown-yellow than the others, a few scraps of mummified flesh still clinging here and there.

"Come *on*," I whispered, holding the light to reveal the rest. This skeleton was curled up to one side of the passage, one leg extended behind it, one arm cradled to its chest, as if it had tried to crawl away and then died right here. I was freaked out for a second, thinking that going this way meant the same for me, until I saw the neat dime-sized hole in the back of the skull. I knew what a bullet hole looked like. In a weird way, I was very relieved. "Sorry," I whispered again, using my toe to move the deceased leg out of my way. "You understand."

The skeleton shifted a little, and I got a better look at the cradled arm, and my stomach lurched. I tried to pretend I was just imagining things, but all the details still clinging to the body fell into place—stringy white strands of hair in the scalp that had been blond in life, the compound fracture in the forearm bone set with three metal pins. I reached down into the gravel, to the flash of silver, and picked up the square metal frames, lenses long ago shattered, that had been Simon's glasses.

Simon. Formerly Benjamin.

And not whoever had been living in my family's house, pretending to be my uncle.

"He left me no choice."

I didn't even jump at the sound of Simon's voice—I didn't have anything better to call him—and the strong beam of the flashlight overwhelming my wimpy candle. I was all out of shock, of fear. Pretty much everything was toned down to a whisper. I had the calm thought that if Simon came at me, I'd bludgeon him with one of these melon-sized rocks.

I wasn't ending up like poor Benjamin.

His shoes crunched the gravel as he came closer, and I turned to face him. I didn't show fear, just squinted in the bright beam until he dropped it to the side, so the lenses of his glasses gleamed like mercury.

"Do you know who I am, Ivy?"

I swallowed, surprised at how calm I sounded when I answered. "Brian. Benjamin's twin brother."

"Very good," he said. "Smart. All you Bloodgood women are so smart. I won't bother asking how you found out."

"Mom saved the birth certificate you tried to burn," I said. I wanted to keep him talking, give myself time to figure out how I was going to avoid joining the skeleton collection in these tunnels.

"That sneaky little witch," he murmured, more to himself than me.

"What happens now?" I said. Simon shrugged.

"That's really up to you, Ivy. I don't want to hurt you. I'm very glad you didn't panic and force me to do something final."

"Is that what happened to Benjamin? Simon. Your brother," I clarified. Oh, I was way beyond panic. I was calculating the odds of me winning if I rushed Simon and tried to make a run for it. He was scrawny, but he'd taken down four people that I knew about, and I didn't know if he was armed. I stayed put. I liked the odds much better if I let him talk.

"Benji was unfortunate," he said. "But I think if you hear my side, maybe you'll understand."

I spread my hands. "So tell me."

Simon pointed ahead of him, past the body of his brother, into the dark. "That way," he said. "Much easier than climbing all those goddamn stairs back to the manor."

Something else clicked into place. The odd acrid, almost burnt-earth smell—the water in the cistern had smelled and tasted the same, when I'd fallen in. I *had* fallen in. Simon had drugged me, changed my wet clothes, but I had swallowed that water, smelled and tasted it.

"What you've been dosing me with," I said. "It's in that water. In the cistern."

"Something in the ground under the house," Simon agreed. "The water comes up from deep below, leaches through a mineral layer, or grows bacteria—I don't pretend to understand, but the effects on an already fragile psyche are pretty remarkable."

"You've been drugging me since day one," I said, not a question. Simon waved the flashlight down the passage.

"It sounds so harsh when you say it like that. Walk. And listen. If at the end of the tunnel you're not convinced, we can discuss our options."

He moved after me, our shadows mixing on the wall. "I was just about your age when Benji—Simon—contacted me. He wanted to get to know his family. His real family."

"I get that," I said. "Pretty normal."

"I was on my own in Portland, sleeping rough, barely

getting by. Hearing that my twin brother had been welcomed into a family rich enough to have their own island was quite a fairy-tale ending, let me tell you." He sighed. "But they wanted nothing to do with me."

"Maybe it's because you creep people out," I said. Simon laughed, the sound echoing. The tunnel was deceptively long.

"Just because Benji got adopted and skipped all the psychiatrists poking in his brain, giving him tests and a couple of stays in the state hospital doesn't mean he didn't have the same diagnosis they gave me. We were twins, after all. Anyway, initially I just intended to use him for quick money, extort a few grand, steal some family heirlooms, and buy a bus ticket to New York or something. Anywhere but Darkhaven."

I kept moving, sensing that he was hesitating on the next sentence. "What changed?" I said.

"Myra," he said.

I felt sick all over again. "What was so special about Mom? Even back then it's pretty clear from her diary she was way off her rocker."

"You know," he snapped, steel in his voice for the first time. "I have had about enough listening to you shit-talk your poor mother. Have a little sympathy, Ivy. Be less cold-blooded."

"Says the murderer," I muttered. Simon put out a hand

and shoved the small of my back. I stumbled, almost going down.

"Less lip, more walking," he said. "Myra was everything to me. She was smart, beautiful, the first person to ever give me her full attention. So I stayed. I pretended I wanted to get to know my brother, even though I couldn't have cared less about his pretense of being normal, his wholehearted embrace of the disgusting, snotty-rich brat Simone had turned him into. When he discovered the truth about my feelings for Myra, he got upset." I saw his shadow shrug. "He didn't deserve all this, you know. He was far worse than I was, really. Back in the orphanage, he was starting fires, hurting animals. If I'd left the island, left your mother and grandmother alone, who knows what he would have done. . . ."

I figured that was crap. Probably a lie cribbed from Simon/Brian's own childhood, and pawned off on poor Benjamin to make Simon seem sympathetic to me. "I understand," was all I said. "So, what? You just told Mom that 'Brian,' what, got abducted by aliens?" I interrupted. I couldn't touch the whole Brian/Simon having feelings for Mom thing. I'd just start screaming. Simon laughed softly.

"It wasn't hard. I said he'd moved on. Gone to California. I sent a couple of postcards from a remailing service in LA and that was that. Everyone on this island thought I—Brian—was a shiftless nobody, so no one so much as asked after him. I walked into Benji's shoes, and to Myra and everyone else, I *was* him. Benjamin. And Benjamin was Simon, and Simon was who I deserved to be, in the end."

"Except my grandmother figured it out," I said, turning back to stare at his black shape in the flashlight beam. "Didn't she?"

"Like I said, smart," he said. "Fortunately, untreated mental illness really *does* run in the Bloodgood family. A few months of drugging her afternoon cocktail, and her evening cocktail, and her bedtime cocktail, and that was that. Involuntarily committed, power of attorney to Myra, any comments about how I wasn't really her beloved Simon easy to discredit." He cocked his head, smiling broadly. "The things that woman told me. She killed her father, you know. She followed him across the island and saw what he did to the Ramseys, and she killed him with a skinning knife, made it look like he cut his own throat. Said she couldn't let that evil keep on existing. She and Liam's father agreed to take that secret to their grave. Isn't that adorable? Anyway, I used bits and pieces of that to suggest some choice nightmares to your subconscious. Bloody footprints, spooky little girls. Classics are classics for a reason."

I couldn't even be relieved that what had happened the night the power went out had been sort of real. I was too horrified by the words flowing from Simon like a poisonous tide rising.

Suddenly the tunnel brightened, and we were standing amid a rock pile in the same woods I'd woken up in when I was first on the island. The seam in the granite was almost invisible—especially in the dark, you'd never see it. Somebody could come and go between the manor and the property line as they pleased.

Simon clicked the flashlight off. "Maybe I was wrong to go straight to that technique with you. Simone had a violent reaction to the drugging, went completely off the rails and had to be hauled away to a mental hospital in cuffs. I didn't plan it that way, but it was very effective. I told Myra she'd died in the hospital. Killed herself, actually. Myra was alone except for me. I knew she resented Simone too much to scrutinize what happened, and we buried a nice urn of fake ashes, and Myra had nobody else to turn to."

Something about the way he said it, the little smug smile that curled his mouth, made me cold. "But then she ran out on me. The drugs didn't have time to do their work. I guess in the long run it didn't matter. She had cracks when I met her, and that vulnerability I loved turned her into something ugly. Broke her in the end." He smiled as he looked into my eyes. "You're made of stronger stuff, though. More like me."

"Oh, God," I said, my legs unable to support me any longer. I crumpled to the pine needles. "Oh my *God*."

"Myra was already pregnant when she figured it out," Simon said. "That I wasn't the twin she thought I was."

The words were echoing inside my skull, like I was next to a speaker turned up way too loud.

The devil.

Your father.

Why Mom had never told me about Simon. Why she'd run as far and fast as she could. Why Simon was so determined to keep me on the island, with bribes of college and a trust fund and a loving family. Why he'd never touched Mom's room, left it just as it was when she left Darkhaven. Left him.

Simon crouched in front of me, putting out his hand to touch my shoulder. I jerked away, the thought of his touch nauseating. "Ivy, I loved your mother. And you. I wanted us to be a family. Myra was so upset she tried to drown herself; did you know that? After she found out she was pregnant with you."

"You mean after she found out she'd slept with a psychopath pretending to be his own brother," I muttered thickly. My body felt as heavy as the stones around us. I wasn't sure what shock felt like, but I figured probably like this. I wanted to run, but I couldn't have. Where would I go, anyway? Simon had the only keys to the boat, and I'd have to go back to the manor to get to them.

"You're upset," Simon said. "I'll make some allowances for your state of mind, but don't keep saying things like that to me." He stood, looming over me. "I don't like it."

"You drugged me," I said. "So you could keep me here. Like you never could her." My brain was still working, at least. I could still talk, still try to con my way out of this. He wasn't any different than a hundred other marks who thought they were smarter than me.

"That is one reason, yes," he agreed. "I tweaked the mixture, distilled it rather than just adding well water to things like I did with Simone. I had to be sure you weren't as volatile as Myra. Fair's fair, she did it to me too—ground up sleeping pills, put them in my drink, and ran out on me. Stole a good bit of cash and jewelry while she was at it."

And then, eight years later, she tried to drown me in a bathtub. Now that I understood the reason behind all of Mom's instability, it didn't really make it any better. I hadn't asked to be born.

"Why didn't she just give me up?" I said. I hadn't even really meant to say that out loud, but Simon smiled again. It was a creepy smile, like one painted on a doll. I got the feeling you could peel off the mask on Simon and the face underneath would be totally blank, like something that had never had any human features in the first place.

"Because of the Bloodgood map," he said. I blinked, the abrupt shift in his tone snapping me out of my daze.

"What map?"

Simon gestured around. "I don't know if you've noticed, but this place is a wreck. House is falling down; I can barely pay property taxes; the IRS has a lien on the estate. Blood-goods haven't been as rich as they want all those rednecks across the bay to think for a long time. But somewhere on this island is all the cold, hard loot Connor Bloodgood earned or stole in his long life. I've spent the last seventeen years scouring the tunnels, but I can't find it without the map. And since in that time I've become sure the map's not in the manor or anywhere else on the island, that leads me to believe Myra took it with her."

He reached down and took my arm, pulling me to my feet easily. He was really strong, and I was glad I hadn't tried to fight him—I'd probably be broken in about ten places. "Which means you have it."

"I do not," I said reflexively. "I am one hundred percent sure on that one."

"Unfortunately I don't believe you," Simon said. "Like recognizes like, Ivy. You're like me. You lie like breathing, and you take secrets to the grave." He shoved me ahead of him, heading back toward the manor. "Let's hope it doesn't come to that, because I do genuinely like you."

"So you drugged me to look for the map?" I said, stumbling over tree roots as he dragged me.

"At first. Then I wanted to make sure you were pliable when I did find the Bloodgood fortune. I'm not one of you by birth. By the terms of Simone's will, all of the actual money passes to the blood heir." He grunted. "Tricky old bitch didn't trust my brother half as much as she made him think, it turns out. If she had died without me locating you, the money would have gone into a trust and I'd lose everything, including my right to live here." He curled his lip. "Only reason I'm paying to keep that bag of bones on ice in Mid-Coast. Dead women can't sign paperwork."

"You're just the soul of compassion, huh?" I said.

Simon laughed. "Ivy, trust me, the woman was a terror when she was lucid, and twice as bad when she was psychotic," he said. "I did the world a favor scrambling her brain and locking her up."

"So nothing is your fault," I said. "It was your brother and my mom rejecting you, or my grandmother's attitude, or anything except you being a cold-blooded killer."

"I know you're trying to get at me," Simon purred. "But yes. I have no problem saying Simone brought this on herself. Now, though, it doesn't matter. I have her power of attorney. All I needed was the last living Bloodgood, and then out of the blue some hick-town social worker calls me and dumps you right into my lap."

He stopped as we came in view of the edge of the grounds. "You could help me, you know. I'd like to give you that chance. Voluntarily give me the tunnel map and we'll be just like a regular family. I've sacrificed a lot to keep the Bloodgood fortune safe. I even put up with the Ramseys. I do owe them, I guess. Liam and his brothers took care of those campers in the eighties, hid the bodies and all. Before my time, but if they hadn't done it, I'd never have been able to become Simon, and wait out Simone and Myra."

"Liam killed them?" I said. At this point, nothing else would surprise me.

"Of course not. They found the cistern, that Peter Ross character drank the water, and he killed them. All Liam and his brothers did was hide the bodies so no police would find the tunnels. Liam's father and Simone had that agreement, you know. Protecting secrets to the grave, be they murder or money." He chuckled. "Liam's never been a hands-on type, at least not with anyone who can fight back. I took care of that idiot Neil Ramsey when he tried coming through the tunnels on our side of the island to do some grubby drug deal. If he'd stumbled across Connor's hoard, he'd tell every last living soul in Darkhaven, and then we'd really have problems."

"Was making me think I'd killed him part of your fatherly sacrifice?" I said. He laughed, shaking his head.

"That was insurance. In case you tried to leave. I'd threaten to tell Liam what you did, and you'd turn to me to protect you."

I felt my face twitch with disgust. "You know, I've never met anyone crazier than Mom, but congrats. You just knocked her out of the top spot."

Simon chuckled louder, shaking his head, then suddenly his hand flashed out and hit me full-on in the side of the face, dropping me like a stone. *"Don't* call me crazy," he said as I sprawled in the pine needles, tasting blood and hearing a high-pitched whine in my right ear. "I don't like it."

I was still gripping the lantern, and as he moved in, offering me a hand up, I swung it up and hit him in the mid-section. He doubled over, air whistling out of him. "Don't hit me," I said. "I don't like it." I hit him again in the side of the head, dropping the lantern and taking off through the trees as he staggered and fell.

I ran flat out, not looking behind me, until I hit a solid mass. "Doyle!" I screamed, as he wrapped his arms around me.

"Ivy," he said. "There's a bunch of skeletons in that hole I fell into. . . ."

"Yeah, I know," I said, grabbing his hand. "Is the stuff wearing off?"

"I think so," he said, as I tried to tug him along. "I feel like crap. My foot *really* hurts."

"I know, but you have to suck it up for a minute. We gotta go," I said, hearing branches crack behind me. *"Now."*

I wasn't fast enough. Simon had a black-handled knife, the kind that opens out of a tube when you press a button, and he slashed Doyle on the arm. Simon turned to face him, glasses askew, twin red spots burning in his cheeks. Blood matted a section of his hair, but he looked way less concussed than I'd have liked.

"I'm not going to mind getting rid of *you* at all," he rasped. "I always hated you."

Simon jabbed at Doyle with the blade, and Doyle stumbled out of the way, his bad foot tripping him up. I picked up the flashlight Simon had dropped, raised it, and brought it down hard on the back of Simon's head, aiming for the shiny bald spot.

He was out cold this time, and I grabbed Doyle's good arm. "We gotta go."

"The woods," Doyle said, taking my hand. We ran as fast as his foot would allow, never letting go of each other. After about thirty seconds I heard Simon let out an enraged yell, and then my name floated through the pines. "Ivy!" he screamed. "Ivy, you get back here!"

"In here," Doyle said, pushing me into the hunting blind.

We pressed ourselves into a corner, me against Doyle's chest. "Are you hurt bad?" I whispered into his shirt. He grunted.

"I'll have a badass scar."

"Doyle," I said, shivering a little. "I'm so sorry. I'm . . ."

"Shh!" he hissed, and I heard someone crackling through the underbrush outside.

"Iiiiiivyyyyy," Simon singsonged, standing not ten feet

from the back side of the blind. "Come on out, sweetheart. Daddy's not mad at you."

I buried my face against Doyle's chest and felt his arms lock tight around me. His grip was steady, but I could feel his heart jackhammering under my cheek. He was as scared as I was.

"Ivyyyyy. IVY!" Simon thundered. After a long pause I heard him sigh. "You have no idea how hard you're making this on yourself. If you'd just help me out, we could forget this ever happened."

I squeezed my eyes shut, like when Mom would get really wasted and start throwing things at me. I used to hide in closets, under beds, shut my eyes, and will myself to be somewhere else. To be invisible and small and still, so she'd forget all about me.

I heard Simon thrash away through the trees, and Doyle's arms relaxed their grip just a tad. "He's gone," he whispered into the top of my head.

I forced myself to peel off from him, trying to make myself stop shaking. "We have to get off Darkhaven."

"No shit," Doyle said. "Let's head back to my place. We can call the cops and take one of my dad's boats."

We made our way through the woods to the edge of the Ramseys' yard, sticking close, jumping at every bird that flew from a branch or small animal that skittered through the undergrowth. "I really am sorry," I said as we walked up the rise to the farmhouse. "I should have listened to you."

"To be fair," Doyle said. "I knew Simon was creepy, but I clearly didn't know the whole extent of it."

Another stab of sickness hit me. "You still don't."

"You're right," Doyle said. "What in the hell has been happening on your side of the island?"

"He was drugging me," I said. That night on the lighthouse, if you hadn't been there, I would have died." And then he could have swept away my grandmother's will and gotten his hands on everything.

As briefly as I could, I filled Doyle in about the will, why Simon was drugging me, the supposed tunnel map my mother had stolen.

"Do you believe that stuff? About the tunnel full of plunder or whatever?" Doyle said as we hit the back porch of his house.

"After the last month? I'd believe anything about my family," I said. And as nuts as the whole treasure-tunnel thing sounded, stealing the only map to it would be exactly the kind of move my mother would pull.

Too bad she'd never even mentioned a map, much less shown it to me. The possessions she'd kept since my childhood could be counted on one hand with fingers left. She shed belongings as easily as she shed boyfriends and aliases.

Doyle unlocked his door and ushered me inside. "Use the phone in the kitchen," he said. "I'm gonna go grab the boat keys and a few things we need."

I took a minute to hold on to the counter and get my breath after Doyle left. I wasn't what I considered helpless by any means, but it had been a hell of a day. Being chased through the woods by a maniac would lead any sane person to have a little bit of a breakdown. I let myself shiver, cry, feel sick and disoriented for one minute according to the plastic clock shaped like a cat that hung above the sink, then I pulled my shit together and reached for the yellow plastic phone hanging crookedly on the kitchen wall. I punched in 911 and waited a long minute as static hissed and the line clicked before finally connecting. It rang four or five times. Gotta love small-town emergency services. Finally an operator picked up. "Darkhaven 911, state your emergency—"

I felt something cold and round kiss the side of my neck, like somebody had put a penny against my skin.

"Hang up," Liam Ramsey said in my ear. I slid my eyes sideways, saw that the thing that felt like a gun was in fact a gun, and gently set the phone back in its cradle.

Liam ripped the cord out of the wall and then backed up a step, keeping the pistol aimed at me. "Walk ahead of me," he said. "And if you're thinkin' of being smart, be *really* smart and realize you can't outrun bullets."

"Look," I said. "I know you and my uncle are—"

"Quiet!" Liam snapped at me. He marched me into the living room, where Doyle sat on the sofa, his hands tied behind him with a thick coating of duct tape.

"Dad," he said. "Come on. Let her go."

"She's more important than you," Liam said, shoving me onto the sofa next to Doyle. "Anything heroic from you, I shoot him." He moved the barrel to bear on Doyle.

A Jeep screeched into the Ramseys' driveway, and Simon jumped out of the driver's seat, running up the porch steps.

Liam tipped his head toward Simon when he came in, never taking his eyes or his gun off Doyle and me. "Thanks for the call, Simon."

"I knew they'd come here," Simon said, panting a bit. "It was that or swim to the mainland."

"Dad, what the hell are you doing?" Doyle snapped. "This is fucked-up, even for you."

"The tunnel map was in our possession once," Liam said. "Bloodgood slaughtered six of us to get it back. Your grandfather told me all about it."

I blinked, thinking the massacre my great-grandfather had perpetrated made a whole lot more sense in the context of a bunch of money rather than a "curse." Effed-up sense, sure, but sense.

"Me, I prefer to let bygones be bygones," Liam said. "For half the cash, I don't give a rat's ass what Simon does on his side of the island. You live here, Doyle. You know how hard things have gotten."

"I know we're broke, but this is really just . . . Jesus fucking Christ, Dad," Doyle said as Liam gestured us both up. Liam slapped him hard on the back of the head.

"Language, you little brat."

"Come on," Simon said impatiently. "I'm ready to be done with this."

Liam herded us into the Jeep, and Simon drove like a crazy person back to the manor house, careening around corners so I half hoped we'd tip over. At least then I could make a run for it.

At the manor, Liam marched us into the front hall. There, he pushed Doyle down to his knees while Simon held me back.

"I'll make this easy, without all the chatter Simon here loves so much," Liam said. "You care about my boy. You hand over that map, or he's gonna suffer."

Doyle stared up at his father, shocked. "Dad. Why?"

Liam shrugged. "I love you, Doyle, but life is about sacrifice. I'm not gonna let almost twenty years of work go to waste just because a teenage girl is feeling stubborn—"

"I don't have it!" I shouted, cutting him off. "My mother didn't give it to me. I don't know if she even kept it—for all I know she pawned it for pills or cash at any one of the two hundred shitty towns we stopped in. She didn't keep things! She didn't even want to keep me!"

"She doesn't have it," Doyle echoed. "Dad, *please* . . ."

Liam turned the gun butt first and hit Doyle in the side of the head. "Hush, boy."

I lunged at him, but Simon caught me. "Ivy," he said. "I'm afraid I insist. The map, or the boy's life. The time for obfuscation has passed. Bring it to us."

"I don't *know*," I said, thinking that this was all Mom's fault. She was dead, and still royally screwing up everything. "She didn't even keep baby pictures of me!" All she had from before my time were some old combat boots, her leather jacket, and her . . .

Then, I knew exactly where Mom must have kept the map. I looked at Liam, then back at Simon. "Okay," I said softly. "I'll tell you."

"Now," Simon said quickly. "Talk."

I held up my palm, showing the scar the old woman in Oregon had inflicted on me. "X marks the spot," I said. "It's a tattoo," I expanded when Simon and Liam looked at me blankly. "Mom made me get it when I was just a little kid. I still remember how scared I was of that needle."

Liam sneered. "There's not a mark on her hand besides that little scar."

"Genius," I snapped, "the tattoo is in reactive ink. It only shows up under black light. But I have it memorized. Mom made sure of that."

Liam and Simon looked at each other, looked back at me.

I just focused on breathing. In, out. You act calm, so you are calm. You sell the lie by never believing it's not the absolute truth as you spin your story.

Simon was a great liar, but I was better. Must be a family gift.

After a minute Simon nodded, shoving me toward Liam, who made me kneel next to Doyle. "If this is some kind of trick . . . ," Liam growled.

"Dude," I said. "You're pointing a gun at us. Why would I trick you?"

He smirked, seeming satisfied. I looked over at Doyle. He had the glassy-eyed look of somebody whose entire life has just imploded in front of his face. I wished I could tell him it was going to be okay, but I couldn't make that promise. Instead, I tapped his leg with my finger, without moving my hand.

"We're going to get out of here," I said softly as Liam and Simon turned their faces away from us, in a whispered conference. "Be ready."

"I'm sorry," Doyle said. "About the map . . ."

"Doyle, there is no map. Not tattooed on my hand at least," I said. "Simon is not going to let you, your dad, or me live once this is over. Our only chance is to run."

Simon turned back to us with a cheery smile. "If you know the map, Ivy, then tell me where the entrance is."

"The cave on the beach," I said. "Let Doyle go. He didn't

do anything to be mixed up in this."

"Oh no," Simon said pleasantly. "Once I know this is real, I'll consider it. For now . . ." He snapped his fingers at Liam. "The beach."

Liam grunted his assent, pulling Doyle to his feet. "Down we go."

Chapter
24

The wind was as strong and cold as it had ever been as Liam and Simon forced us down the slippery, groaning steps to the beach. I lost all feeling in my fingers and face as I tried to hold on to the splintery railing.

Liam cursed as my foot slipped. "The time we can be rid of you can't come soon enough," he grumbled.

"That's Simon's call," I said.

Liam grinned unpleasantly. "After what you did to Neil? Hardly. Our family is going to make you pay in blood for every second of that poor kid's suffering."

I stopped on the step, turning to face him, grabbing the opening. "Oh, that wasn't me," I said. "That was all Simon."

Liam's brow crinkled, and he whipped sharply toward Simon, who was bringing up the rear behind Doyle. They'd cut the tape off his hands, but his arm was still bleeding, bad enough to soak the sleeve of his henley, and he looked pale and unsteady, his broken foot dragging.

"What's she saying?" Liam snapped at Simon.

Simon shrugged. "Lies. She's unstable; who knows what happened to Neil."

"Neil was looking for the tunnel," I said. "Simon took exception, so he killed him in the woods and planted evidence in my room so he could control me too. Birds, stones, all that."

Liam's face darkened even more. "That better not be true."

"Neil was exploring the tunnel system," Doyle added. "He had a contact in Canada who was selling him wholesale pot, and he was looking for the old bootlegger mooring to bring the stuff in."

I held Liam's gaze, projecting confidence I didn't feel in the slightest. "Who on this island do you know has killed before? Who would be capable of cutting Neil down without a second thought?" I pointed up at Simon.

He started to open his mouth to deny it, but Liam aimed his pistol at him.

"You rotten son of a bitch!" he roared. "How dare you use him like a prop? Nobody touches my family!"

Except him, evidently.

"Liam, calm down," Simon started. "This gets neither of us what we want."

"Hell yes it does!" Liam shouted. "I have the map, and now I don't have to split what it leads to with your murdering ass!"

I nudged Doyle. "Go!"

We took off, half sliding down the staircase as the two men's shouts grew louder behind us. We were almost to the bottom when shots starting pinging off the rocks around us, sending chips of granite flying like tiny missiles. I heard Doyle give a short yell, and saw him sprawl in the sand, clutching at his shoulder.

"Doyle!" I screamed, dropping to my knees beside him. Halfway up the steps, Liam raised the pistol again, but suddenly his arm sagged and a look of confused pain crossed his face. Simon stepped out from behind him, withdrawing his knife from somewhere in the vicinity of Liam's kidney. Liam didn't go down, though, and as Simon started down the stairs, Liam got off one more shot, catching Simon high on the leg, making him crumple just a few feet closer to us.

Doyle was groaning, but when he took his hand away, no blood bubbled from the wound. It looked clean, through the meaty part of his shoulder.

"I think you're gonna be okay," I said, sagging with relief. "It's through and through."

"Fantastic," he grunted. "That totally makes up for the agonizing pain."

I got Doyle by his good arm, laying it across my shoulders and helping him stand up. The two of us staggered awkwardly up the steps, gingerly avoiding Simon's prone form and Liam as he lay across two steps.

"Should we help him?" I said. Doyle's lip curled.

"I'll call him an ambulance when I get to the mainland."

That was just fine by me, and we kept going, until at the top of the steps I paused, groaning. "The boat keys."

"Huh?" Doyle said, leaning against one of the stone walls

that marked the edge of the formal grounds.

"Simon has the only set," I said. "They're on his key-chain." I'd have suggested we take the Ramseys' boat, but Doyle was in no shape to trek to the other side of the island. I sighed, not thrilled at the prospect of having to get that close to Simon again, when Doyle's eyes widened.

"Ivy——" he started.

I spun, and almost smacked into Simon face-first.

"You," he hissed, grabbing me by the shirt, "are in a lot of trouble, Ivy Bloodgood."

I shoved him, but his grip was like a vise, and we both stumbled toward the edge of the steps. Simon hit one of the railings, and it cracked, rotted wood and rusted nails tumbling down the steep cliffside. I grabbed the portion that was still steady with my free hand, crying out as splinters and jagged metal bit into my palm. Simon swayed, losing hold of my shirt but grabbing my hand. We hung there for a split second, and then he smiled at me. "Go ahead."

I blinked through the fog of pain and adrenaline. *"What?"*

"I knew we had more in common than DNA!" he said. "You're like me, Ivy. Not Myra. She was weak. You're a survivor. You know what you have to do." His smile got wider, so wide it seemed to be pushing his face out of shape. "You want to let go. You'd enjoy it. It's okay, Ivy. I understand. We're the same."

He suddenly reared back toward the edge, putting all his

weight on me, yanking my arm so painfully I felt a joint pop. "Come on!" he shouted. "You're my daughter. You hold on to me, you die!" He scrabbled at my wrist as I felt the railing slipping out of my grasp, tearing at my flesh. My upper body was out over open air now, and I could see straight down to the beach. "Maybe that's how it should be," Simon sighed. "Father and daughter, together. Maybe that's just. I did those awful things to your mother, after all."

"You're wrong," I said. "About everything except this." The railing creaked even as I held on for dear life, and I felt the timbers shudder as they started to give.

"Ivy . . . ," Simon said as he tipped out over the cliff, only the toes of his shoes still on solid ground.

"I am a survivor," I told him. "And you're not worth dying over."

As the railing snapped, I opened my other hand and his sweaty palm slipped free, gravity sucking him away from me as quickly as breathing. I thought I was all right for a split second, and then I was sliding over the edge, trying desperately to grab anything I could to slow my descent.

A hand locked on my ankle, and a strong arm pulled me backward, until my center of gravity was back on the cliff top, and I could crawl away from the edge.

Doyle sprawled on the ground near me, white as a sheet, good arm reaching for me. "Is he dead?" he asked, panting.

I stood shakily, going to the edge of the cliff and looking over. At this distance, Simon looked like he'd just decided to lie in the sand, peacefully, while the waves lapped at his one outstretched hand. "I hope so," I said, and turned my back on the cliff. Doyle was trying to stand, and I helped him.

"I guess we never did get those boat keys," he said. I pulled out the ring I'd grabbed from Simon's pocket when he'd first appeared at the cliff top and tried to manhandle me. Pickpocket skills don't just go away because your psycho uncle-slash-father is trying to throw you off a cliff.

"Have a little faith in me, Doyle," I said.

He groaned in relief. "Good, because I really think I need a hospital. And a transfusion. Maybe like six or seven."

We limped back to the Jeep, and I drove us to the dock, helping Doyle into the boat and making sure he was strapped in before I pulled out into the bay. I didn't look back at Darkhaven once.

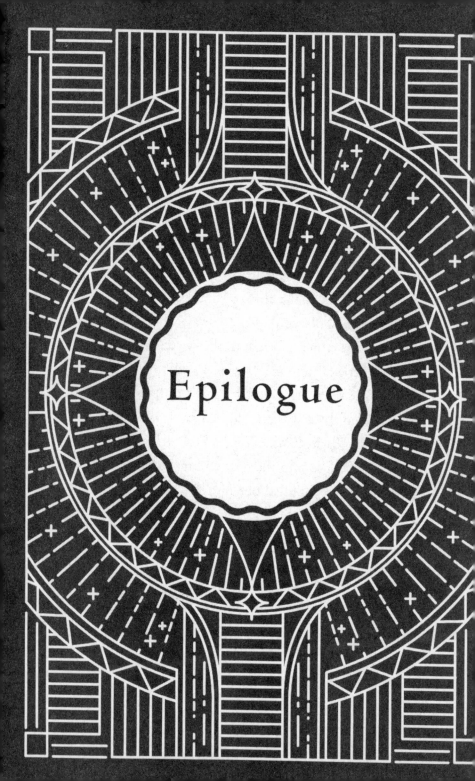

Epilogue

There were Christmas lights stringing the docks in Darkhaven Harbor when Doyle and I took the boat back to the island, but none when we approached the dock at Darkhaven. I hesitated before climbing out, thinking back to when I'd first arrived, with friendly Officer Brant, and the first meeting with Mrs. MacLeod.

She'd be spending her golden years in jail, fortunately, for going along with Simon's drugging me and who knew what else. He'd glossed over the details of my paternity, promised her money, and just like 99 percent of people, that was all it took. I hoped the prison cafeteria served nothing but meat loaf and stew for her entire sentence.

Doyle touched my gloved hand with his. "You okay?"

His arm was still in a sling, his wool coat only draped on one side, and he shivered a little. I pulled him close so he wouldn't get too cold. "Are *you*?"

"My dad got charged with accessory to murder, most of the rest of my family are in jail thanks to the state police swarming all over the island and finding their stash, you almost died saving my life near this very spot, and I'm headed back to the manor of a psychopath who drugged and killed people for fun," Doyle said. "I'm fan-freaking-tastic."

"You saved my life too," I reminded him. "If you hadn't

attacked Simon, we'd be turning into skeletons number five and six in that creepy cave."

Doyle grinned at me. His bruises had entirely faded, and he looked happier, less like he was carrying weight on him, than he had in the time I'd known him. I guessed putting your abusive asshole father in jail had that effect on a person.

Simon had been buried in the state-run cemetery near Thomaston. I didn't go to the interment. I'd said everything to him that I needed to say.

Before we went up to the manor, I drove past it to the little cemetery, and I put a wreath next to Mom's grave. I didn't say anything to her either, but I figured once I'd had another month or two to process everything that I could come back. It wasn't like she was going anywhere, not this time.

"Nice," Doyle said. I shook my head.

"Mom hated Christmas, and wreaths, and anything sentimental," I said. "So this would have totally pissed her off."

Doyle stuck close to me as we went back to the manor, turned on a few lights, and headed out the rear door to the beach steps. The railing had been repaired, blond two-by-fours where the rotten old railing had been, complete with a new sign that read: Dangerous Cliff—Stay Back 10 Feet.

"We don't have to do this," he said as I carefully brought out Mom's velvet-wrapped tarot deck.

I shuffled until I found the Devil card and held it up. "This was so Mom," I said. The cards were all dog-eared and worn from decades of use, and I slid my thumbnail into the crease at the corner, peeling the two thin layers of card stock apart. Inside, on vellum paper so thin it was transparent, sat a tiny folded map. In all the questions from the cops after we'd made it to the mainland, the meetings with Simon's lawyer, all the papers I'd signed to be the legal owner of the property on Darkhaven when I turned eighteen, I'd kept this to myself.

"We absolutely do have to do this," I said to Doyle. "After everything we've been through, I am not just leaving this tunnel thing alone." We took the steps down, and I flinched when I saw the dark bloodstains on the two steps where Simon and Liam Ramsey had gone down. This time, I'd brought lanterns and a satellite phone and everything else I could think of that we might need for exploring bootlegger tunnels and possibly finding a cache of loot hidden by my ancestor.

The map branched off from the tidal cave, through a sliver in the rock so small you couldn't see it unless you knew to be looking for an opening. It was deceptive, though, a sort of L-shaped atrium to a network of dry, carefully excavated tunnels, and it didn't take long, following the turns on Connor's map, to find the small hollow at the end of the chain.

Doyle shone his lamp inside. There was a crooked stack

of chests and crates in one corner, a pyramid of wine casks that looked like they were probably as old as the house, and a lot of odds and ends from centuries of occupation.

I put my hand on the lid of the top chest. Doyle gave me a grin. "Ready to be rich for real?"

"I'm ready to figure out what Simon was willing to kill me over," I said, and flipped the lid.

It was empty. I opened the next, and the next. A dozen chests and as many crates, all empty. The only thing that wasn't broken and used up was the wine and a small stack of spare bricks, piled in the corner along with other odds and ends from mansion construction—sheet metal, old tiles, boards eaten up with dry rot.

I waved away the ancient dust, sneezed, and started to laugh. "All of that, and it's all gone," I said. "I guess Simon was more right than he knew."

"So Connor Bloodgood was as much of a grifter as his descendants," Doyle said, also starting to laugh. I choked on the dust and picked up the flashlight.

"Let's get the hell out of here. And maybe chuck one of those bricks through a window before we go."

Doyle laughed. "Can't blame a con for doing what comes naturally."

I hefted one of the bricks. "Heavy," I said, surprised at the weight. "Maybe I can sell these on eBay or something." I dropped the brick back on the stack, and then started at the dull metallic *thud*. The red-brown outer layer of the brick flaked off where it had hit, and something gleamed underneath. Doyle's breath caught.

"Ivy," he said, scrambling to hand me his pocketknife. My hands were vibrating with excitement as I scraped away the thin layer of clay, the shimmer of silver reflecting my flashlight beam around the tiny room.

There were thirty silver bars in all, heavy and handmade, the spoils of Connor Bloodgood's life melted down and hidden away for the future. They wouldn't make me manor rich—private island rich—but they'd definitely pay for a couple of plane tickets to San Francisco. An apartment. Even college, if I wanted it. I could stop, and live, and be normal. If I still wanted to take off, given that I did, after all, have something holding me in Maine.

We locked up the manor and drove back to the dock, silver weighing down our backpacks. I cast off the lines while Doyle started the engine. I was getting pretty good at knowing my way around boats, and once some snow fell and things got quaint and festive, Maine wasn't so bad. Valerie's mom was letting me live with them while I finished out the year, Officer Brant had let Doyle move in with him in town, and neither of us had to go into a foster home, so in my book that was as happy as an ending got. Betty and I went to movies almost every weekend, and I'd even let her talk me into playing "Girl on the Beach" in one of her own works, so she could build up a reel to apply to film school.

And there was Doyle. He held my hand with his good one while I steered us out into the bay, and gave me a smile when I looked over at him. I could see myself with him, at least for a longer time than I'd ever seen myself with anyone, anywhere. Darkhaven had felt temporary. Doyle didn't.

I looked back once at the looming manor house, the crooked light tower, the stark gray cliffs. If I never saw the place again, it would be too soon. The creditors could have it, sell it to pay the family debts. I'd been poor when I walked onto the island, and I didn't need all the trappings I'd found there. The little bit left of Connor's fortune would help me take my first step as an adult, but I didn't need money in the visceral, desperate way Simon had. For a long time, I'd convinced myself I didn't need anything.

But that wasn't true anymore. I opened up the throttle, and the boat skipped over the waves, aimed back toward the mainland, and the first place I'd felt like I could *maybe* settle in my entire life. San Francisco was still out there, no longer an end goal but a new chapter. After that . . . I really could do anything I wanted.

Doyle smiled at me, and I smiled back. He put his arm around me, and for the first time I stood on my toes and kissed him, quick, tasting salt on his lips. He leaned in, and we stayed close, arms around each other as the lights of the mainland got closer. I didn't know if I'd stay in Maine forever; I didn't know if I'd get together with Doyle officially, and, if I did, if I'd stay with him beyond the end of the school year. I didn't know if I'd go to college or even if I'd be on the track team next year. But for the first time in seventeen years, I knew I could stay in one place long enough to find out.

ACKNOWLEDGMENTS

This book could not have come about without the Maine branch of my own family tree, who I spent summers with as a kid on an island, for better or worse, just as small as Darkhaven. You either love island living or you hate it, and unfortunately even though I have a lot of good memories of those summers, I admit my feelings about it are close to Ivy's—too long surrounded by water and I feel claustrophobic. Still, five or six generations of my family managed to hang on in a tiny town on what is essentially a granite rock covered with dirt and a few trees, and without the deep roots they put down—and the stories my great-grandmother Hazel told about being adopted after her entire family was wiped out by tuberculosis—I would not have been able to write the story that became *Dreaming Darkly*. So thank you to Hazel, Edwin, Grandpa Keith, and the Snow family—I owe you.